Beauty or the Beast

Beauty or the Beast

by PHILIP LINDSAY

SAMPSON LOW
25 Gilbert Street London W1

First published 1950

Made and printed in Great Britain
by Purnell and Sons Ltd
Paulton (Somerset) and London

Dedication

for

MOLLIE and CHRISTOPHER OWENS

Dear Mollie and Kit,

This book must be yours because it should have been Blasco's. So enthusiastically and exhaustively had he studied the Overbury case for the verse-play he intended to write, and so often did we discuss it, that, even after the tragedy that robbed us of him, never did I once consider using the story in a novel. It was Blasco's and therefore sacred. But one evening at the home of my friends, Michael and Joy Russell, at Bodhiam, Michael lent me that fine scholarly work by his aunt, Swallowfield and its Owners by Lady Russell (Longmans, Green), 1901, and suddenly I realised that here was the tale I had always longed to write; yet it is also the tale that I would a thousand times have preferred not to have written had only Blasco completed his play.

In Swallowfield and its Owners, *the tragedy is only briefly examined, which is natural enough as the book deals with the Russell family, but Lady Russell had included an excellent reproduction of that lovely portrait of Frances wearing the pearl earrings and the stiff lacy ruff while showing her almost naked bosom. Seeing that portrait again was like falling in love. Her face fascinated me with its supercilious amused half-smile and the quizzical eyes and I knew then that I must write about her; and with that book propped up before me open on the portrait have I written it, turning from Frances to my typewriter and back to her again to be met always by that smile, as tantalising as Mona Lisa's, the lips closed scornfully on some supercilious secret, mocking perhaps the painter because he, too, loved her as she sat in her heavy embroidered gown opening to show the pressed-up breasts almost, but deliberately not quite, revealed.*

The best history of the affair remains Sir Philip Gibbs's King's Favourite (*Hutchinson*), 1909, *although he vainly attempts to wash James of much of his callousness, while there is a typically brilliant study of Overbury in Charles Whibley's* Essays in Biography (*Constable*), 1913. *Otherwise, apart from a too imaginative work by Sir Edward Parry, little has been written about the case in modern times. A book, however, which I found of extreme value was Gladys Scott Thomson's* Life in a Noble Household 1641-1700 (*Cape*), 1937, *and Miss Thomson was also kind enough to answer my questions about the appearance of the earl and his countess. I might add that the pamphlets quoted are all contemporary.*

There was one detail that troubled me greatly, the accents of Somerset and Archie Armstrong, both of whom, like King James, talked broad Scots. Although of Scottish descent— indeed, some of my relations insist that our tree is the only genuine Lindsay one and, like true Scots, will produce pedigrees to prove it—I cannot unfortunately speak the tongue and feared lest I parody it, nothing being more exasperating in a book than dialect unless written by an expert. Somerset and Archie, therefore, speak like the English characters. Even after I had decided on this, I was afraid to begin work, the ghost of Scott watching me from the reproduction of Landseer's portrait on my wall, reminding me of his mighty novel, The Fortunes of Nigel, *with its inimitable picture of James. After that book, it would be more than audacious, it would be lunacy to attempt to create that king again, so superbly has Scott revealed him to us. This worry I eventually solved by working out a construction which kept him off the stage, as you will find when you read the tale.*

Doubtless it will disappoint you. Anything must disappoint those who know the structure Blasco was building. But I am certain that, despite its faults, you will accept this book with my love and in memory of that great man and poet whose loss was truly irreplaceable to us all.

PHILIP LINDSAY

Sussex

Contents

Contents

Beauty or the Beast

CHAPTER I

The Path of True Love

YEARNING to clasp her in his arms yet not daring to move, Will gazed at Anne, his hands at his sides. And what he feared he could not understand. Her scorn? Nay, not that! Anne was too compassionate a girl—or she had greatly changed—to scorn a lover. Or did he fear her mockery? Or her gentle yet firm rejection of his kiss? Nay, none of those he feared because he knew she still loved him as he loved her. Words were not needed to express the strength of that love. It was a more subtle barrier which kept them apart: the barrier of time. When last he had seen her, Anne Carr had been a child and it had been a child whom unconsciously he had expected to meet again in this old Chiswick manor: instead, he found a woman concealed from him not only by her green velvet gown but within a proud reserve that drew back the plump shoulders, raised her chin and hooded her large blue eyes. She had been taught womanly restraint, the prudent bridling of her feelings, and therefore now in silence which jailed her from him she stood after she had risen from her curtsey and waited first for him, the man, to speak; and Will's tongue was dry in his mouth. Nor did he really wish to speak, so precious to him was this moment of re-meeting while he looked on her, dazed with longing and dazzled by her loveliness; and although he knew it not, he smiled in his chestnut beard.

Flinching before that smile, Anne drew away, yet she too smiled in answer, although she cringed within.

" You smile, sir ? " said she as though amused.

He did not answer, not wishing to lose this moment of meeting, realising that never again, however greatly their love might feed on loving, would he know such ecstasy. Through years of exile from her had he lived, taunting his self-pity with images of her in other men's arms, mocked by a ghost who had become strangely more real than was this living girl who breathed before him now and watched him warily. Her ghost or the girl herself, which did he love ? Or did he love them equally ? This was a girl of bone and flesh, the other a phantom of his own creating, an image built from loneliness and love-longing. He had but to stretch out his hand to touch her hand and that dear ghost would vanish in the fever of their meeting. Therefore, wishing to prolong this delicious torment of anticipation, he examined her from golden head to hidden toes, mingling his memory of the girl she had been into the body of this woman.

Tall she was although not so tall as he : neatly would she fit into his arms ; golden she was and pale while he was tanned, and golden was her hair while his was brown ; and that gold was like gossamer, shimmering to silver where the dying sunlight glossed the curls and the fringe across her forehead. Her gown did not dip to show the swell of breasts in the fashionable cut but was frilled with lace over the bodice ; although much of her shoulders were bare—those at least her envious tire-women had not hidden—her arms in the puffed bejewelled velvet sleeves rose monstrously, ribboned across the elbows to draw them in, making both upper- and lower-arms seem as though bitten by giant bees that had left their honey on the cloth in golden lace and buttons. High-waisted yet showing nothing of her shape, the skirt drooped loosely. Little indeed of the girl Anne Carr could be seen, apart from dimpled hands and chest, with her shoulders, her perfect throat and perfect face. Her shoulders, face and hair—may God and those devils of tirewomen be thanked !—could Will gloat on while he wished this moment were eternity, for he would never tire, he felt, of watching her, while with her father's pride and her mother's beauty, she held up her chin and stared with a shielding smile into his eyes.

"Sir," said she at last, trying to speak merrily but there was a catch as of tears in her voice, " have I passed inspection ? Would you have me turn that you might tabulate my back ? I do assure you, sir, that there is naught concealed save what modesty commands. Mayhap I am not so bold as the French ladies you are used to, nor so fiery as the Italians ; nevertheless I am all female, warranted so, unless my women lie . . ."

"Nan," he whispered, "don't . . . You've not forgotten me ? "

"Fie ! " said she with a faint titter, " I see so few gentlemen that I'd find it impossible to forget even an ape in breeches. Besides, I heard your name when it was announced and although my memory, being a woman's, is fickle enough . . ." She paused and licked her lips. " I have small opportunities to forget," she cried on a sob, " being ever locked in here like a bird in a box. Not a dozen times have I been allowed to go to court, while you . . . you have been ranging the world. Paris, Venice, Rome, mayhap the Hesperides and perhaps Ethiopia where even queens are black."

"My world," he sighed, " lies here, globed in your arms, Nan. Wherever I went, whomever I met, I saw only you."

"What ! " cried she. " Are foreign ladies slovens ? Am I so ordinary a thing that I'm to be met by the hundreds in Padua and France or wherever it was you roved ? That is an uneasy compliment, sir. But what know I of compliments, a simple silly wench who sees none but servants and the gallants passing on the river ? Should I curtsey and say *Thank you, my lord* ? "

Mockingly, she dipped in her skirts, glad to look down that she might suck her lip and shut her eyes to squeeze back tears. Then she shuddered at the hot touch of his hands on her bare shoulders ; she shuddered and looked up with doubt and wonder and felt his mouth on hers, her chin tickled by his beard.

Almost on to her back she tumbled and she had to press one hand to the floor lest she fall while she choked as she sighed and felt her corsage swell, being dazed with joy and triumph to know that after all her fears he had not forgotten her in the bodies and eyes of other women, those foreign devils. Then, as he lifted her to her feet and hugged her in his arms, Anne wept. Tears of anger and humiliation long held back could flow now for happiness and would not shame her proud young womanhood. Dimly behind her she heard the clucking of her women and the hissing of their skirts but she cared not what they said or what they did. Rather was she delighted to be able to flout their teachings with a lover, so long had they treated her like a child, ignorant and ugly.

" It has been eternities," he whispered against her teeth, his hand fondling her head through the curls. " I was afraid you would forget me."

" I forget you ! " she sighed, gazing wetly into his eyes merging to one tremendous god-like eye watching her fondly ; and scarcely aware of what she did, she ran her fingers down his back and strained him to her. " You wandering the great world," she said, " with all its temptations of beautiful ladies, and I . . . I . . . O, how could I forget you, living here ! "

" Mistress Nan ! " wailed her ladies. " For God's love, Mistress, remember us ! "

4

Anne scarcely heard their frightened voices or the fluff-fluff of their skirts as they hovered about her, imploring her not to be wanton lest her father hear.

" You mustn't, no, no . . . or I'll tell the earl ! " cried one.

What did Anne care whom they told ? Even her father, that man of angry moods and occasional almost frightening gentleness, could not terrify her now while she held her love in her arms. Brooding through the years, alone with her ageing women and with only memories of childhood-tumblings with this lean boy who had lived nearby until he had vanished when the plague neared Chiswick, she had begun to doubt the reality of the lad's oaths and the power of her own beauty, having no other girls with whom to compare her mirror. Even Will's passionate letters smuggled to her, re-read though they had been until they had become tattered and his writing smudged under her tears and kisses, had seemed rather messages from a wraith of her own begetting than a man. Yet now, with no warning, nine years later, he had ridden back to claim her for his own, a damsel of nineteen in no golden tower guarded by no dragons yet as desperate for liberty as any such prisoner awaiting Jove's shower to open her to love and to wash away fretful imaginings of what she feared might never come.

Long into Will's eyes she gazed after, taking a deep breath, she leaned back in his arms, seeing her own chubby face minute in either pupil smile happily at her. Babies in their eyes, both saw images of themselves as though in kissing they had drunk their love's souls to keep them caged forever.

" I feared you'd never come," she sighed.

" I have dreamed of nothing else," said he. " All the time I was waiting, waiting for now, for you, my love. And the moment I was back I slipped my people and rode here."

5

"O, mistress!" sobbed one of her women. "This is madness. You know you can never wed!"

"Why?" asked Anne, turning cold-eyed, still in her lover's arms, to look at the woman. "Why can I never wed?"

The woman shrank back, hands covering her face.

"Why?" repeated Anne, her voice trembling while her heart beat fast. Then she noticed that one of her attendants was missing and she cried in dismay: "Where did Betty go?"

The others did not answer but shrank together, gown folding lispingly into gown. Only the sound of her own blood beating could Anne hear while she glared from woman to woman, half-turning in Will's arms. All had become silent in that dim gallery which was so rarely opened that it seemed inimical with that damp breath of places too long neglected. Anne had always hated it. Its gloom seemed threatening to her youth, jealous of her vitality, with its boards going rotten, hangings damp and lustreless, no rushes on the floor, and the creeper outside darkening the crusted painted glass of the windows, even the heavy furniture appearing sullen with neglect. Like a tomb resenting her rebirth through love it seemed, wanting to clamp her in its own decay, and she feared and loathed the place and her women soured in untapped maidenhood.

"Why can I not marry?" she cried again and was startled by the harshness of her voice with *Marry?* echoing in a dying fall, sadly, along the dark gallery into which the afternoon sun could filter only frail tendrils of colour. "Am I not like other women?" she demanded. "Tell me, I command you, tell me!" She swung round again in her lover's arms and stared at him with terror and desire. "What do they mean, Will?" she whimpered.

"No matter what they mean," said he into her mouth, "you will be my wife, Nan, my wife."

6

Yet even in his eyes she seemed to read a mist of doubt.
" There's something you've not told me," she cried
shrilly. " I know it ! Always I've known there was
some secret hidden from me and that's why I've been
kept here, away from the court and other ladies, but I've
not dared brood on it. I've heard it in the servants'
hush when I approached them. In my father's sighing
and silences ; in my mother's slow sickening and painful
death, I felt it. Hearing her cry out against a Thomas
when no man stood near her, I felt it. Something I've
not yet been told and which makes me different. Am
I diseased ? Did the stars darken at my birth or the sky
rain blood ? I am nineteen now, I am a woman and I'll
be bubbled no longer. Why have I been reared here,
hidden from the court, given no friends to love ? You
must know, Will. Tell me ! You've coasted the
world. Tell me everything . . . No ! no kissing now !
It is the truth I want ! "
" I . . . I've heard tales," he muttered, looking aside.
" Tell me ! " she cried.
Back against his arms she swung and glared into his eyes,
her teeth showing between lips curled back in anger and
fear ; her hands were on his shoulders, under the lace
collar, holding tightly. Frowning, he leaned over her,
sick with desire and with dread of the future while he
saw her wet lips curl away and the cloth of her bodice
tight-stretching when she breathed deeply.
" I have nothing to tell," he sighed. " I've been too
long away and I was a boy when I left, although of
course I have heard rumours."
" What rumours ? "
He shrugged. " Lies probably," he said. " Who
can trust what courtiers chatter ? And I was only a
boy."
" What did you hear about me ? "
" Nothing about you, nothing, only about your
parents, about some crime, or sin, or something. What

7

it was I neither know nor care. What are your father and mother to us who are young ? Can you trouble about what happened before we met ? Let them snigger and lie, what matter that when we will be together ? We are not babies, Nan, and I swear I'll never give you up. Have I spent my youth in dreams of you and our marriage to be cheated at the end by some old scandal which cannot touch us ? I'll not have it, I say : I will not have it ! "

His voice broke in his fury. To hold Anne at last in his arms again and to have her swing against him out of kissing's reach was anguish that made him sweat. That her parents had committed some grave sin he had heard often enough, but the scandal had always been hushed in his young presence and he had shrugged from it as a sample of old folks' intolerance and liking for bawdy revelations of others' doings. Anne's mother was dead and her father a hermit. If they had sinned, they had atoned for it : that was sufficient, although at thought of his father, that cold-voiced puritan, he shivered, dreading what in his righteousness he might say against his love.

" Come away with me now," he urged. " Ride with me to London. Let them chatter and be damned, a fig to their talk when we are married ! "

" You've not told me yet," said she. " I've long suspected there was a curse on me but my women tell me naught. They treat me like a child when I'm a woman. I am nearly twenty. Most girls are married and are mothers long before then. Yet here I rust, a lady nobly born, while others dance at court or have their husbands. What have I done that I should be treated so ! I'll have no further lying, I am weary of it. Often I saw my mother weep and when I asked what ailed her she'd not say ; and when I asked who was this Thomas she called on in the night she would only whimper and cry out she was ill and that talking

8

hurt her, and then send me off. I have been reared among dumb folk but I'll have no more of it ! Mary, Rosalind, Clarinda. What have you hidden from me?"

Into the shadows sank her waiting-women as she glared at them ; and only the sighing of the wind and the rustle of the creeper on the glass could be heard in that long gallery.

"Tell me ! " Anne almost screamed. No revelation, however terrible, could prove so sickening as the fears she suffered and she felt that unless she were told this secret she might swoon and die, so fast-beating was her heart. At last, this secret now lay in the open and could be spoken ; yet none would tell her what it was. Ever since she could remember she had suspected something hidden. Her having been reared at home with private tutors, seeing no children of her own age, had made it plain that she was different from others. Yet no one would tell her in what fashion she was different that she must be locked away like a leper. The servants and her women had avoided her questions, lightly pretending there was nothing to conceal ; her father she had never dared ask, and her ailing mother had either rebuked her curiosity or had mocked at it ; then when at last after the old king's death her mother had occasionally taken her to court—her father still not moving from this house —she had sensed amongst the ladies and gentlemen a kind of amused curiosity which many a night had driven her sobbing to bed. But none had she dared in her timidity to ask, her pride keeping her reserved, and she had been happy to return to Chiswick to her books that conjured a dream of love with the memory of the boy, this man now holding her about the waist, who had stolen upon her one day in the garden a thousand years ago and had wooed her boisterously, boastfully, yet with sudden unexpected shynesses, amongst the brambles and bushes far from the house. Yet always, hidden under the pretence of arrogance she forced herself to maintain,

9

behind the haughty swagger which she had trained her
legs to use and the cold smile into which she had set her
lips, had lurked this horror of being different from other
girls. A footpad behind her eyes, without warning
it would strike her to appalling doubts which had made
her lean against the wall or grip a chair-back lest she
swoon when she had heard laughter beyond the window
or had seen on the river men and women singing and
fondling as they rowed by. That was a gay world
inexplicably denied her because of some secret sin, some
ancestral taint in her blood, for which she could not be
blamed although she had to bear the curse of it. A
leper at least knew why she was shunned, but Anne Carr
had never been told. Only the love of this youth had
held her from death, she felt, and if today he had
spurned her as an unclean thing she would not have
been surprised—indeed, she had expected no less—but
she was certain that afterwards she would have crawled
under the curtains of her bed, never to rise again. Then
would her last hope of happiness have faded and life
been robbed of beauty. But incredibly, Will had
returned ; incredibly, he still loved her and wanted to
hold and kiss her, this tall, dark, beautiful man who in
his travels must have seen thousands of other women
and had yet returned to claim her, a ghost from the
garden of his boyhood . . . That again she might lose
him was an unbearable thought, dazing her with panic ;
yet her women said she could never marry.

" I'll have you whipped ! " she cried. " Dear God,
I am going mad but I'll be cheated with lies no longer.
I *will* marry ! Do you hear me ! I'll not be mocked by
ghosts of before I was born. What have I done that I
am different from other girls ? "

Then, before her scream had faded to an echo, she
heard the latch click and she saw the door open and her
father enter, her woman who had run to warn him
smiling malevolently at his back. Slowly, Robert Carr,

Earl of Somerset, closed the door, then stood with his beard pressed into his lace collar, staring at his daughter in a man's arms. For a long minute he did not speak and none dared move ; even Will in his surprise felt unable to release his beloved burden, while the man with bowed back and his hair cropped in ancient style stood in the shadows.

Suddenly, abruptly, the earl moved, sighing. He padded forward, the light from the many windows flickering multi-coloured over him and turning one eye for a moment into a blazing jewel before he stepped again into the shadows. The women crouched within their skirts, curtseying, while Will let Anne go and she almost fell but managed to keep her feet, hands on her bosom.

Tall was the duke and although grey-bearded, his face wrinkled, it could be seen that once he had been beautiful. A few gold hairs glistened amongst the grey and his blue eyes were bright, undimmed by the years, and when they looked at Will the lad felt weak and humble as though he stood before a king, so majestic was the man's mien and walk. Dressed in black from toe to shoulders, save for the narrow white ruff about his throat and the white lace at his wrists, Somerset seemed a solid ghost with marble head in which only the eyes flickered alive ; and in his walk there was an easy grace that proved him to be one long used to command and to have those commands immediately obeyed. So softly did he step that he made no sound, his velvet body vanishing into shadows to show only the marble head with gleaming eyes, that he seemed a ghost until he spoke in a harsh voice difficult at first to understand because it was long unused and had a Scottish sharpness.

" Who are you ? " he demanded, staring into Will's eyes. " What would you do with my daughter that you steal to her here like a thief ? "

" I am no thief," cried Will, " unless it be theft to lose

one's heart and to wish to marry honestly ; and I am of gentle birth, my lord. You need fear no disparagement. . . ."

"What is your name ? " asked the earl in a high-pitched crackling voice, still staring with never a blink into Will's eyes.

"I am William Lord Russell, my lord," said Will ; and before he could speak further, he caught his breath to see the earl stagger and blink and raise his hands as though to ward him off.

"A Russell, a Russell, a Russell ! " cried the earl ; and at each repetition of the name his voice skirled into a squeak of fury. "Get you out of here, you liar ! " he cried. "Get you gone before I have you beaten, bobbed and kicked ! Out of this house, liar and villain, that you must cloak yourself with that dog's name and think to fang my daughter from me ! Lord Jesus, this, this . . . Nay, it's not true ! Or have you come to try me. Have you, fellow ? Or is this Villiers' doing ? Out of the grave. Can the bitch bite his way back to taunt me ? Even beyond hell to send you here ? Or is it the king's unkingly doing to mock me when he has me crazed under his royal revenge ? Is he not satisfied that he would steal my reason with my money—if I have reason yet and am not mad, Sirius-mad, barking at a moon ? Russell did you say, sirrah ? Russell would be older now and yet, by God, you are his own damned butter-print with the same sniff of virtue in the nostrils and his obstinate eyes. Can it be that you . . . ? Nay, never. You are not Russell's son ? "

"My father is the Earl of Bedford," whispered Will, trying to speak calmly, but this madness in a man who at first had appeared sane scattered his own wits so that had not Anne been near he would have turned coward and fled as from a ghost.

Trembling, the earl moved away and walked a few paces. Then he sprang round and glared at Will as though he had expected to find that the lad had vanished, a demon, on the turning of his back.

" Still here ? " he whispered and licked his lips. " I live so much alone and there are so many ghosts, friendly and otherwise, how can I tell which men be real ? But Bedford's son . . . for Bedford's son to steal my daughter ! This would be a rare jest were it true ; but such things do not happen, therefore I know it for a trick. Yea, a trick . . . and yet . . . Boy, what does your father say of this ? "

" I . . . I have not told him yet, my lord."

Slapping his thighs, the earl roared. He laughed until he had to lean against a chair, then slowly he slid on to the seat. His was no merry laughter but a shrill cackling unpleasant to hear, and Will shivered at the sound, no longer questioning that the man was mad. Was this the secret troubling Nan ? Why, it was so small a matter that almost he could have joined in her father's laughter, his relief being great. The earl was mad and that was why he was kept away from court ; and that was why no suitor had taken Nan, she being a madman's daughter. Will turned and saw her white-faced, trembling, leaning against the tapestry at his side, and he put out his hand, took one of hers and clasped it. Lifeless it seemed, and ice-cold, and he noticed that she scarcely appeared to breathe and that her blue eyes were distended in their lids and were expressionless, like glass.

" My love," he whispered.

Low he whispered yet the earl heard him and abruptly his laughter ceased. Into the coloured light from a window he screwed his head and appeared to be listening, leaning to one side, but his bright glance rested unblinkingly on Will, the beard twisted by a mocking grin.

" Boy," he said, " come here. Into the light."

Dropping Anne's cold hand, Will stepped forward, trying to calm his fast-beating heart, and stood before the old man. Now that he saw him closer, he was surprised to find that although the hair was grey with a few golden threads and the brow wrinkled, the earl did not look old. His skin was soft and rosy as a boy's, although dirty, and his blue eyes were clear ; it was as though a youth masqueraded in wig and false beard, and his voice, too, was young as though not fully broken into manhood, not retaining the one pitch but running suddenly into high notes, then without warning dropping into gruffness.

" Yea," said the earl after staring long and intently into Will's eyes, " you are Bedford's brat. The same smirk, the same air of virtue to cover craft and greed, envy and wickedness. Now, boy ! No lying. I may live here now alone without splendour, but once, by God's heart, I was the greatest in Britain and all cringed before me. Perhaps you know that though. Of course you know it ; my name must yet ring somewhat in the world to have a lecher sneaking behind my back to smouch my daughter. Is she not fair, my child, eh, boy ? Has she not an uncommon beauty and a mien that makes her more than woman, being the child of one who had no peer for beauty and who was so loved by a king that he had merely to flick his fingers, like that ! to have a thousand golden coffers opened ? And her mother . . ." The pointed beard twisted as though with a spasm of disgust or pain and the high-pitched Scottish voice grew rasping. " Whatever might be said about her mother," he growled slowly as though rolling the words through his broken teeth, " she had loveliness enough on her outside to send men mad, yea, sufficient to win a prince who until then had shown himself a monk amongst the ladies, to have him crawling to finger her skirt-hem ; and she had me, too. Think you then to sneak here mouse-hunting the daughter of such a goddess ? And I warn you. Anne will have no dowry worthy of her form and lineage, her parents having been misfortunate, the victims of a coxcomb's envy, of a snot-bred lout who won his place in the king's lap by sorcery, I doubt not, acting Ganymede that he might spit a love-potion into the royal cup, a clown in scarlet whose name will stink in histories for ever ! . . . May God bless Felton who cut down the dog! . . . Ah ! I talk treason, but that's an outcast's privilege. What should I talk save treason ? That is why they keep me here, outlawed, because they Fear me. Even though the fleering Buckingham be gone to hell, men Fear Me yet. There-fore must I stay here, alone . . ."

The harsh voice with its sing-song note, its drawling vowels, ceased on a snarl as the earl gripped his beard, and Will saw that his hands had plainly not been washed for years, being black between the rings. Yet his beard was perfumed.

"I'll not speak of it ! " howled the earl suddenly. "All can be left to that liar history to record, for I am history. But you would breed other history, you two together, would you not ? You, boy, indenizing a Russell to a Carr, smouching my daughter in the dark . . ." His voice sank to a husky tenderness as he turned to Anne crouching against the tapestry. "My child," he coaxed her, "my golden daughter, come to me. You do not fear your father, do you, bantling ? By God's blood, girl, I love you beyond rubies. I could not say how much I love you if I knew a hundred tongues. For I am damned and lost without you, a husk of history drained of life, grimacing at a mirror of the past when I and my world were young ; but you are future, bone of my bone, flesh of my flesh. You are me, Anne, and only that I might guard and love you, shielding you, have I kept living. Otherwise, like her, I'd mayhap have let the rats in my belly gnaw me to my grave. Ah ! would that I had died, for what is life but memories and memories mean regrets ? . . . But all that is dead, forgotten, while you're alive and a woman, too . . . Come, tell me, Anne, do you love this fool here ? "

Trembling so that she could barely stand, Anne whispered, " Yea, father, with all my heart."

" Do you know," said the earl, " that he is son of my most merciless enemy yet living ? That this accursed life, nay ! living death to which I am condemned was wrought on me by him and others of his kidney fawning on Buckingham ? Do you know that of all men living few do I hate as I hate that fellow's father who conspired and lied to ruin me and would kill me now if he could ? He slavered on my tracks and licked up poison to destroy me, lies, all of them lies, and he knew it. Yet all the time he spanieled on me. Such is this boy's father. Yet you would marry him ? "

" I . . . I love him, sir. What his father did, I know not."

" Do you think he loves you ? Or can it be chance that he is Bedford's son ? That of all men in this land he should seek you out ! Can that be chance ? Or devilment ? Or God's work ? " He paused and pursed his lips, repeating with an air of wonder : " God's work ? Strange are His ways beyond our petty understandings, and would it not be heaven's justice for Bedford's boy to love Somerset's bairn ? I thought there was no justice left, having in innocence suffered for the guilty, but now . . . Who is to tell if this be not God's holy work ? "

Back in the chair he lounged, pointing his grizzled beard towards the beams, his eyes open as though he watched and listened to unseen familiars, while his hands drummed softly on the chair-arms. No one dared speak. Crouching together, Anne's women held their breath and tried to slink within their clothes ; Anne leaned against the musty-smelling tapestry, panting and terrified lest Will be outraged by her father's daft talk and spurn her ; while Will stood with bowed head, narrowly watching the madman, although enraged at these insults at his father, one hand on his silver sword-hilt.

"Well," said Somerset slowly, "it may be so and who am I to gainsay heaven's doings? Who am I to say nay when lovers meet, although my heart would break to lose her? Then will be I utterly alone, abandoned, daughterless, unloved. Ah, me! Nay! not alone! With voices yet about me, may Satan damn them into hell! Such is man's fate, to know glory and to atone for pride. And I'll not hurt my poor motherless bairn should she crave love like other wenches. May God forgive me, how could I who suffered so for love withstand it now whatever guise it wears, even the visage of a Bedford? Yet can I trust you, boy? How did you smell me out, eh? How did you discover my unhappy bairn? This love of yours could not have broken suddenly at a blow of her eyes from a window. You have huggled in sin together, no doubt, she being her mother's child . . ." and again that abrupt spasm twisted his beard and wrinkled one eye. "The young are wicked," he groaned, "not foreseeing the future and are reckless even of nine months' watching of the hour-glass, the best with the worst of them, hot-blooded and venerial. But if you've harmed my bairn's name, boy, with my own hands I'll strangle you, though they hang me for it."

"My love, sir," said Will with dignity, choking on his anger, "is honourable and has kept alight these nine long years, it being three or four years before that when first we met. We were younglings then, my lord, and my home was nearby. One day I climbed your wall, and thus we met and loved and swore our troth. The plague drove nigh and my father left for Welbeck, taking me and his family with him, but in secret Anne and I corresponded and when I could I came to London and visited her, meeting her in the garden, until my father

sent me abroad to study and to visit foreign courts. By
that, I do believe, he thought to cure me of my love
which he suspected. He questioned me about it and I
doubt not, servants had spied on us and squeaked of it.
Therefore he sent me off. Yesterday I returned and
today I rode here to redeem my troth. That is all, my
lord : before God, I speak truth."

" Is it so, my child ? " asked Somerset, turning to
Anne.

" Yes," Anne whispered.

" And you would be fool enough to wed this fool ?
Well, I'll not say you nay, but . . . One moment !
My poor blessing you may have for what it's worth, but
will you get your father's, boy ? "

" With or without it, I will marry Anne," said Will.

" Bravo ! " jeered Somerset, yet there was joy in his
eyes. " It seems I've wronged you, lad. Go to it !
Ask your father, ask him, yea. But I must have your
word, should he forbid it, that you'll not come snooving
here to rob me of my daughter. She's an earl's bairn
and her mother was a Howard ; she's no chance
trullibub to shake sheets with any lout that whistles, even
though he be the Earl of Bedford's eldest son. If you
would have the girl, you must marry her, else you can
mowl like a cat and I'll shoot you should you touch her
skirt-hem ; d'ye understand me ? "

" I am a man of honour, my lord . . ."

" Honour honour honour ! " shrilled the earl, and
spat. " I mislike such words. I have lived too long at
court to trust a word like honour. 'Tis lisped by every
whore who locks the bedroom on herself and lover ;
'tis the password to a courtier's treachery. When man
or woman prates to me of honour I conceal my purse
and dare not turn my back lest I be stabbed. I'll not
heed your gab but I'll take care after my fashion that
you act honourably for all that your blood be hot and
you a Bedford. From now, you'll never see my bairn

alone, not till the priest has said *Go to it*. So get you gone and return only if your father says you may." He laughed. "'Twould be a jape indeed," he groaned, "were she any man's daughter but mine own, for it's not good to see a girl's heart broken as hers must break ; he'll never marry you, my child."

"Before God, sir, I swear I will !"

"Why won't he marry me ?" Her terror of her father Anne conquered in her eagerness to learn the secret. Towards him, pleadingly, she stepped. "I am no longer a child, sir," she said. "Pray look on me and note that I'm a woman, and I must know why, why, why I am different from other girls ? Why do my women say I'll never marry ? Why do you say it, too ? Am I not made of flesh and bone and am I not healthy and honest in my ways ? I have done no ill, please God, and cannot understand why I alone of women must be set aside and have no husband. Why ? Father, you must tell me. Why ? "

"Your belamour shall tell you," muttered Somerset, nodding towards Will.

"He knows no more than I," she cried : "or little more, he's lived so long abroad." She stumbled towards him, blind with tears, while Somerset cocked his head, looking at her but not seeming to listen. "I have been so long alone with fears," she sobbed, "that I can bear it no longer. Ever since I can remember I have been alone. I have had my women to wash and dress me, but never a confidante, no one to whom I could open my heart. Even you, father, father . . . O, God, I don't, I couldn't doubt your love, but I've been always watched and felt myself mistrusted. Silence ever about me, and old folk. And it will drive me mad. I am going mad now ! Only Will's love has kept me sane through these years and given me the strength to live ; and now this Secret holds us apart as it's held me from others. Please, father, you must tell me what it is."

At her father's feet she fell while he looked down into her face until that spasm again twisted his beard and from head to feet he shuddered ; then, hands gripped in her yellow hair, he pushed back her head and stared into her eyes.

"So like," he murmured, "yet so different. Can similar visages hide such contrary souls or is there no truth in physiognomy ? You have her eyes, my child, her shape, her nose, her hair, her lips, yet are not her, may God be praised. Pray God that that be so ! That you are different-souled and not dangerous like her with her beauty and her cunning. Tell me, daughter," he whispered, leaning down until his mouth was almost upon Anne's while hungrily he glared into her eyes, "hide nothing from your dad : Have you behind that white visage secret and abominable desires ? Do you suffer such passions and hankerings that you would kill were they to stay unsatisfied ? If I told you that you could not marry this lad, would you pluck the purple nightshade and squeeze it into my glass and, while I lay sick, would you fawn about me and smooth my brow and feed me pap in which was stirred henbane, vitriol, aqua fortis, powdered diamonds, arsenic, cantharides and such witch's broth ? What man can read the souls of these lovely devils with bodies soft to house hard hearts and lusts and wickedness beyond our dreaming ? You are her daughter as well as mine. You have her beauty ; and mine, too. You are both of us, yet neither of us, so seeming fair, so fond, so kind, and yet . . . you are a woman and I have cause enough to fear all women."

"Tell me," Anne sobbed, staring back into his eyes and gripping both his knees, "you must tell me everything."

"There is nothing to tell." He pushed her hands away and spurned her with his knees. "The world will chatter if you ask it, but not I. What use my lonely voice of truth against the clamour of lies from which through the years I've tried to shield you? Boy, look long on her for you will look your last . . . I, too, was a lover once though now I'm old and grey. There were few lovers like to me who, for a harlot-Helen, burnt more than Troy, by God! And I can remember enough of what it is to love to leave you here alone a while, with only her women to watch that you do not sin. So kiss her and begone. Get you back into that busy world from which I'm banished, ferret the truth if truth can still be found ; then, if your virtuous father permits, come back to her and claim your bride. But should you think to steal what he forbids you to marry, you will die, for only by honest marriage can you have her."

" Father," cried Anne, " will you not tell me the truth even now ! "

" Let him tell you," said Somerset, " if he should come back."

As though with those words he forgot to whom he talked, he stood to his feet, pushing Anne aside, and walked swiftly to the door. His head was up and his step jaunty, but once that door had closed behind him and he found himself alone at the stair-head, Somerset stood stone-still as he clutched the carved rail, suddenly feeling old with a bent spine. Thus for many minutes he remained, unmoving until he sobbed ; then on slow feet, stiffly as though his legs were brittle and he were blind, he stumbled down the stairs and entered his own apartments.

Into his study he walked until he kicked a chair, then he drew it to him in the twilight and sat down.

" Frankie," he whispered ; " Tom Overbury . . ." he said, and his beard twisted up while his eyes wrinkled, " . . . and damned Buckingham," he growled and, leaning his head on his arms on the table, he lay, weeping. Nor did he move when from the night outside he heard the sound of a horse stamping and the jingle of its bridle and young Russell's strong voice cry confidently : " Have strong heart, beloved, for I'll be back. By God's dear body, I'll be back for you."

Then did Somerset laugh, choking on sobs, as he lifted his head to grimace while he spat into the shadows crawling towards his feet.

" He will come back ! " he jeered. " Dear God, have I not suffered enough that You would drive my child into my hell ? Why should she suffer, too, to wait and wait and wait alone, . . . like me, for death ? "

CHAPTER II

Dark Homecoming

AFTER Somerset's Chiswick manor shadowed by hatreds, regrets and despairs, Woburn Abbey seemed gay to Will when he rode home ; bright with light it seemed, although the sky was leaden and rain fell softly ; and he would have been content, eager to work with his father, had he not been haunted by the memory of that white-bearded man with youthful face and filthy hands cackling at him while Anne had knelt at the fellow's feet, imploring him to reveal that secret which tormented her. Now was Will also tormented by the thought of that secret although determined somehow to unlock it from its Pandora-box that he might possess the girl he had loved since boyhood. That, when discovered, this secret might prove terrible enough to shatter his dreams and to drive him in horror from Anne he could not believe. There was nothing on earth or beyond it, he swore, which could kill his love which possessed him wholly. To live without Anne was an impossible thought : therefore, being a serious, resolute youth incapable of accepting defeat, Will never considered such a possibility, save to dismiss it. He would marry Anne if he had to wait fifty years for her. He would marry her even should his parents curse and disinherit him ; he would marry her even though her father were a lunatic and her late mother had been wanton. Parents were creatures to be revered yet often scorned. They lived in a dying world that could have no conception of youth's passions and tendernesses ; money and power alone were able to excite them and it was impossible to believe that such people had ever been young. This exhilarating world of adventure in which he lived could not, he felt, have been the same before his birth. Girls then had never been so beautiful nor men so wise and courageous. They could not have sung songs nor written poetry nor fed on dreams of beauty day and night, eating, drinking, breathing the loved one, meeting her in dreams, meeting her on waking, seeing her, a ghost more real than the dull fools around one, wherever one turned, wherever one looked. Anne. Anne was in those wet trees shaped sensuously, a dryad smiling at him ; Anne was that pool in the garden and she was those chubby clouds ; she whispered to him in the gentle rain. Unforgotten, unforgettable, Anne never left him, and while he talked or walked or ate and behaved as though he were normal, he was not really listening to what was said and only dully noted what others did because with inner eyes he was watching Anne and rediscovering her beauties, revealed and unrevealed, until there was no inch of her from crown to toes that he had not explored and found desirable.

Over Woburn his father escorted him, showing him what had been altered or built while he had been abroad. At that time it had not been finished and the manor had been noisy from dawn till dusk, the workmen singing while they worked amongst their pulleys and cradles and puddles of water and mounds of bricks. Now was the place completed and the earl was like a boy again in his pride and joy at showing his eldest son this home he would in time inherit.

" For you, my lad," he said, squeezing Will's shoulder, " for you and your bride when you wed—we must speak of that anon—have I built this home for your children and your children's children, for Russells down the centuries."

Then before Will could blurt out his confession, his father rattled on about further improvements he intended to make and talked gravely of the Italian designs he had discussed with Inigo Jones. Unsmiling, seeming in his gravity the elder of the two, Will sighed and held his peace while being hurried into the gardens to admire the herbs, the triangular-shaped flower-beds scrolled within pebbled walks, the domed fountain, the sundial—and at it the earl squinted, one eye on the hidden sun and the other on the dial, while he muttered about the speed of time. But not again did the opportunity come to Will to mention Anne and marriage.

Even into those rooms he remembered so well, his father conducted him, pointing out old beauties of which Will had wearied years ago. As though he were a stranger, he had to gape into the great hall and to peep into the eating-parlour and the smaller parlour opening from it ; he had to mount the stairs to see again the five state rooms overlooking the park which now was misted under rain, and he had to twist his neck to admire the golden stars painted against a purple sky of the Star Chamber's ceiling, a room of which his father was particularly proud and into which he admitted none but most important guests. Indeed, all this west wing, the more ornate and luxuriously furnished part of the manor, was rarely seen by the family. It was kept locked as a man might lock away a mistress he fears to show lest she be ravished.

In the north wing the family lived in bleak apartments which even forests thrown to burn on the hearth could never have warmed. But here was the earl's darling, his grotto, a room so chilly that within the minute of entering it one froze. Nothing, however, it seemed could freeze the earl in his enthusiasm. If the west wing were his haughty mistress, imperious and rarely visited and then only with gifts, this grotto was his favourite wench who liked cheap toys, being common and easily satisfied. Almost entirely covered were the walls with gleaming shells arranged in different shapes, the design unfolding here and there into intricate figures and stalagmitic forms. The furniture was gilt and far from comfortable. And here, as though he would welcome all admirers into his mistress, the earl disdained to hide her behind either doors or windows so that all might enter, the north wind with them, through a three-arched loggia in front of the garden.

Footsore yet uncomplaining, Will attended his father into each of the ninety rooms of the house. Even into his parents' sacred bedchamber he was taken, and into servants' rooms, his brothers' and sisters' rooms ; and at times he felt uncomfortable as though by chance he had stumbled on a woman at her toilet, the beds being often unmade, garments tossed to the floor or lying with a disconsolate and sullen air over stools and boxes, the pots unemptied, and washing-water yet in basins and scummed with grease and ringlets. Such things his father did not appear to notice or, if he did, he dismissed them with a wrinkling nose and a wave of the hand. But warmer than the wood he touched, more friendly than the furniture, the presence of those who lived in these rooms was to Will, and he felt as though their outraged spirits rebuked him while imploring his tolerance when he glanced at disarray or dirt which strangers should never have seen.

Into the heat of the kitchens was he taken to meet the greasy cooks polite although inimical, and the smut-faced kitchen-boys at the jacks gaping at him ; and all the while, no matter whither his feet led him and on what his eyes looked, Will walked with Anne and sighed for the opportunity to break the tidings of his love to this garrulous parent. That opportunity, it seemed, would never come while he had to sniff the cooking foods and even to be taken to the lowlier servants' quarters, the vast hall for men and the other for women.

" I'll have no mingling of the sexes," growled the earl ; and with trepidation, Will noticed the puritanical set of his father's lips under the greying moustache. " They sup apart and work apart as I pray they sleep apart," said his father, "and should I note any immodesty, there's an end on it. Out they go, no matter their length of service. 'Tis a wicked age, my son, and daily it grows wickeder. But I'll have no sinning at Woburn. An abbey stood here once and as those monks lived—or should have lived according to their profession—so must my servants live. Sinless."

Before the portraits in the hall to which they returned Will would have liked to linger, but his father loved the building more than the paintings and he shrugged them aside. There in his frame Will saw himself stand as he had been fifteen years before, at the age of six, and he found it difficult to believe that that boy in the pink robes of the Bath, the badge of the Order around his neck, was himself as once he had been. A foreigner had painted it, a spitting fellow quizzing him from behind the canvas and chattering to himself as he worked, while Will had stood in misery, mourning the sunlit sport he missed at having thus to remain indoors. There to this day he remained on the wall, with moping eyes, his long-feathered hat in his hand, his gloved left hand on his sword . . . Thus had he looked while he had dreamed of Anne . . . as he yet dreamed of her, only now with a man's desire for her possession.

And possess her he would. Somehow he must quiet this tall, talkative father with the thin mouth, must catch him in a tender mood—if he ever had such moods—and beg his blessing. He would roar, no doubt ; but in his roaring he would be certain to reveal the secret that had sent Somerset into rustication and had kept Anne from the corruption of the world. Even his fear of his father's wrath could not stifle Will's curiosity, yet he shivered at the thought of what the old man might say and do, not doubting after what Somerset had said that he could expect no calm acceptance of Anne as a daughter. But Will had inherited his father's stubbornness and courage, therefore he could not doubt his final

27

success if only he could find some way of entering the old man's heart through that exterior of forbidding virtue. Only the plump white and brown-splashed spaniel gave him hope of winning, for when the dog, trotting ever at its master's heels, looked up with melancholy eyes, the earl would fondle it and his long face would soften, the heavily pouched eyes losing their indrawn sharpness, their icy suspicion, and lightening into tenderness.

Almost did Will tell his mother first because it seemed she knew about his love or, at least, suspected it. In the evening, while his father talked, growling at the state of the nation as he sipped his watered wine or, with sudden change of mood, expatiating on further beauties to be added to his mansion, Will could sense his mother watching him with troubled eyes of sympathy. His impulse was to confide in her but his pride held his tongue. That would have been a boy's act, to go to his mother, as though he had stolen comfits and feared a flogging ; he was a man now and would discuss the matter with his father as with an equal. Love his mother though he did, that plump, faded lady who had yet a girl's shy movements, he could not consider her, a woman, as being fit for masculine confessions. Yet it was evident that she wooed him to confess, leaving sentences half-uttered while waiting with an air of gentle expectancy when she fell silent, her head to one side like that of the little yellow bird she always carried with her, perching it on her shoulder when she sat or bearing it on her finger when she stood up.

"You must marry soon, my son," she said coaxingly one day. "Your father and I have talked of it often and now that you're a man and your brothers and sisters are grown up, or nearly grown up, we'd like some more babies in the manor."

"I intend to marry," said Will harshly, annoyed that she and not he had first mentioned the precious subject.

" Of course, of course you intend to marry," chirruped his mother eagerly. " Perhaps you've already set your heart . . . No ? Well, there's that sweet little Elizabeth Cecil now. She'd make a bonny mother and is ripe for marriage. I'd like her for a daughter, indeed I would." Then, seeing her son flinch, the skin seeming to tighten over his bones, she added quickly : " Or Lady Dorothy Sidney . . . you remember Dorothy ? "

" I am told," growled Will, " that the Lady Dorothy and that poet—what's his name ? Waller—do more that sing together in the dark, whatever else they might do in the daylight."

" O, fie ! " squealed his mother, " you must never say such things ! O, the wickedness of people to say such things and she so good and modest a girl and she but nineteen, too ! As if any girl of nineteen . . . You don't understand girls, my son. Nineteen ! And you can listen to such abominable tales because, and it's natural when one's young, she likes to have poems read to her."

Will snorted a laugh. " You can't read poems in the dark," he said and, with a curt bow, fled from further questioning and probing, feeling in truth ashamed of what he had said, the Lady Dorothy being, for all he knew, as virtuous as his sisters . . . but then, he groaned, he scarcely knew his sisters. . . .

They were younger than he ; therefore he treated them with amused tolerance, but now, his eyes sharpened by love, he watched them with new interest, noticing when they blushed and trying to overhear their whispering and becoming angry at their continual giggling, and he wondered : Did they, too, love ? Was it possible that lads stole into this garden, as when a boy he had stolen into a Chiswick garden, to kiss and huggle such hoydens ? Impossible. They had not Anne's gravity, for all that they were womanly as their bosoms proved, and plainly they had no interest in anything save sewing and dances and clothes. With his brothers also he could find no companionship, their minds being set on sport or study, things he had outgrown since love obsessed him and made all else seem petty, childlike. To none of these could he unpack his heart and confess the trouble darkening his days, making the tick of the clock at times unbearably monotonous, fretting in his blood as if demanding that he loiter at Woburn no longer, his beloved waiting for him in that haunted house in Chiswick with a mad father hooting laughter at her.

Yet days and sleepless nights passed and Will could never find a propitious moment until, unable to bear the torment longer, he turned one evening to his father when they were alone in the withdrawing-room, and said :

" Sir, may I . . . will you . . . I . . . I've something important to tell you."

" What is it, my son ? " asked the earl quietly, laying down his pen and with both hands pressing flat the pages of the account-book on the table before him.

Then to his horror, panic drove Will's wits away. He gaped, the blood burning his cheeks, and no words issued from his lolling tongue. As though he had become again a boy waiting to be beaten, he cursed himself for having spoken and wished that he were out of the room and running through the park. As loud as the clock sounded to him the ticking of his heart, while the snapping of the fire was like the crackle of approaching thunder.

" I am waiting," said his father.

" I . . . I . . . I want to get married, sir," gasped Will, and set his teeth, his body hot under the clothes.

" A very laudable desire," said the earl. " Young men should marry early to keep them from temptation that might lead to sin. I am glad to see you have grown into a serious man, my son, and are no coxcomb like many youths. I had feared, I confess it now, that while abroad you might had learned the vices of the age, the levity which takes no heed of holy matters and can see no woman but, like Satan himself, must long at once to ruin her. I speak no evil of our king who, in his honest living with our queen, shows an example the kingdom might well follow, now that his evil ghost and prompter, the Duke of Buckingham, lies dead ; but at his court lounge fellows who think of little but frivolity. They drink and gamble, dance and wench, make songs and seek debauchery. I've heard them, I've seen them, and such an age of wickedness cannot long continue . . . But we'll not talk of politics. I can only say that I am most happy to note your serious intentions and I'll not hide from you that your mother and I have often spoken together of your marrying. There are two ladies who appear to us worthy of such an honour, being young, virtuous, wealthy and well-born. One of them was indeed suggested to us by her mother, the Countess of Leicester. I refer of course to Lady Dorothy Sidney ; and although we would welcome her gladly as a daughter, your wife, our preference lies more with the Lady Elizabeth Cecil. But we'd not press you. The choice is yours to make, my son. . . ."

"No, no, sir," stuttered Will, "I have liking for neither of those ladies who doubtless are all you say. There is another . . ."

"Who ? " asked the earl in a flat voice.

Will swayed on his chair, his jaw seeming fixed in its hinges so that it would not open, while desperately he sought for inspiration in the hangings and paintings on the wall, at the carpet at his feet, at the wine on the table, and at the fire in the grate. Then, in a choking voice, he mumbled :

"The Lady Anne Carr, sir, I . . . I . . ."

Before the ice of his father's eyes, his voice stumbled into silence and, sighing, he sat back, his courage gradually returning now that he had spoken. The long silence that followed did not fret but rather pleased him, giving him time in which to become calm and resolute, for he knew now that a quarrel must break out.

"Whom did you say?" asked his father coldly.

"The Lady Anne Carr," said Will firmly, defying him with a glance.

"At first I could not believe I had heard aright," murmured the earl, sitting very erect. "I knew that when you were younger and even a greater fool, that you hankered after some such wench, but I had believed and prayed that the fantasy had been set aside with other childish toys. You are no longer a boy, but are a man with a man's responsibilities. Yet I'll be patient with you, because you must understand that such a marriage is impossible, utterly impossible. . . ."

"I am going to marry her," said Will.

"I repeat: it is impossible," cried the earl, his voice rising. "We will not even talk of it. You had better go, my boy, because I'll not talk to you until you have reconsidered your . . . your insanity. You have my permission to depart; and when you have thought better of this fantastic idea of yours I will listen to you. But not before."

"Then," said Will, "you will never listen to me because I am going to marry Anne Carr."

"Even though I forbid it?"

"Even though you forbid it, sir."

Sick with horror, trembling at this defiance of his authority, the lean learl, who had carefully trained his features to conceal his feelings, strove to remain calm, but his impatience with this young fool and his fantasy made him shake and it burned his cheeks with colour.

"You know nothing of the woman," he stuttered at last. "What you felt when a child is not what you should feel now you're a man. Memories are often liars. You've made an idol in your imagination and forgotten that feet stink. It is not a woman but a dream that has gulled you. Should you see the creature again after all these years you'd probably turn from her in amazement. . . ."

" I have seen her again," said Will. " I saw her the day after I reached London. And I swore my troth with her a second time."

The pen snapped in the earl's gnarled fingers. Otherwise he gave no sign that he had heard what his son said, but the colour darkened his cheeks and his eyes glittered.

" That," he said, " was most unfilial of you. You should have ridden straight here, to your father and mother ; instead, you turned aside in hot lust after this hoyden, this witch's egg, for like her mother, doubtless she's a witch and has entrapped you with some hellish art. How else could she have drawn you back after all those years ? She's given you a stinking apple to eat which she's carried under her armpit to soak in her Circe-sweat, or fed you on cockle-bread obscenely kneaded. Her mother was a witch most damnably armoured by Satan with a mask of beauty, a creature of lusts and hatreds to turn men sick. I saw her foul toys produced in court, that ruttish couple shaped in clay, like stallion and mare but man and woman, I saw the devil's babies she had had made in postures . . . O, that such things should be ! . . . No ! you will hear me out, my son. This is witchcraft. I'll have her hanged for it rather than that she should marry you."

" Beauty," cried Will, " is all her witchcraft."

" Poor fool of a boy ! how cunningly she's snared you in a moonlit web for her spidery satisfactions ! cozened you with her spittle or scratched you with an envenomed pen shaped like a phallus ! I know their wanton tricks from which no man is safe without the help of God, Satan being everywhere seeking whom he can devour, silly youths like you tangled in a golden curl or spellbound in a glance. I tell you they were shown in open court, I saw them all, and lightning struck the court, the timbers shook and snapped and people screamed, that the devil's work should be revealed . . ."

" I care not what her mother was or what she did," said Will. " Anne is good and chaste and modest . . ."

" Like mother like daughter, maggoty, bred in a whore, fathered by an ingle turned stallion, a man who'd kill his friend and kiss him while he killed him that he might earn a harlot's commendation. Those were her parents, the vilest of that vile crew that gathered about the late King James and turned his court to Sodom and Gomorrah. None were safe but villains. Poisoning, adultery, murder, blasphemy, drunkenness, all manners of debaucheries there were, naught was too vile but they must experiment in it, dabbling in muck and laughing in the face of God. Yet such a woman, a satyress, and such a man as he, you say, could breed a lily ! "

" Lilies have grown on dung . . ."

" Yea, dung they were, and lilies can stink of death. You'll not marry this witch's spawn. If I have to kill you you'll not marry her. A Carr to wed a Russell ! Carr's evil brat to bed at Woburn, to bear your children, suckle them with her milk of sorcery ! Never ! I tell you : Never ! "

" Yea, yea," shouted Will, " I tell you : Yea ! "

Both men were on their feet, glaring, their love for one another forgotten in their fury. They gasped, spit on their beards, showing their teeth, each the mirror of the other, save for the wrinkles and greyness of the earl.

" No," moaned the earl and clapped his fists against his temples, " this marriage must not be, my son ! Listen to me . . . I, I will be calm. Sit down and hear what I have to tell you, the history of this wench's parentage."

" I'll not listen, I'd not believe you, so puffed with prejudice are you. You hate her father and therefore hate his child . . . O, God, forgive me, father, that I speak with disrespect, but all my future, all my hope of happiness, my very life itself, rests on my love for Anne and I could never give her up, never, even for you. Tell me that her father has been a murderer and her mother a punk and I'll yet whistle and go seek her, for what care I for them ? "

" Worse than a punk," moaned his father, " worse than a murderer."

" I snap my fingers at your tales."

" No, son, listen . . . If you'll not heed me, your own father, there are others to advise you. You've not far to seek to find the truth, the whole world rings with their infamy, books were printed and ballads made about their evil living . . . By God ! why do I sit here and plead with you, insolent, disobedient boy ! Get you out of here, get you from my sight, that you should beard your father thus with that whore's name ! "

" Whore or no, I marry Anne."

" I'll kill you first ! " roared the earl.

Will wrenched open his doublet, snapping the coral buttons to bare his pink satin shirt, and stood erect.

" Stab for the heart," he cried, " else you'll not kill my love."

Gasping, the earl sank back into his chair and his teeth chattered while, eyes closed, he gaped towards the ceiling. With horror at thought of parricide, Will feared he was dying and ran to him. Then he saw the wrinkled eyelids flutter to show rims of white, and in the beard the thin lips twitched.

" Wine," croaked the earl, " wine . . ."

But after Will had poured the wine and pressed the glass to his father's lips, the old man would not drink. His eyes opened and the glazed balls rolled to look at his son, and he gasped :

" Get out, get out . . . For the love of God, go ! "

Reluctant to leave him in his seizure, yet fearful of remaining lest his presence work greater harm, Will set the glass back on the table and tiptoed out, gently shutting the door behind him. And at the click of the latch, the old man slowly awoke, his beard waggling as though he talked in silence with himself. Then he took up the glass and tried to drink, but much of the wine shot over his shoulder and some drenched his beard and collar while only a little reached his lips ; and with sudden strength he crushed the glass in his hand and flung the splinters against the wall.

" Never," he muttered, " never . . . I'll not have it, not that creature . . . never . . ."

Slowly he lowered his head to rest it on his open hands and began to pray. Against witchcraft there was no other remedy, and it was evident that this young witch had captured Will. How else could he, God-fearing, ageing, passionate yet staid, believe that so good a lad could possibly defy his father and sell his soul merely for a young girl's love and her golden hair ?

CHAPTER III

Mothers Have Also Been Young

WHEN the countess hurried into her eldest son's bed-chamber, she entered with anger on her tongue, but when she saw him lying face down on his bed, his arms outflung and fists clenched, her anger at his rebellion fled before pity for her child. The earl's shaken state was forgotten in sorrow for her son, and she stood in the doorway uncertain whether to enter or retreat. Fear of being repulsed made her pause, else she'd have run to comfort him, but since his return from the continent, Will had withdrawn from her inside himself and his cold reserve frightened her as she had believed only a taciturn lover could frighten a woman with dread of his thoughts. Hiding himself from her, alert to frustrate her love and sympathy, he had become a stranger, a creature of moods ruled by some dark planet. Then when she had found her husband flushed and choking, gibbering with fury, threatening disinheritance while muttering of whores and witchcraft, her irritation with the lad had flamed to anger and she had raced upstairs, prepared to shame him out of his unfilial behaviour. Only to find him thus, outstretched, sobbing into his pillow, no longer a haughty man but a boy in need of comforting.

Softly she closed the door and tiptoed into the room, then stood looking down at him, tears in her eyes. This chamber had she tended with such fond care, allowing no servant to enter, while he had been abroad, and heedlessly he had tramped into it, tossing his mail and kicking it under the bed ; unhitching his travelling-cloak, he had let it drop to the floor and had not glanced once

37

at the flowers she had plucked to welcome him, or at his swords and pistols she had kept polished on the walls, or at the gay curtains her own hands had embroidered in green and red, his favourite colours. Surly, ungrateful, he had pecked her with a casual kiss, such as he might have given a strange woman, never even looking into his eyes to see the love shining there ; but now she understood his behaviour. . . . He was bewitched by a wanton and therefore he needed her.

"My son," she whispered tremulously and knelt beside the bed, "tell me, what is it that troubles you ? It breaks my heart to hear you weep ; and what have you said to your poor father to make him so unhappy and angry ? Tell your mother. Never fear to tell me anything, my darling, but do not break my heart with silence. No matter what you've done or what you ever do, let me share it with you ; I'd not upbraid you, so tell me, please, my son."

He lifted his head and looked at her, his cheeks glistening, his beard damp.

"I have done nothing," he growled, "nothing but what man and maid have done since Adam lost a rib. I am in love, mother : is that a sin ? To love a girl pure and nobly born who loves me, too ? Yet father cursed me and abused her whom he's never seen ; and her father cursed my father, yet he was kind, he carried no malice and blessed us and told us we could wed if father'd let us. And by heaven, we will wed ! I care not how the world might smirk and even though father and you, my sisters and brother, hate and despise me for it, I will marry Anne ! "

"Why shouldn't you marry Anne ? " she asked.

"Why ? " he gaped at her, bewildered. "You . . . you're not against us, too ? " he whispered.

"I against you ! " she sighed. "You jest, my son, but 'tis a jest that hurts. Why should I be against you when all I want's your happiness ? Should she be a girl from the Exchange or an innkeeper's daughter, I'd not say you nay if you were happy in her company."

"Then you don't know who she is?" Defiantly throwing back his head and staring into her eyes, he cried: "She is Anne Carr, mother, the Earl of Somerset's child."

He saw her flinch and bite her lip, yet she maintained her stiff-lipped smile although her cheeks paled under the paint.

"Is she pretty?" she asked. "Ah, but of course she is! or my boy'd not love her. And is she good, modest, and kind?"

Incredulously, Will gaped at her, unable to believe that at last he had found one who did not shudder or curse at mention of his love; then, smiling, he clasped his mother's hands and kissed them, and pressed them to his cheeks; and now that he was no longer watching her, the countess dared unguard herself and she swayed, eyes shut, while she murmured a prayer. But when Will looked up, she was smiling fondly, although she wept.

"Tell me," she whispered, "what is she like, this Anne of yours?"

He sighed. "I am no poet, dame," he said, "but when I read poetry I think of her, for she is all the poems that poets ever made. That is what she is to me. Everything that's beautiful. But I'm not apt with words. If you could see her you'd love her, not only for her beauty, but for her goodness, her sweetness. . . . Yet father says we must not marry! There's some secret, something evil in the past, which holds us separate. What is it, mother? You must know. Tell me."

"No," she said, "no. I know nothing."

"You do," he cried, "and I must know."

She twisted from him, to escape his eyes, then she said slowly:

39

"I have been long out of the great world, my son, caring more for my home and family than for the court. Rumours I've heard, of course, the usual gossip, but I was never one to take heed of scandal and no one could believe all the naughtiness one hears. People will tattle, words can be wicked things and they breed further words until a lie once spoken is puffed to something monstrous. Who am I to judge? I wasn't there all the time. I saw nothing, or very little. Only heard about it and dismissed it, although your father swore . . . he was at the trial of course . . . but you mustn't ask me! You must ask him. He was there."

"I'll ask him nothing. He is prejudiced. I am asking you and you must tell me. My love, my very life, depends on knowing."

"Please." Swiftly she stood to her feet and walked away from him, wringing her hands. Then with her back turned, she whispered : "What is it that you want to know?"

"Everything!" he cried.

"But I can't tell everything, I don't know everything. . . ." Suddenly she swung round again to face him, and smiled. "Come," she said, "I'll tell you nothing wicked for I know none of it, nor would I have you hate me afterwards as one who fouled your loved one's mother's memory. But I can tell you merry things ; let the bescumbering be done by others and not I, and you'll hear all the wickedness you want when you go to court, God knows. From me never have you heard any sinful tattle, so I'll speak only of your Anne's mother when she was young and O ! so beautiful."

"She, too, was beautiful?"

"Never was there a woman so lovely." The countess smiled and settled herself on the stool beside the bed while her son sat up and, hugging his knees, leaned against the wall. "Whatever was done afterwards—or said to have been done : God knows the truth of it—none can say she was not beautiful," said the countess, happy to see that her son was smiling. " Yet it was not so much any particular feature, it was all of her. Feature by feature, she was just a woman. Her nose, for example : it was no shapely nose, yet not too fat, nor too thin : it was but a nose, the nostrils slightly heavy and broad that no sweet smells should be lost to it. It was, indeed, a nose which on another woman might have been considered coarse. Fie ! here's the cat in me ! but I'll begin with the lady's defects, or what in others would have been called defects. Item : her nose : a waggish nose, one that curled up in laughter, yet had scorn under its nostrils, and pride and, as I said, coarseness, being sensual. In that nose lay her wickedness, mayhap for it was wide to snuff out lechery, broad-nostrilled that nothing might escape it, a greedy nose, such as one sometimes sees on naughty women and on country-wenches during harvesting when more than the hay tickles under their clothes."

" So much in a nose ! " he laughed, his misery already forgotten at finding his mother so waggish ; and she laughed too, happy in having made him happy. " Go to, dame ! " he mocked her : " you are a soothsayer and should sit in a booth at Bart's Fair and read the maps of clowns at a penny a guess ! "

" And I'd make gold at it, I warrant," she laughed, " faces being beacons from which we should take heed. Ferret-eyes and narrow lips and we have dangerous folk ; hang-dog chaps and we have murderers with tiny ears ; while wenches that gape as though catching flies and have thick nostrils be notoriously wicked : or so I'm told. These are all marks placed by God for the wise to read. I've a book on it somewhere that I must give you. Such noses as Frances Howard's, not ill-shaped so much as unshaped, and strongly marked, here ! where the nostrils curl like a horse's : such are coarse and naught can disgust them while much can tempt them. But I was only a girl when I met her and had not learned such wisdom then. I thought her so beautiful I'd have died to serve her. I worshipped her and sighed when I saw myself in a mirror."

" Was she all nose, this paragon ? " he scoffed. " And even the daintiest of noses, even Anne's, I'd not consider lovely."

" Noses are character," said the countess solemnly. " And Frances's nose had character. But enough of that ! I have shown that she was sensual and in-quisitive, according to this nose of her, a sniffer after sensations. Now we come to Item Two. Her hair. She had an angel's hair like spun gold. Such hair that makes other ladies' look like wire. For hers was living hair and when one ruffled it, it seemed to crackle with sparks, as I've heard tell it did whenever it was brushed. It was not red nor gold nor brown, but all three, changing with the light. And well she knew its beauty and was proud to show it, curling it in folds from her forehead to reveal her ears."

" What of her ears ? What did her ears tell you, mother ? "

" They told me naught, yet they were big enough to overhear a man's heart thump, although not too big, and they were pink, the lobes being dragged down by the heavy jewels she hung from them. Pearls she liked most. Pearls, fat heavy tears they seemed. And that finishes Item Three. Now Item Four : her brows. But she had no brows, it being the fashion to pluck or shave them off. So, Item Five : her forehead. It was high and rounded and unwrinkled and it glowed ! You must have seen such women with skin which seems not skin, being too white, transparent one might say, and so delicate. There is no word to use, for glowing makes one think of heat, and her forehead and chest and bosom were ice, yet they were not ice because they lived

and shone. Ah ! I can't explain, but she was beautiful
and one wanted to touch her all the time to see if she
were real. Nor had she need to paint her veins, like
some women, so delicately violet they were."

" Item Six ! " cried he. " A fig to forehead and
shaven brows ! "

" Her eyes next," sighed the countess. " Here memory
proves indeed a cheat. Strange is it not that eyes which
we love most and trust the most are easily forgotten ?
Or is it that they rarely have one colour but change
like cats' with the hour ? I have seen blue eyes look
black in candlelight and brown eyes twinkle to gold.
Frances's eyes were blue, I think ; they were gay in
strong lids tightened merrily at the corners, and very
large, and always seemed about to laugh at you. In
them lay much of her beauty : in those eyes. I can see
them now."

" Yet know not their colour ! "

" Because they were all colours, starred with laughter.
But now to Item Seven. Her mouth," she laughed,
" and, marry ! 'twas merely a mouth, well-shaped
enough the upperlip, not needing paint to point it,
while the lower was full and pouting and was pressed out a
little. A kissing-gob I heard a man once call it. But
being a woman, how could I tell ? True it was that all
men liked to kiss her and lingered when they should
have but pressed her lips lightly at meeting. There ! I
cannot tell you further. Her throat, for here is Item
Eight, was long but rarely seen, it being the mode those
days for ladies to wear stiff ruffs of starched lace on
wires. These concealed our throat and shoulders."

" Lower, mother. Below the throat ? "

He saw her shiver yet she made pretence to laugh and
to look aside. " Marry ! " she cried with false gaiety,
" would you make a bawd of me, your own poor
mother ! Frankie was a woman and therefore had a
woman's shape, but I'm no poet to sing of it, although

none of us girls could compare with her there . . . But marry ! You will have me blushing although in those days we did not blush, which is strange. One generation will think naught of showing what would shame their mothers ; then the next race of women hide what their mothers revealed and reveal what would have horrified their mothers. Such is our sex's modesty ! In my youth, shoulders and arms and all were hidden, even our throats by the ruff, but below the ruff the gown gaped wide as though we were all, even the younglings, wet-nurses who had forgotten to pin up our bodices, and we were not ashamed. We were proud of it . . . But you have me rambling into wickednesses and forgetting where I was, being lost in my youth . . . Ah, me ! I'll talk no further of it ! "

" Nay," he cried, holding her wrists : " you must continue. You must tell me more. I have this Frances Howard now before me, with her naughty nose and her kissing-gob, her bare bosom and her shaven brows, her rainbow-eyes and with fire for hair. You must tell me how she used these snares for helpless men."

" Little good did she do with them, poor child," sighed the countess, " and little happiness they brought her. She was too beautiful and I think it made her mad. I have been told—it was common bruit at court —that she would sit hour upon hour before her looking-glass. A basilisk, the ladies sneered ; but if so, it was a plump and pretty basilisk, by my fai' ! And she trapped more than herself. There would she sit, exploring all her skin like a soldier planning a battle or a sailor charting a voyage into dangerous waters. And she would practise her wanton wiles—her ladies told me so—pouting and rolling her shoulders and puffing out her bosom and tossing her head to see which way she looked the best. Therefore, my boy, take heed : the flirts and winks and eyelid-fluttering which foolish fellows believe show innocence have oft been learned

with care and practised in a glass, and many a silly man's
been trapped under a lowered eyelid which hid mockery.
But mayhap, only in her mirror could that golden girl
find one worthy of her loving ; and despite all that she
did for love, it was herself at heart she liked the most.
Who can tell ? Vanity, self-adoration, can bring a girl
to her ruin as surely as a man's whispering. I have seen
it happen. The poor wench surrendering to the lover
under her eyelids before a man so much as asks her
leave to kiss her . . . There are many wicked women,
my son. No men can be so wicked, as I pray you
never find . . ."

"No sermons, dame ! Leave the lady's mirror and
tell me what happened when she looked elsewhere."

"Much happened, alas ! " The countess shivered
and looked down at her wrinkled hands in her lap.
" Yet who can blame the lass ? It was not right of God
to have made her so lovely. Her beauty doomed her as
surely as a wound can kill. In the insolence of her
youth she believed herself at first too dear for any man's
possession, yet always her big eyes were open and
sluttish for any handsome gentleman. But she did no
more than look, I swear it, not then ! She liked to show
her power, to have men hungry and unsatisfied. Therefore, to feed her pride with conquests, she could be
shameless and her gown, being often parted to be no
gown on top, was tempting to most men. Yet who can
blame her when she was a wife and yet no wife ? "

"What riddle's this ? " cried he. " A wife and yet
no wife ? "

"Ay, so she was," smiled the countess. " All this, of
course, I only heard, for she was a mere child when she
married, being no more than thirteen, I believe, while
her husband was about fourteen. She was the Duke
of Suffolk's daughter and her husband was Robert
Devereux, the present Earl of Essex, for he is living yet
and should go on his knees to thank God for it."

45

" Why, she'd never have murdered him ! "

" Hush ! don't say such things ! I told you I'd speak only of jollity when she and I were young, before . . . When she was young, and I too ; and hers was a beautiful wedding at Whitehall with a masque specially made for it by Mr. Jonson and Mr. Inigo Jones. But all indeed was a masque, a pretty play with the actors afterwards to disrobe to dress in ordinary garb and part, for although wedded, the couple did not sleep together. They were too young it was pleaded, too young to consider what they did although old enough to consent to the doing of it. Scandal tattled that Frances had wept and kicked and swore she'd have naught to do with the lad who, as he is to this day, was mumpish, serious and with few graces and less words to win a pretty lady, particularly one so vain and head-strong and capricious as his bride. But whoever was the cause of that no-bedding, wicked it was and the breeding of villainy to come, for who can doubt that had Frankie been taken and mastered in her youth, she'd mayhap have been tamed and have learned content at home with babies in her lap ? But that was not to be. The stars had worked a different course for her and had conspired to part husband and wife after the ring was on her hand, but whom the stars used to bring about that parting I cannot say for certain. It could not have been the little earl's doing, for clod though he be, he must have burned for such a wife when he saw her step towards him in her golden hair. Hers was a transcendent beauty full of fire, her form comely beyond most women's and her countenance demure, when she wished it so, sweet and bewitching to melt a dragon's heart with longing. And true he proved it later, her husband loved her. Yet he was a sad lad, unable to forget how his rebellious father, Queen Bess's darling, had lost his head. And as though he feared to lose his own, to this day he seems content to smoke his

46

pipe at home, a stinking custom worthy of such a boor. But we must remember how he suffered and forgive his foul ways. Few who knew Frances well did not suffer for it in the end, God's pity on them all.

" This husband who was no husband was sent abroad to learn soldiering and study—as you went, Will, although, thank God, without a wife at home to ruin you. It was dangerous of him but he had no choice. Dangerous would it be thus to leave any girl who felt herself quit of maidenhood although a maid, even though she had the face of a pie, for who could blame her if she began to believe her marriage had made her free of modesty ? And that court to which Frances came in the glory of her youth and beauty was a monstrously wicked court. You who have seen our present king's court, so quiet, so sober, so tedious, all ceremony and hush hush, can have no conception of his father's times. If it be treason to speak so of the royal dead, I nevertheless say that King James was a wicked man, a nasty man and a drunkard, a creature of forbidden lewderies, a drooling, ugly, mis-shapen beast with a tongue too fat for his gob so that he was ever dribbling into his beard ; and he never washed but at the most dipped his finger-ends in perfumed waters, yet he had a skin as soft as satin, softer than most women's . . ."

" Never washed ! " cried Will, remembering another man who did not wash although his skin was soft as satin.

" No," said she, widening her nostrils with distaste, " the late king never washed and commonly he was so drunk he couldn't stand yet, being a pedant, he would drool on for hours and hours, slobbering while he talked in Scottish-English, his language being so bawdy and blasphemous that it was said that he frightened even himself at times because of what he'd said. He had weak legs, too, so that, even on those rare occasions when he was sober, he must have some man to lean on ; and he would lean on him like the wickedest of women, eyeing him and simpering until one had to look away for very shame. For he loved men beyond the love of men for women and once I heard him say that he wondered not so much that women painted but that men could love them even after they were painted. He was the foulest creature, though a king, and his court was Sodom and Gomorrah over again with no one, it seemed, ever sober, but grave men and little boys both ever tippling and staggering and cursing horribly. We women feared to go there and only went when we could not escape, and then we locked our doors. Should we venture out we were certain to be assaulted or insulted, the men jeering and laughing at us, and trying to tumble us, with never the king to rebuke their impertinence but only to laugh the louder at our tears and blushes.

" I tell this you, my son, that you might know what kind of a court, a bed of corruption, it was to which this young wife who was yet no wife came in the pride of her beauty, a child and woman both, wise beyond her years, although yet innocent, and avid for delights. And this must I say of most of our sex. We have different minds at different ages, each so different that, when one is shed, we are quick to forget it and can become honestly indignant when reminded of it. We are a different person then and feel we can't be blamed for what that other creature who had once been us had done. So easily we forget unpleasant things and the torments and the curiosities of our youth. But watching over your sisters, I've been reminded and at times have feared."

" Nay, dame, never ! Not of such honest girls as they ! "

" They are innocent, praise God," said she, " for I have kept them ignorant ; yet there are stages dangerous to girls and women. And when young, too often they become inquisitive. Then it is that, should any wicked

man or woman chance on them, they can be easily
debauched, having no true knowledge of what sin
means. Besides, they feel the future too distant to
trouble them and believe they will be young forever.
And it was in such a mood, turning from girlhood into
womanhood and wondering at the change, avid to learn,
that Frances came to the wickedest court in all the
world . . . Can she then be blamed for what she did,
having none to counsel and guide her, her mother
a monster and her father prepared to sell his soul
for gold? I blamed her once. Not now that I am
older."

Fiercely she spoke, her teeth set and her eyes glaring
at the empty wall; and Will was startled by her
vehemence, for the first time seeing her not as his mother
but as a woman capable of passion. As though he had
stepped into a secret-house to stumble on forbidden
things, the revelation frightened him and made him
uncomfortable so that he shifted on the bed and looked
away. That she and his father could ever have been
lovers had not before occurred to him. How could that
man of iced fury, his father, have wooed a woman?
Theirs must have been an arranged marriage, a mercenary
union from which had grown affection but no desires.
This conclusion faintly comforted him although he yet
felt disturbed by the energy with which his mother had
cried that she'd no right to judge the wantonness of
Frances Howard, as though in defending the dead
woman, in some fashion she defended herself, too. With
new interest, with suspicion yet with sympathy, he
watched his mother, and noticed with surprise that she
was still attractive, although wrinkling and faded.
Much of the girl remained in her with her shynesses, her
readiness to blush and giggle, and in the half-finished
gestures she made when words died or she felt she had
neared a dangerous subject; and Will thought: How
beautiful she must have been when she was young!

Feeling the intentness of his gaze, the countess blushed and began lightly to talk again as though with merriment she hoped to conceal something which she feared to admit. With sharper eyes Will watched her, noting the occasional flush at memories, the biting of her lip, the brightening or the dimming of her eyes, the flutter of her bosom, the twisting of her hands, as the tale she told excited or saddened her. And he tried to reach beyond her words, to mingle with her in her past, while in his mind he saw her a slim wench with that golden girl, that hoyden, Frances Howard.

Had she envied Frances her freedom of being wife and yet no wife, of possessing a married woman's privileges with a girl's curiosity, being permitted to meet men and to talk with matrons as an equal, while enjoying also the self-completion of virginity, able to titillate herself with the power of denying men while luring them to denounce them as beasts? Doubtless all other ladies at court had envied her beauty, her wealth and her absent husband, and probably his mother had been no different. Yet it would seem from the accounting of her charms that Frances's fascination had lain more within her spirit than on her face and form, exquisite though that bare young bosom must have looked squeezed between filigree-lace ruff and bodice and sliced invitingly with shadow. Will had seen such tantalising ladies and knew their spell without being able to explain it, for he had stood apart from lechery, armoured in love for Anne, but nevertheless at times had he found himself enchanted by the magnet of some lady's being which drew him willy-nilly despite his virtuous resolutions. Some rare women did possess this vital flame, this jewel of the spirit, shining through their eyes and skin, which made everyone, women as well as men, turn towards them, startled by a miracle of desire made flesh.

Thus must young Frances have been when first she came to that drunken, lewd yet learned court of

James I, in the prime of her girlhood, ambitious for power and for proof of that power through love. Will could imagine her clearly : Anne without Anne's softness, a vixen Anne, having the same haughty walk, the same brave bearing to conceal timidity, as though to hold off the malice of the world with outthrust bosom and belly and shoulders back—only Frances's bosom, catching his breath with wonder, Will recalled, would have been almost bare ; and he flinched because in this image he was building of this Anne who was not Anne, he feared to disrobe her of modesty, if only for his own sake and the tight hold he maintained on his desires. Back into his room he blinked himself awake to see again his mother in the damp sunlight and to hear her placidly recall past junketings, feasts and masques in which both ladies and gentlemen had dressed in fantastic garb, and the bawdy roistering of that court which must have been so different from the present king's.

Often, she said, these masques were never finished, the ladies and gentlemen becoming too drunk to remember the poetry and sometimes rolling amongst the broken meats on the floor, giggling or spewing. There was one she recalled which made Will catch his breath, both fascinated and appalled by the description she gave.

"There was King Solomon's temple builded," she said, "and it was after dinner with food still about, and it was to show the coming of the Queen of Sheba. The king was there and all the court and they had feasted well : and so, too, had the players. But, alas ! one might have laughed had it not been filthy, the lady playing Sheba's part had to carry precious gifts to the king who was on the halpace but she forgot the steps leading up to him and overset the carpet into some of the guests' laps and fell at their feet. Much was the hurry and confusion, as you may imagine. Cloths and napkins were at hand to make all clean. One gentleman

would have danced with Sheba but he fell down and
humbled himself before her and had to be carried to
an inner-chamber and laid on a bed of state which was
not a little defiled by the presents Sheba had bestowed
on his garments—wine and cream and jelly and beverages
and cakes and spices and such good things. But the
entertainment went forward while most of the presenters
went backwards, or fell down, wine so occupying their
upper-chambers. In rich dresses came next, I remember,
Faith, Hope and Charity. Hope tried to speak but
wine rendered her attempts so feeble that she withdrew
and hoped the king would excuse her brevity. Faith
soon followed her in a staggering condition, and Charity,
being left, came to the king's feet and seemed to cover
the multitude of sins her sisters had committed. In
some sort she made obeisance and brought gifts but she
said she would have to go home again as there was
no gift heaven hadn't already given his majesty. She
then returned to Hope and Charity who were both being
sick in the lower hall.

"Next came Victory in bright armour to present a
sword to the king, but he'd not accept it and put it by
with his hand, such craven terror had he, being unmanly
of the bare sight of steel. But Victory didn't triumph
long, for after some lamentable utterances she was led
away like a silly captive and laid to sleep on the outer-
steps of the antechamber. Then Peace entered and
strove to get foremost of the king, and I grieve to
remember the wrath she showed to her attendants,
contrary to her semblance, for she made war on them
with her olive-branch and laid on the pates of those who
would have carried her out . . . Ah, my son, I tell
you these filthy things that you may understand what
that court was like to which young Frances came when
she was no more than fourteen or fifteen, if that, without
husband to guard her and she as beautiful as a child-
goddess . . . "

Always thus, after laughing until she looked a girl again when recalling some merry episode, suddenly his mother became aware of her own sinful delight in sin and she set her lips and nodded her head and said that she told such tales only to remind Will of the wickedness of those times. To him, a serious youth devoted to study and theology, those times seemed indeed wicked beyond belief and while he tingled to hear them, lascivious images making him sweat with horror, he thanked God that virtue was king of King Charles's court and that his Anne would never be unloosed amidst similar temptations.

"Jealous although most women were of her," continued his mother, "for that was only natural, none of us thought even to compare ourselves with so rare a squirrel, and amongst ourselves we trembled and wondered whose lover she would steal. For we had lovers . . . but you must not mistake me, Will, they were lovers only in name. They meant nought to us and we never saw them save in company. For our silly girlish self-respect we had to have some courtier at our heels, and the fellow acted his part too and pretended . . . It was all pretence, but we didn't want to lose our gallants, of course. It would have been humiliating ; but we needn't have feared Frankie. She scorned to steal any ordinary gentleman. Had there been a visiting god at court, that god she would have pursued and she'd have caught him, too ! I swear it, so marvellous were her fascinations. For that reason, I believe she never truly loved, not even Somerset, but cheated herself and thought she loved when it was only pride that drove her, her over-mastering need to show us all that men could not escape her . . . Alas, alas ! for vanity . . . For if hers had been true love she'd not have chosen the greatest at court to snare, love not stealing on us in that fashion, but taking it would seem haphazardly this man there and that woman there and

setting them alight without reason. That's why I feel
that poor Frances who came into this world a pet of
Venus, being given all that any woman could desire,
not only wealth and position and looks, but this strange
jewel, this lodestone for a heart, never truly loved,
although she suffered all love's pangs in time. Had the
king been fond of ladies she'd have netted him, I swear,
for all that he was bandy-legged and slobbering and
dirty. So failing the king, she took the prince ; and
that was a triumph to startle all the court, Prince Henry
being thought a despiser of our sex.

" He was the love of England, that young Harry, and
ah ! a handsome lad he was, if solemn in his ways,
preferring dogs and hunting and military exercises above
love's interchange ; his hound, his horse and his sword,
he boasted, he liked above any woman living. That
was his challenge which Frances took. Mayhap disgust
at his father's drunkenness and painted lads drove him
to this hardiness, this loathing of things feminine. He
was happiest, it was said, in the cold Tower studying
under old Sir Walter Ralegh, for the king, jealous of
that great man's glory and wishing to please Spain that
feared his courage, had locked him away. ' Only my
father,' I heard the prince say once in scorn ' would
keep such a bird in a cage.' Yet the prince was no
puritan and in his palace of St. James, he gave banquets
as luxurious as his father's, only at his table none dared
get drunk or talk or act bawdy. And this godly youth
who scorned ladies and had never been known to
converse with one in private, became the slave of Frances
within a week. Such was her domination over men.
How it was worked, God knows. It is an art, if devilish,
an instinctive skill, although the woman must know how
to use it, as with all arts, this stealing of a man, for a
lady dare not be bold with a lover, nor too cold ; she
must not speak first lest he think her immodest and despise
her, nor must she lure him with beckoning smiles and

promising words. Not such a man as that virtuous prince.

"Yet Frances did it. Amazed, we noticed that he sent her many loving glances as ambassadors to her ; and although we envied her her victory, we also felt we shared it with her and, I doubt not, became in our delight more imperious towards our own poor lovers. It was whispered that all was a plot and that Frances had been set to it by the Earl of Northampton, her uncle, to capture the prince for his scheming. Mayhap there was truth in that, such being the intrigues at court that none could tell the rights of anything, but certainly it was a plot to suit her mettle ; and right merrily she went to it. Soon, often was she at the prince's palace and he was giving banquets and masques to honour her. Nobody ever mentioned her husband, that moody, unhappy lad learning warfare on the continent and no doubt dreaming all the while of her and of how he'd love her when he was home again. He was forgotten, yet he was Frances's future. But the young have no thought of the future, feeling certain that it will be glorious, so assured are they that until the end they will stay beautiful and always vital, always fascinating . . ."

She sighed and her eyes were dark with shadows. She was thinking of her own youth, not Frances's, thought Will with a pang of jealousy ; she was thinking all the time of that world of love into which he could never enter, a world of violence and lust, ugly, drunken, debauched, and she amidst that debauchery, doubtless enjoying it all . . . What was she thinking of? he wondered : what lover of her youth, what drunken gallant bedded now with her in her mind? Had she, too, God forbid ! like Frances, stripped herself to the buff in these riotings, open to men's fingers? By God, he groaned, and bit his nails.

"Was she the prince's mistress ? " he cried harshly.

"Of course," said his mother. "What woman—

what young girl, I mean—could hold against a prince if he beckoned her ? Just as ladies dress to out-dress other ladies, so often do they take a lover just to spite their friends and to triumph over them, not so much for liking of the man, although that often follows. Of course, we were young and reckless, each trying to capture more lovers than the others . . ."

" Dame ! " cried Will, gripping the edges of his bed and showing his teeth, " who would have thought that you, that you, you could have wantoned like that, half-naked, with men ! Yet they dare call this Frances a whore ! All at that court were whores, it seems, but she, being the greatest, came to symbolise you all ; and that I swear's the truth of it ! She had more offers, that was it, being damned in her own beauty. Is there no bottom of goodness even in a mother that you could lick your lips on those foul memories ? Are all women rotten at heart, likerous, craving the apple, lying to men with their faces oiled with hypocrisy, lying with them, living a lie, with thoughts of lechery behind your modest mean and shrinking gait ! . . . This is too much ! that you . . . yet you'd judge Frances Howard ! "

" I never judged her ! "

" You dare not judge her, being yourself no better ! Was ever son so damned to hear such tales from his own mother's lips ? By her triumph, said you, you became haughty towards your lover. Who was he ? Or had he many names and different shapes each night ? But not being a prince, he did not matter. No, no. Only must Frances be damned because she ravished a prince from his honour. You dare prattle with such relish of those Babylonian days, glorying in wantonness, stripped to the waist, no doubt, for sweaty encounters at White-hall or Hampton Court or Windsor or St. James. I wonder what's my father's name. Must I ask even that ? "

Aghast, he shrank from her, and she looked suddenly very old, haggard with red-rimmed eyes.

" I . . . I meant no ill," she sobbed. " I talked to help you, to make you understand your lady's mother . . ."

" And thereby damned yourself, gloating on those bestial nights with wagtail women and their stallions ! Who was your lover ? Or were they so many you can't name them all you, were you the common couch of courtier, groom and squire ? And you my mother ! Does my father know of this ? Nay, he is too good a man ; yet you could marry him and have such memories, shutting your eyes upon his noble face with devils under your lids to make you kick ! This is too much indeed . . ."

" Will, please ! " she moaned, " you don't understand. I was never wicked, never once. I swear by all my hopes of heaven I was honest and a maid when I met your father. You must believe me."

" No," he cried.

She gripped his legs when he stood up, and, weeping, clung to them while with cold fury he glared down on her greying ringlets.

" Let me go," he said.

" I'll not let you go," she wailed, " not like this, not when you're angry with me, and all for nothing, because I tried to help . . . yes, to help you, my darling, that you might not hate your lady's mother. You must not blame me for that. I was a child then but I did no wickedness : before God, I swear it."

" Women were ever liars," he said. " You just told me so yourself. They'll take men without the excuse of love, you said, that they might tyrannise over them and jet with pride before other ladies . . . But they are not all like that, please God . . . not all . . ."

" Of course they aren't. Many might be wantons but most are true. I . . . I have been true, always

. . . O, do not look at me like that ! How can you doubt me when you see your mirror and your dad looks back with his own eyes at you ? . . . Will ! where are you going ? "

" Out of this house," he said, dragging her after him to the door, "into the air to wash this bawdy clammyness away . . . Stripped to the waist, lady-harlots, women in name but satyresses in the dark ! And my own mother, too ! "

" I didn't, I swear it on the cross ! I was lying to please you, trying to speak well of Frankie for her daughter's sake and I only damned myself in doing it ! "

" Ay," he said bitterly, " damned, indeed ; and you've damned me as well, for I've lost something so precious I would that I could die . . . Whom can I trust from now ? "

He caught her fingers and bent them back to free his legs while she wept and wailed for him to listen to her ; but he dared not listen lest he beat her. And that would have been a sin beyond forgiveness, no matter how evil-living she might have been in her youth.

Not from her so much as from himself he fled, slamming the door on his mother sprawling amongst the herbs she had scattered to perfume his chamber ; and down the stairs he ran, almost tumbling over his sword, until in the garden he stood with clenched fists, tears behind his lids, and found himself alone. And from now must he ever be alone, fatherless, motherless . . . with only Anne in Chiswick waiting for him to claim her. And Anne, after all, was woman concealed under her modest airs. But nay, nay . . . He must not, dared not doubt her : else he'd have gone stark mad.

And then, stiff with terror, he wondered if he were going mad.

CHAPTER IV

Enemy of the Rose

To the family mansion, Bedford House in London's Strand, Will rode from Woburn Abbey which, so enchanting in its welcome with memories of his boyhood, had grown hateful to him. From a gallop, he reined his horse to an amble when his fury ebbed, and he grew ashamed, although yet shaken by his mother's story, wondering whether he had been unjust towards her. But it had not been so much her words conjuring a vision of semi-nudity and of women taking lovers to feed their vanity in that court of corruption under James I, it had been something in her voice and eyes that had appalled him. Gentle and husky had become that voice, purring, while she had smiled and her eyes had darkened with a kind of wistful completion as though she had been recalling lovers at her knees, suppliants at her bed-curtains, and herself the mistress luxuriating in her body's power and taking lovers only when it pleased her. Momentarily, the dead woman and his mother had merged in Will's imagination. The wantonness of Frances with her prince had seemed but a reflection of his mother with some lesser gallant, and his disgust at Frances's behaviour had fallen on the ageing woman sighing at youth's passing.

Even if, as she had sworn, she had exaggerated her part in those junketings that she might make the hoyden Frances Howard seem less a whore for his love's sake, the fact that not only had she been present at such saturnalia but had worn the almost bosomless gown of the age without shrinking, and that she could speak of such immodesty without a blush as though they had been

happy days and nights, childish gambollings, could not
be easily forgiven by a son who loved good books and
hated sin. No, not so much her words, he kept repeating
as he rode that his anger might stay hot to justify his
cruelty towards her, but her enjoyment of such ruttish
memories was what had sickened him. She was a
woman he had adored, seeming modest and gentle, and
this sudden new picture of her when young seemed to
Will as monstrous and unforgivable a betrayal as though
she were his wife whom he had caught in adultery. If
thus, secretively, she cherished lubric memories, he
wondered how much of her past his father knew or
suspected. That thin-lipped man with the weary eyes
who would tolerate no lechery amongst the lowest of his
servants, dismissing them at the faintest rumour of sin,
would have been struck dead had he heard such talk.
Only to him, to her son, had she unlocked this portion of
her past ; and the secret, their secret, would remain safe,
Will swore, his father never discovering it from his lips.

Yet every mile that sped him from Woburn until at
last, dusty and weary, he entered the noise of London
again, diminished Will's anger and brought even a
quiver of pity that he had left her unforgiven. He would
write to her, he decided : a brief note, one that would
appear innocent should others chance on it but one
which she would understand, telling her that he was no
longer angry. For his conscience's sake, if not for her
peace of mind, he must do it . . .

Heartened by this decision, the moment he arrived at
Bedford House he sought for pens and paper, yet found
the task no easy one and put the letter by, saying :
" Tomorrow, I'll write tomorrow : I am weary now ; "
and surprised, found that he was indeed weary, not only
bodily but spiritually weary with a disgust of humanity
and a dislike of the task he had set himself of uncovering
the history of Anne's parents. When from his mother's
lips he had learned the tale of her venerial gambols and

of her seduction of the noble Prince Henry—for he could not doubt that she had snared that virtuous boy—and the suggestion of yet other lewderies when she had been still a girl of sixteen or so, he wished to dig no further into that grave of corruption. But thought of Anne, pale in that Chiswick house under the shadows of her father's madness, steadied his resolution. Whatever depravity he might find, Anne, he was certain, could never be touched by it ; to believe otherwise would have made to him life impossible.

He could not sleep. Hotly he tossed through the cool night, stifling within his bedcurtains, being haunted by indecorous shapes, by big-bosomed wenches tempting him ; and when he did sink into slumber, soon did he wake again, sweating, heart beating like a gong, while he shut his eyes on the horrible beauty that had sprung on him in dreams. In that velvety darkness lit only by the red eyes of the charcoal in the perforated box at his bedhead, he felt certain that the dead woman had returned to haunt him. In his panic, he even believed—and his hair stiffened at the thought—that he could smell her ruttish presence ; and he chattered a prayer, conjuring shapes out of shadows and in the moonlight through the window, watching chairs and table and curtains come to life. That this Frances had sampled magic he knew by what his father had said of the figures that had been produced in court ; and who was he to question the power of witchcraft and the perpetuity of conjuration ? Behind them, even after they have been slain, the wicked can leave the spoor of their wickedness to entrap others. He had known houses which had seemed to catch him by the throat with the almost tangible presence of evil, the blasphemies of those who had once lived there remaining like a stink in a still room, and he did not question that witches might be able to live after death, by Satan's will, to corrupt others that they might drag their souls to hell.

Yet his mother had said that Frances had intended no evil, that only her young vanity had driven her to wrong-doing . . . that may have been true of her youth ; but what of afterwards, after the love of the prince had waned, to whom and to what had she turned for other sensations that to this day the mention of her name brought squeaks of horror and revulsion ? To what satanic depths had she crawled in search of obscenities and devil-worship ? Impossible was it now for him to give over his mission, Will realised with despair yet with excitement. The need to learn the truth for his own satisfaction was becoming greater even than his need to discover it that he might free Anne from her parents' past ; and he cursed the years abroad when he had heard no scandal. But these things had happened long before then, during his childhood when he had been too young to be interested in his elders' doings, and in a way it was best that he should come fresh with no preconceptions to the task.

But where was he to begin ?

Alone in that mansion on the Strand save for the few servants left to keep it aired and to tend the gardens, Will brooded, not knowing whom to question, so few were the friends he had in London or at court, and he was furious that, instead of abusing his mother, he had not asked for letters to people who might help him. But he salved his conscience by writing her a brief note of forgiveness, then he sat in the gloom of the mansion, trying to read but finding it impossible to concentrate while he wondered how to begin his search. No longer could he find delight in the magnificence of his home's furnishings. Such things of the flesh mattered no longer. He might as well have lodged at an inn for all the heed he took of the paintings and hangings on the walls or of the sight of the noisy Strand to be watched from the gallery with its hangings of green cloth and gilt leather and its red velvet furniture. From such sights almost he shrank, hating to see people free of his phantoms, the travellers on horseback or in coaches, or the throng of ordinary passers-by ; happier he felt, even in the cold, on the raised terrace or in the exquisitely laid out garden at the back of the house with its high wall beyond which could be seen the spire of St. Paul's and the tops of Covent Garden piazzas.

In nowhere could he find rest, neither in books nor in beautiful things, the perplexity being knotted in his soul, and this maddened him who was a youth unused to indecision. Amazed at his own indolence, restlessly he roamed the mansion, taking up books only to put them down again or staring hours away into the fire. The thought of going out again into life had suddenly become repugnant and at every attempt he made to leave, he shivered and sat down again.

" I am bewitched," he thought and he peered into the shadows over his shoulder, half-expecting to see that bare-bosomed devil from the past who haunted him ; but there was never anything to see beyond familiar things. Often he considered riding to Chiswick, hoping that Anne might exorcise her mother's ghost, but he feared to go with so few discoveries to reveal, and this will-lessness maddened him who had always hated and despised indecision in others. Yet whither should he turn ? He could scarcely wander abroad, asking strangers to tell him the history of the Earl and Countess of Somerset ; besides, whom did he know to trust, for tales would have to be tested against other tales and the speaker's malice discounted ? The prospect of re-entering life, of again meeting people masking envy and rancour, frightened him, much of his belief in human virtues being now gone with faith in his mother's innocence when young.

Yet he could not remain forever indoors and at last he forced himself to roam abroad, eating and drinking at taverns in the hope of meeting by chance somebody who might without prejudice uncover the mystery ; but he met no one save other lonely bachelors, drunkards, harlots, gamesters and indolent gentlemen sharpening witticisms against one another's skill in bawdy talk ; and the court at Whitehall differed little from tavern-life save that it was ceremonious and more tedious, none daring to relax while all were wary and jealous and quick to wound. There could Will make no friends. The unreality of such an existence he despised, the courtiers and ladies in their silks and satins and laces and ribbons seeming phantoms beside the bold reality of that dead woman who followed him no matter where he went. More living than the living, this mother of Anne gave him no peace. Awake or sleeping, she obsessed him. Luring yet mocking him, teasing yet enticing him, she was ever under his eyelids so that at times it was with surprise that he remembered that she was dead, for continually was he half-expecting to meet her while, like an impatient lover off to a tryst, he roamed the royal apartments and the gardens in continual disappointment. Beside this enigma, living ladies appeared insubstantial, false in looks and false in manner, their ogling and simpering too crude allurements which repelled him ; and the only way whereby he might be quit of this ghost he realised was to find the truth of her life and death and why Somerset remained a prisoner in his own house and his daughter moped in loneliness.

It was not difficult for him to hear tales of the man's disgrace. That remained yet a jest to many and the king kept his hatred of Somerset warm by, whenever the detested name was mentioned, silently staring at the thoughtless one who had spoken. This, Will soon learned, was apparently because Somerset and Buckingham, the king's murdered love, had been fierce enemies and the king could never forget nor forgive. But the cause of Somerset's disgrace was not so easily discovered, everything knowing the scandal so completely that they

did not trouble to discuss it, speaking of it only casually
as a notorious matter. That there had been a murder
and a great betrayal, with poisonings and magical
conjurations, was all he could learn ; and he feared to
reveal his interest by open questioning. His love he did
not wish yet to be told, not for shame of Anne, by
heaven! but because he knew how these oiled and painted
ladies would snigger and how their perfumed gallants
would smirk that he should be so great a fool as to wish
to marry the child of a disgraced favourite. From no
one at court could he expect sympathy for love. Only
the king himself appeared an honest lover, adoring his
proud and insolent queen. Other men mocked at love,
discussing women with a contemptuous familiarity that
made Will tremble on occasions. Nor were the women
any more generous or delicate. Either they were
hoydens or they went masked with ostentatious virtue.
They'd never understand his love's perplexities . . .

Then one day he chanced to stroll into the rose-garden
at Whitehall to escape the titterings of those indoors and
there he stood amongst the last autumnal flowers, the
weather being too cool to entice others out of warm
rooms. At first, he believed himself alone, then he
heard a giggle and up before him rose a fat, little, large-
headed fellow with plump moustaches and a tuft of
beard, and questioning brows over eagle-eyes. So
unexpected was the man's appearance and so wild his
looks that instinctively Will clasped his sword-grip
before he recognised him as Archie Armstrong, the
court fool. And a canny, grasping, bitter-mouthed fool
he was whom men avoided and women feared.
Notorious for gathering and hiding what money he
could, dressing—save for state-occasions when he donned
cap and bells—in cast-off clothing begged from courtiers
who dared not say him nay, knowing him to be
vindictive and unscrupulous and privileged in any lie he
told, Archie strutted whither he willed, even into the

king's privy chamber, arrogant, jeering, knowing all secrets and being capable of revealing them for the pleasure of watching a lady blush or seeing a gentleman turn pale.

" Whisht ! " said he, scowling and pushing his snub beak into Will's face, " quick with you, fool, down here ! "

" I'll not ! " cried Will.

" Would you spoil a jest, you loon," growled Archie. " If so, I'll spoil whatever sport you're at. Down when I tell you ! "

For a moment Will thought to resist, then he shrugged and submitted, feeling too dispirited to argue. Behind an arbor he crouched with the jester and they had scarcely settled themselves before a gentleman came from the palace, treading delicately in his high-heeled rosetted shoes, and leaning with amorous avidity over a lady while, with lowered lids and pucked mouth, she smiled up at him. Into the rosery, the gallant led his darling and before one bush he paused. On that bush, Will noticed, one flower had been covered by a silk kerchief, and he heard Archie snort beside him as though the jest were too tickling to be endured in silence.

Whatever had been under that kerchief when, bowing and with a flourish, the gentleman whisked it from the flower, plainly it was not what either he or his lady had expected. Her cheeks turned scarlet and her eyes glittered as though she had been smacked and was about to cry. She stamped her foot and spat and cried words so furious that the man slunk back ; then with her long fan she hit him in the face until she snapped the sticks while her lover could only gape and stutter, holding out both arms imploringly. Then she threw the broken pieces at him, lifted her skirts, and scampered off, leaving him bewildered, hand to his brow as though he were stunned.

So swiftly had the lady acted, and for no apparent

reason, that Will felt as bewildered as her lover, while
Archie's fingernails dug into his biceps ; and he dared
not cry out lest the gallant hear him and believe he had
committed this base jape, whatever it might be. Not
until the fellow had tottered back into the palace did
he speak. Then he turned furiously to stare into
Archie's wrinkling eyes and to damn him for a base
fellow to injure poor lovers.

" Poor lovers, indeed ! " shrilled Archie, speaking so
rapidly that Will found it difficult to understand his
Scottish accent. " Why should I pity those who lose
their wits and get no payment for it beyond the spittle
of a minx," he cried, " or a blow, mayhap, on the gob
as that pretty fellow just suffered ? If I were king, I'd
sentence any that prattled of love to a week in the stocks
that I might tickle the lust out of him with a peacock's
feather on his feet. And as for females, it'd not be poor
honest whores I'd have whipped at Bridewell but she-cats
who ape virtue. Ay, I'd do the whipping myself till
I whipped blood from shoulder to hip ; I'd have every
sly dame at court carted there once a month for the
good of her flesh and the peace of her husband's mind,
that bad blood be flogged out to keep them quiet for a
while. You're young, you've not been long at court,
but you'll learn. Women'll teach you. They are
tantalisers when they are not whores and I'd rather pay
my pennies at Bankside than lock the door on such a
greasy-polled mincing piece of laced mutton as that
she-ape we just saw who'll not·forget in a hurry the gift
her lover gave her in the rosery."

" But what did he—what did you do ? "

Archie's sly eyes shifted and he shook again with
merriment while, rising slowly to his feet, he looked
cautiously around to make certain that the gallant had
gone.

" I saw that loon," said he, " and a monstrous conceited kite he is who turned his back once on a jest of

mine while all the court was laughing, even the king, who laughs not often ; I saw him steal here and place a love-token in that rose and cover it with his kerchief and tiptoe back to call his whore. I changed the gift, that's all. Ask not what I put in its place, but it was not what he or she expected, as you probably noticed. He'll be no bonny boastful gallant after this, methinks, the devil ride off with him, he and his slut together ; and I warrant she's having the vapours now and scheming how to be revenged on such an insult. Do you call that love ? Two beasts who'll soon find other riders. There's naught that goes on here that Archie doesn't hear, and I know the pair of them from their dirty toenails to their lousy scalps . . . Ay, I am the father-confessor of Priapus and from the servants I learn all the tattle and I go everywhere, for I'm invisible, a fool, a zany, but those fools' master . . . But you, what seek you here at court ? Is it a wench you want ? They are too cheap to purchase, but a coin or two in Archie's palm'll lead you to their secrets. And once you have a woman's secrets you have all of her, for she dare not say nay then lest you blab to her husband. I'll tell you which one leaves her door unlatched and which one's husband, with the apothecary's aid, sleeps the soundest. I tell you, boy, that there's no secret here that Archie does not know, for Archie sidles everywhere and no one minds him for a daft loon while the ladies chatter and scratch themselves and worse when I am by as though I were a blind dog. Ah, I see things that you might look through keyholes till you're blind in the eye and not discover. For a few wee bawbees I'll unroll bed-sheets for you and bring the list of patients that the leech has for the French disease. You could find no more industrious friend and guide than Archie and it'll not be too expensive ; for are you not Russell's son and he a wise, careful man amassing gold for you to squander like a brave heir when the old loon shuffles off. Yea, tell me,

lad : what d'ye wish ? I'll lead you into such temptation, and not too expensive either, as will make you bless
me for Aretino's ghost . . . "

" You are a wicked old man," cried Will and would
have flung away from him had not Archie's talons been
hooked on his sleeve.

" Wicked, ay ! " grinned the jester, " but not so old,
laddie, that I can't frighten a wench in the dark. You
have a damned conventicle countenance, and I see that
I mistook you for my brother. 'Tis neither the wenches
nor the wine-pot you hanker after, yet 'tis something.
I've been watching you some days now, seeing you stalk
like a glandered fowl enough to frighten the females,
your nose in the air and your eyes under your lids.
Hey ! how the females laugh when you are past. Would
you not like to hear what they call you ? "

" No ! " shouted Will.

" Then I'll not tell you," said Archie : " it might
undermine your faith in women and that is no good
thing at your age, it being evident you are in love."

" Evident ! what do you mean ? "

" Ah ! " grinned the jester, delighted to find by Will's
anger that he had hit the truth. " You have the
semblance of a lover, my lad : the miserable chaps, the
creaking sighs and the hungry gape of one who feeds upon
a wench's eyelid and munches her memory like a cow.
But there's a mend-all for that distemper, and a gay
one, no matter how impishly snout-fair she be, and
impertinently high-priced in her own ignorant opinion.
Whisper me her name and cross my palm with a few
gold bawbees and I'll light you the way to her chamber,
be she widow, wife or maid, if such as maidens be these
naughty times. For I tell you, lad—and I'm no liar, if
a rogue—there's naught of which I do not know and
not one person, man, woman, dog or child, at this court
of whom I've not sniffed a secret, for a man must look
to his future and some day, and not so long now, please

the Lord, I'll be buying myself an inn and taking a good cook with a young face for wife to see to my digestion. So, if you'd care to lighten your purse for a little information at small expense, I'm the very fellow for you . . . Who is the little bellibone ? Come, lad, you may trust fat Archie, a true friend of lechers and a lover of good insects. Who is she ? "

" There is no woman, fool," cried Will, " and if there were, your long tongue'd be the last I'd weight with such a secret . . . You know so much, you say ? "

" I know everything," said Archie, nodding his round head and shaking his greasy curls.

" Then . . . mayhap . . . There is something I'd like to know." Uncertain how far he dared confide in such a mercenary rogue, Will paused. Not to take advantage of this chance meeting seemed to him dangerous, a flouting of the stars ; such an opportunity might not come his way a second time, for it was certain that of all people at court, this jester knew the most of others' doings. Yet he feared to be open with such a babbler, remembering his reputation as one remorseless in squeezing money from a victim under the threat of making him a mocking-stock in a jest. Therefore cautiously he said : " I've been long out of England and would like to learn something of the histories of others."

" Of whom ? " demanded Archie. " I'll leave her not a stitch on her past, be she ever so virtuous, if you'd let me peep into that purse of yours."

Ashamed of his weakness in buying such a rascal, Will slipped his purse from his sleeve and took from it a gold piece which he held up before the jester.

" I have no need to pay for what I want to hear," he said, " because my interest lies in nothing secret but in a public scandal. Were my curiosity strong enough I could learn it in a dozen questions anywhere, but you are present and are garrulous. So let you tell me of it. I'd like to know why the Earl of Somerset is forbidden the court. What was this crime he did that no one speaks his name without contempt or hatred ? "

" What ? " cried the jester, snatching the coin, " you would hear the tale of Robbie Carr, eh ? Well, I'm the lad to tell it, being myself a Scotsman, although not so misfortunate as he . . . But talking's parching work and the tale's a long one. You have bawbees there enough to open any tavern-door, so let's over the road to a cheap den I wot of where the wench is bedsome and cheap and the wine's not cidered. Or are you ashamed to be seen boozing with me in my homely garb ? I can tell you that greater men than you, lad, have been proud ere this to take my arm and have not stinted the wine and gold to buy my confidence . . . "

Gripping his victim's arm lest at the last moment he escape him, Archie hurried Will through the garden to a door in the wall, with a hitch of his tattered cloak, ignoring the guard's grin, and over the muddy road to a tavern opposite the Wall Market beside the water-steps. It was a small yet surprisingly clean place with a few watermen in thrum caps and woollen jerkins playing cards under the window, and a fat bar-girl who at sight of Will in his expensive doublet curtseyed so low that her knees creaked when she stood up again. The little jester smirked at her and rolled his eyes but did not pause. Through the tap-room he hustled Will out on to a wooden balcony jutting over the river. Then, with a great sigh of contentment, he sat on a bench beside the table that was wetly ringed with previous drinkers' cups.

" The best red wine you have in your cellars, my moppet," he cried, " and never consider the expense. My rich friend will be paying and he is an honest gentleman as you may mark by his simple countenance. And be yare for I have a thirst like a furnace. Ah ! " said he when the girl placed the pots before him with the air of one deaf and blind while he peeped into her

71

bosom, " that is excellent, lass. Sit you down, my
friend. There is an afternoon ahead of us and much
to tell. Look you, sir," he added, forcing Will on to
the bench beside him while he craned to watch the girl
return to the shadowed taproom, " she is a nice pigeon,
although a little expensive. Yet you cannot blame the
wench for marketing her goods at the best price offered.
'Tis the braw young gallants who ruin sport by over-
paying for what an honest wench should be pleased to
offer with a thank you ; but men are fools and have
no conscience when a pert wench gives them a dainty
leer . . . But 'twas not of such as her that we would
talk, but of that popinjay, the Earl of Somerset, was it
not ? And there's an excellent example to you of a
man who liked one wench too much, and she as dangerous
a parcel of lusts that ever bit one body. But he's learned
better now. He had his lesson under a cruel teacher.
But what would you have me tell about the stinkard ? "

Ashamed now and angry that on impulse he had
chosen this arrogant Scotsman for a confidant, Will
sat silent, staring at the muddy waters rippling about
the steps ; but having chosen him, he felt it would be
both foolish and dangerous to withdraw. The fellow
would blab and tell everyone what he had been asking.
He was determined, however, to hide all mention of
Anne and therefore he spoke cautiously.

" A devilish curiosity," he muttered, " has pricked me
to it, but I've been abroad and am country-bred. The
titterings I've heard since my return about this Somerset
and his countess have interested me, I know not why,
but I'd like to learn their histories, that is all, from
the beginning, from the lady's coming to court."

" You have met the right fellow for that," said the
jester. " I was there, of course. I saw her with her
puffed-up bubs and her big wicked eyes that looked so
innocent at a man while they pulled him on to her.
She was that kind of a trullibub that you knew not for

certain what she was thinking, save that it must be lewd ; but she seemed like a child, save for her body, who tried to act the woman and did not understand how lasciviously she could peep out of the corners of her eyes. There was not a fool at court, save me, that wasn't biting his whiskers to snatch her ; and she . . . Nay, she was beautiful ; and the bitch knew it."

"Her nose was broad, I hear, shapeless . . ." murmured Will.

"I looked not at her nose," growled the jester, " nor did other men, I warrant. We looked further down, my lad, and then we didn't look away, because we couldn't. She was as lecherous as a sparrow and she made men lecherous, too, just to watch her, even the good prince being burnt in her ogles. She was a great sinner but cannot be blamed for that, being so well adorned with what every woman needs . . . Ah ! my adorable," he cried, slapping the serving-girl as she returned to refill their cups, "what a pretty child we could breed together, if you could forget your mercenary instinct, my lass ! For she is mercenary," he growled after she had left him with a toss of her rump, " and has no ideals in her. You'd think you were buying a dozen Jews the way she bargains. But whisht ! we were talking of Frankie . . .

"Yet what can I tell you, lad, who never saw her buxom beauties ? You know, mayhap, that when little more than a bairn she was wedded to that lump the Earl of Essex, but never slept with him and came to court a maid in all save her imagination and made our Harry her lover . . . ? "

"Tell me from there," croaked Will, his hand shaking while he lifted his cup.

Watching him shrewdly, irritated because as yet he failed to understand the lad's interest in a stale scandal, the jester lounged against the wall and rested his short legs on the table. Then in his whistling, sneering voice, while he watched the boats rock over the grey river, he said :

" From there, my lad, 'tis the history of a whore. She bedded with Prince Harry whom every wench had sighed for as though he were made of sugar and worth a lick ; and indeed, he was a bonny lad, if solemn, and none'd believe it at first, he always despising women as though he knew them from the bottom up. But it was different when Frankie fluttered her lashes at him and took a deep breath that he might see what she had to offer. Forgotten were his virgin-oaths with his dogs and his horses for the sake of a salt bitch in a low gown. He was like a man mad and was forever giving feasts and masques at St. James's and elsewhere, and very welcome, too, they were, he being a generous-fisted lad, unlike some that I know, and as different from his dad as a cat from a cow. For the king his royal father was a slavering, cowardly, pedantic loon, crawl to him though I did like any good hound, but the prince was as long-legged and handsome a lad as ever turned a woman's innards with love-longing, but he scorned them till there were times I felt that I could beat him, were he not a prince and very strong, for the opportunities he stepped over. But he despised them all, and serve them right, say I. Would there more lads of his conceited spirit that females might be taught their places and prove kinder to us who have no such advantages as Harry had. But Frankie tripped him. Then she tripped Carr with equal ease. It was edifying to watch and very humbling, and Carr a Scotsman who should have known the price of a dinner."

" Carr ? " repeated Will.

" Yea, him that became Somerset, but Carr he was to me, and Carr he stays. A pretty golden-headed lout who came out of Scotland as penniless as any of us after our king, but soon he had the treasury for a plaything, so doting became the king of the ingle that he'd have

74

chopped off our heads at a nod from him. But Carr was a fool and never so clever as Buckingham, that lovely monster who destroyed him, for Buckingham'd give no man the smell of a ringlet unless he were well paid for it. What Carr like a loon often gave away, Buckingham sold : he sold not only titles and lands but men and women too ; and he squeezed and killed any that rebelled. He was a lad, was Buckingham, but Carr was no true Scotsman and, although he sold titles and such enough, he also gave when the silly mood took him. He was a fool, having naught but his good looks to hold him in power, it being common fame that his familiar, Tom Overbury, guided him."

" I know that name ! " cried Will.

" Who does not know it ! " said the jester. " Tom Overbury was a wit, a slanderous talker and a slimy gentleman. He sneered. He sniggered. He looked down at you as though you stank, as mayhap you did, but no man likes to know it ; and above all, above even gold, he loved power, liking to have his betters cringe to him. Yet he suffered for it in the end. May God rot him.

" On the king's love, Carr rose, and Overbury rose on Carr's back, neither of them having much money. There was a rime some rascal made, telling how Carr got his chance, for he rose by falling down, tumbling off his horse in front of the king who was so pitiful for the red-headed dog that he had him carried off to his own bed. It went like this :

" *Let any poor lad that is handsome and young*
  With Parle vous France, and a voice for a song,
  But once get a horse and seek out good James,
  He'll soon find the house, 'tis great, near the Thames,
  *It was built by a priest—*Wolsey, ye ken—*a butcher by*
    calling,
  But neither priesthood nor trade could keep him from falling.

75

And as soon as ye ken this pitiful loon—the king, mind you!
Fall down from your nag, as if in a swoon,
If he doth nothing more, he'll open his purse
If he likes you ('tis known he's a very good nurse).
Your fortune is made, he'll dress you in satin
And if you're unlearned he'll teach you dog Latin.

But Carr learned little Latin, I warrant. He'd not the wits for that or he'd never have been gulled by Northampton, for Northampton it was, beyond argument, who set his bitch to bite him as first he'd set her to biting the prince to drive the fool's wits away. And soon—yea, she was so apt a pupil of Satan and lechery—soon she had both the fellows at her skirts, both the prince who hitherto had turned his nose from females and Carr who never looked at them save to snigger with Overbury or his sweet dad, as he called the king. Yea, she had both spanieling at her heels. You should have seen it, boy ! Such a double-conquest as'd have made Cleopatra jaundiced and Helen drown herself from very spite. Had you known Harry and Carr you'd understand the greatness of what she, a young girl, did. No other lass could have done it, and so quickly, too. I drink to her for it. By Beelzebub, I do ! . . . Hey, Hebe, more wine ! "

So intent was he on the past, leaning against the wall with his brown-hosed legs on the table, that the jester even forgot to pinch the girl when warily she refilled their cups. Pulling at his snub nose, he sat staring at the distant Surrey bank, and he nodded his head and sighed.

" Fortunate was I," he said at last, " to have been unworthy of her cozening, although the thought of her robbed me of sleep many a night. I warrant that wives at least made merry those nights and many a lass found her gallant trebly ardent while he thought of Frankie. There's been no such wench since Helen proved what a whore could do. And had this been Troy, doubtless she'd have lighted it and burned us in our beds, such being her bold spirit, insatiable, orgulous for flattery. She fattened on our sighs and licked our tears, growing more beautiful like a vampire while we wilted under her contempt. Such women should be forced to act like taverns and be free to all comers, it being iniquitous for one man to keep such a one to himself. Yet she was no bed-gadding harlot. I heard of only those two men— and had there been others, I'd have known it—but they were sufficient for any woman. For soon, although the prince's mistress, she was after Carr and in her vanity she thought to keep them both and bubble them together ; and true she made Carr her fool but never Harry.

" 'Twas dangerous juggling ; mayhap that's why she liked it, relishing the risks. There was her husband abroad, there were her lovers, the prince and Carr at home, and there were the king and Overbury who might not like her doings. I wondered who would fall the first . . ."

Over the river, on the marshes, Will saw a falcon rise, then he saw men, tiny from that distance, running with their heads in the air. He saw the falcon dart down but not its prey tumble under it, some wretched heron probably slain by the bolt from the sky, and sudden impatience fretted him at these hours wasted over a wine-pot with this harsh-voiced jester jeering at his side and, like that hawk, slaying beauty with his beak. For Frances had been beauty doomed like a heron to envy's claws ; and at that thought, Will started, realising that no longer did he feel disgust at her wantonness. Somehow, by attempting to degrade her, Archie had uplifted her, making her appear helpless, pathetic, before the birds of prey at court, men taking women not from love but that they might enjoy their conquest, and the women longing to destroy in others the innocence themselves had lost.

Almost a child, Frances had entered that world of sensual temptation in which the king had been rarely sober. And a court was always the mirror of its king. As Whitehall now under Charles I and Henrietta Maria had become sober, modest, devout, so did the men and women behave courteously and with outward decorum, and so under James had the court been one of debauchery. With none to warn her, none to defend her honour, but rather with many avid to despoil her, her mother lustful and avaricious, her father lazy but ambitious, and her great relations brooding only on power, Frances unknowingly had been used, baited for bed, that the Howards might become great again. That so chaste a prince as Henry had loved her was surely proof that, at the beginning at least, no matter how time and lewd examples altered her, she had been honest? And could one blame a girl who surrendered to her prince? But Carr . . . why had she turned from the prince to Carr?

" He was the beautifullest man that ever I saw," snarled the jester, " and him a Scotsman, too ! Ah ! but a fool ! He had the mind of a horse in the body of a god. Had it not been for tiptoeing Overbury ever whispering in his ear, even his beauty could not have kept him great and the king himself must have wearied of this peach with a worm in it. But Overbury was a serpent in cunning, a university wit, who liked to wound that he might show his power. And he had naught save that wit to support him, when with his dad's chief clerk, as I've been told, he went on a voyage to Edinburgh—ah ! there's a city for you, lad, to which your London's but a pile of petrified soot—and there he met an old friend from Queen's College—Oxford, mind you : a well-educated fellow was Overbury, like most rogues, and little good it brought him, not teaching him the difference between venom and fruit in a tart. And boozing round that proud city whom should they stagger

into but pretty boy Carr with his red hair and little else
to sell ?   And they loved each other and swore brother-
hood as lads commonly will, being drunk and ambitious
and thinking they'll be friends forever with no witch of
a Frankie to sidle with her wagtail-ways between them.
Then when Carr fell off his horse and the king nursed
his broken leg, who must he have with him always but
his sweet Tom Overbury ?   Soon he had the witty
mongrel made one of the gentlemen of the household and
then he got the king to knight him, too.   I was there
when Jamie took him to his queen, for he'd have no lads
about him unless his drunken spouse approved them
first.   In the privy-garden he took Overbury and he
said : 'Look you, this is my new server,' and Annie
goggles at him and without so much as a hiccup, she
says : ' 'Tis a pretty young fellow.'   Then we knew that
Overbury would be another of our masters and those
who'd been ready to trip him louted low and bit their
tongues.

"But 'twas not for long.   None could like Overbury
for long, save pretty Carr, the fool, such being his
insolence and braggart glances, and he made the queen
wince when he laughed that cackle of his and she
speering at him from a window at Greenwich and seeing
the pair sportive in her garden and laughing.   For she
thought they laughed at her and so she had Overbury
clapped into the Tower and we all danced to hear it :
even I, although I had the measure of him as a greater
fool than myself, he not having my licence to jape at
royalty.   But the peacock thought he could crow where
he listed ; and so he could, damn his liver, for Carr goes
weeping that they were never laughing at Annie, God
forgive 'em both for liars !   but at remembrance, he
said, of a joke the king had made at dinner.   'Twas
Overbury thought of that, you may be certain, Carr
never having the wit for such a trick ; and soon the
arrogant ape was back again, more upstart than ever and

79

ruling the kingdom, too, he being Carr's master as Carr was master of James. So there was England balanced on the nose of a twopenny knight from Oxford, a squire's son and a lawyer and poet, too, with all the great men having to leave their daggers at home lest they lose their tempers and use them on a dark night.

" Fit pair were Carr and Overbury, being so different, one the fool and the other the scholar. Reared in France, Carr understood a courtier's trade and how to tickle a woman or to beguile a man with flattery ; he had beauty and knew how to bedeck it, the cut of a doublet or the starching of a ruff being portentous to him ; but Overbury had learned cunning at the Temple and the Inns of Court, he was one of the tribe of Ben, companion of that pot of a poet, Jonson, who lived on whom he could and scorned the world. Although later Ben hated him, as all men hated him once they knew him well. Nor was he discreet but wrote what he thought of others. Love, he once wrote, he considered men's affliction, and he put down man, woman and the devil as the three degrees of comparison. He jeered at holy things and it was said whenever the pair were sighted : ' There goes Carr and his governor ; ' for Overbury had full governance over the fool. Men stooped and crouched to him, for through him came all favours from the king. The sneering couple made a play of all the world beside themselves and had cyphers and jargons for the king and queen and the great men of the realm.

" David and Jonathan, Damon and Pythias, they were till Frankie's coming ; and here's the jest of it—or so 'twas said at the time—Overbury spurred his friend to mounting her. God knows the truth of that. Even I cannot be certain. But there was hatred between the prince and those whom the king fondled and mayhap Overbury—'twas like his malicious humour—thought it merry to steal the prince's mistress from him. And he'd not be the first I'm thinking who dug his grave with his own teeth, writing love-letters for his comrade to gull the wench, women being notorious fools in believing what's writ to them. True it is that Overbury had a pen he could dip in gall or honey. Read his *Characters*, laddie, and you'll find the subtlety of the man, even Ben Jonson, before they quarrelled, saying he was a poet to equal himself. Many a time have I seen Frankie sitting in the garden or by a window reading those poetical letters writ by Overbury which she thought were Carr's, until you could see her heart beating through her breast, for she hid little from a lecherous eye : nor much from some men's fingers either, if all's told. There she was sighing and windy with love, wet-eyed and unjointed, reading poetry when Carr had a ploughboy's hand and she thinking the sentiments came from that bullock. It was those letters, letters dictated by Overbury, that won her even more than the shape of Carr's legs or the curl of his beard and his golden hair."

" Then all the more cause to pity her ! " cried Will. " She was gulled and trapped."

" Yea, trapped by honey, like many a wench and a wasp before her. She read what she desired to read, a mirror for her vanity. For 'tis often themselves they see in a man's eyes that women love the most, their own image in his flattery and lies ; and thus it was that Carr through Overbury stole Frankie from the prince. Many a time I've seen them laugh together at how they'd made a mock of Hal, but, although they knew it not, it was the laughter of blind men walking on the edge of a precipice, for more than Frankie it was themselves they cheated by it and the prince was lucky to lose a whore."

" I will not have this word Whore ! " cried Will and found that he was trembling as though, not a dead woman, but his living love had been abused. " She was a child and loved her prince, and who can blame her for that ?

Then two rascals, skilled in cheating, gulled her and how can she be blamed for their wickedness ? "

" 'Snails ! " cried the jester, " you'd think you loved the wench, and she rotten these many years ! "

Loved her . . . Through Anne, yea, he loved her, this symbol of all girlhood, of Eve with the apple, a nymph amongst satyrs. Yea, groaned Will to himself, he loved her ; and the realisation brought a sense of lightness as though a knot which had bound him fast in misery were now untied and he was free. What right had he to condemn her when he had never known such temptations, and she a girl and therefore without a man's strength and mastery over his emotions ?

" I pity her," he said, sighing while the jester poured more wine into his glass.

" Rather pity her victims," cried the jester. " Think you the prince did not suffer, that lovely boy ? Think you that in the night he had not often awoken to hear her breathing in the shadows of his bed, snuffing the perfume of her unbound hair and her skin in that airless cavern of the curtains ? He was an honest, God-fearing youth, a virgin, I swear it, until she tempted him. Like Samson must he have felt, the strength of goodness sucked out of his heart, his soul surrendered to the spider of lust which fattens on its own success. Ay ! I can see that unhappy boy, loving him as I did, and I weep for him as I weep for all lovers with girls the way they are, teasing when you want them, clamorous when you're weary of their company. Only when you don't need them do they try to capture you, as Frankie had captured the prince, not for love of his bonny face but because his chastity was to her an affront, a challenge that had to be met even though she lost her soul in doing it and damned him, too, to triumph over him and all the other ladies who had failed to tempt him. For there was not a woman at court who'd not laid her traps to trip him, spiteful as wasps to see him happy in his own honey.

And he despising them all. Think you his noble heart
did not break when he knew himself love's fool like
any other man, snared in a wanton's web, trying to
escape her but beating with wings that could no longer
fly ? It was not in those early days that Frankie had
the devil's help, having as yet no need for his dark arts,
but devil's work it must have seemed to the prince that
he could not escape her. Like a man mad he was,
even his attire becoming careless, being bewitched and
bedamned. God keep you, lad, from such a female ! "

Too late that prayer ; already bewitched, Will loved
the dead woman and felt that she was at his side. More
vital than the jester drinking and creaking malice, more
living even than the plump wench continually refilling
their glasses and adroitly keeping out of Archie's fingers,
that ghost of Frances Howard sat beside him and he
could almost feel her touch his hand.

"But it could not last forever," said Archie. "The
prince was too wise and honest a lad to remain her
gull for long, particularly when he found that his rival
was the man he hated, his dad's minion, and knew that
behind Carr stood his loathsome ghost, Tom Overbury,
dipping his pen in treacle to tangle Frankie's feet.
Besides, there are always kind friends to warn a man of
his jill's behaviour. Such people—women no doubt—
told the prince of letters passed and of meetings in the
dark, and Harry rose from the slumber of his distemper,
fiery as a lion yet hiding his anger with a serpent's guile ;
ah ! if he had only lived to reign instead of his
brother ! "

The jester gaped and his plump face turned yellow
while he glared about him, startled that he, usually so
cautious and cunning, should in the delight of listening
to his own voice have let his thoughts escape him.
Behind him, he peeped into the darkening tavern but
the drinkers were busy at their talk, the wench was
amongst the barrels, and none had heard his treason

except this loon at his side whose eyes were glazing and whose head was nodding. Young fool, thought Archie, refilling his cup from the pot : they did not even learn how to drink these days.

" I was saying," said he, nudging Will with a sharp elbow to keep him awake, for he hated to lose a listener. " I was saying, if you'd but listen to wisdom, that the prince knew Frankie's treachery. He'd not share even a woman with such a popinjay as Carr, so proud-gutted was he, the brave boy. And it was at a masque one night when there was dancing afterwards, all being a little drunk and very merry when Frankie dropped her glove and somebody picked it up and gave it to the prince to return to her. But as though it were unclean, the good prince spurned the perfumed doeskin embroidered with gold and silver and whatnot. ' It has been stretched by another,' said he and turned his back.

" Around the court his words were whistled and even Frances blushed. It became the jest of all. ' Stretched by another,' they tittered, and wherever Frankie went, gloves were waved and toyed with and stretched and raised with two fingers as a sign of cuckoldry. She outfaced—or should I say, out-breasted —all the japes and jests with that tight smile of hers which didn't show her teeth. For what cared she what they said when she had Carr for her spaniel ? Ay, she was never one to be satisfied with common victims : the prince who curled his nostrils at females and then the king's minion whom no woman before had taught to suffer, both she mastered. What more could any orgulous lady ask ? But there was a worm in the bud— are you listening, friend ?—there was that husband of hers, young Essex, and he was sailing home to claim her.

" Abroad he'd proved himself a man and a warrior and did not seem the kind to become a tame wittol with his wife the leman of a lout with red hair, even though

he were the king's own darling. For two years had
Frankie lived as she wickedly willed with none to beat
her whatever she did, and she had learned pleasures
concealed from most girls ; and now was the ogre
returning to lock away beauty, to chain her in matrimony
to bear his children, and to sit at home while she itched
to be off, dancing or whoring—'tis oft the same thing—
and she'd not have it. Distraught she was when she
heard—I saw her—with dark smudges under her eyes,
not only from boozing and amorous nights, but fretting
because she must learn at last to behave herself like a
true wife. Now had come God's revenge, the time for
her, in her turn, to feel the lick of pain. She who had
been haughty to men, liking to see them in pain with
longing for her kindness, knew now their anguish, being
scatterbrained and desperate with love for Carr. She
was the man in that, I wager, the dominant one : he
was the woman, she the lover ; he the passive accepter,
being flattered yet frightened under her passion, and she
the tireless, caressing adorer. Often I saw him maggot-
pated as in a daze before her while she ate him with her
eyes as though she were an insect, gloating in him, as
a man might look at a roasted goose. She'd not leave
the loon in peace, but like a man with a woman, must
be ever fondling him, patting his knee, squeezing his
biceps, kissing and coaxing him to play. The words
that Overbury had wrote, sniggering to himself, no doubt,
had acted like acid eating through her pride and I have
seen her tremble as if pierced with a sword when Carr
came into the room, and tiny beads of sweat would
start out on her underlip for her to lick away. It was
not decent, I tell you, one so beautiful as she to be so
slavish to him, a fool in a pretty doublet. And now
was her rightful husband coming back, a stranger to
her, and she had not liked him when he was a boy.
He was a man now of eighteen or thereabouts ; and she
swore she'd kill him. I heard her. Rather than bed

with him, she'd kill him, she said. Already, yea, was there murder in that wicked little heart . . . "

" No ! " cried Will, " no ! " He rose to his feet and stood swaying, suddenly realising that he was drunk when, as through a mist, he saw the fat face of Archie, pointed with malice, grinning at him. " Not murder ? " he moaned.

" Yea," smiled Archie.

" Liar ! " cried Will.

" I'll not be angry with you, boy," said Archie, shrugging. " You're drunk, my lord."

" Drunk or sober," cried Will, " you're yet a liar ! "

" Now, now," said Archie coaxingly. " I cannot return a man's insults after he's bought me such excellent wine . . . You had best pay the reckoning, my lad."

" There is a greater reckoning for us all to come," groaned Will in a sepulchral voice, feeling tears behind his eyes when he thought of the wickedness of the world and the slanderous tongues of men.

" Give me your purse and I'll pay," said the jester. " 'Tis a little expensive, this wine, but good, for Archie'd let you have none but the best. Wench, pretty wench ! " he cried, expertly slipping the purse from Will's sleeve, " bring me the reckoning and no cheating because you think my friend's drunk. I've made a mark with the dagger on the table for every quart we've had. And call me a pair of sculls. My poor friend is taken with a wee sickness and I must ferry him home before he falls down . . . "

CHAPTER V

The Jester in the House

IN his own bed at Bedford House, Will awoke, sick and
ashamed. Never before had he been drunk, but
unthinkingly, fascinated by the jester's tale, he had not
noticed how often his cup had been refilled, and the
wine, unwatered, had been unusually strong. And he
shuddered more because he could not remember coming
home, save in scraps, a picture here and there, and all
of them shameful. His last distinct memory was of
Archie Armstrong's little-eyed round face, red with
malice, close to his while he had denounced him as a
liar for saying that the girl Frances had ever had murder
in her heart when threatened with her husband's return
from Europe ; after that, darkness fell with blurred
memories of sliding over slimy steps, of a wherry rocking
under him, then of streets of laughter peopled with
curved and bulging shapes pointing at him while he had
been sick on the cobbles, somebody slapping his back
and Archie's grating voice bewailing the waste of so
much good wine at so much the quart. After that he
recalled nothing until now when he awoke within the
shadows of his own embroidered bed-curtains and
shuddered to think that Betty Buskin, the woman left in
charge of the house and an old and privileged servant,
must have seen his return, and must with the help
of her fat kitchen-maid have undressed him and put
him to bed in this perfumed silk nightgown. He would
be unable to look either of them in the eyes again ;
and he swore that from that day forward he would
avoid the court. What he might have blabbed to the
jester he feared to think and he prayed he might

87

never see the evil creature again with his lies about
Frances . . .

Lies ? No. Will knew that Archie had told the
truth, however he might have coloured it, and he tried
to sort his tales into sequence. The virgin-wife arriving
at James's debauched court to be herself quickly
debauched, first becoming the prince's mistress and then
Carr's ; and he found that her acceptance of Carr stuck
in his throat. That she should surrender to the prince
his loyalty made him accept with only a faint wince, all
the tales he had heard of the tragically short-lived
Henry having been in praise of the lad whose sudden
death from fever at the age of eighteen years eight
months, about four years after his adventure with
Frances, had so shocked England that many to this day
believed that the king his father, jealous of his popularity,
had poisoned him. Difficult would it have been for the
most honest woman to have resisted such a prince, and
Will was grateful that the present king lived so chastely
with his queen that men could take their wives and
daughters to his court without fear of them being
insulted or ravished. But under James it had been very
different. Himself despising the sex, the king had
thought it merry to embarrass ladies with gross conversation so that nothing might seem sacred, their secrets
discussed and laughed at, and the most carefully reared
and ignorant girls must have become depraved after a
few days and nights at Whitehall, Hampton Court or
Windsor, with their elders' examples before them. Like
a knight of Queen Elizabeth's gallant days, Prince Henry
had remained aloof from his father's pranks and
ribaldries, being tutored by the great Sir Walter Ralegh
in the Tower where the envious James had locked him
that Carr might steal his lands. For Frances to have
loved so godly a youth was to her honour, even though
in excess of adoration she had acted dishonestly to her
good fame, princes being above ordinary men's con-

demnation ; but that from such a prince she should turn to the young Scotsman with naught beyond his beauty and his knowledge of tailoring to commend him and to raise him to greatness made Will sick with anger and shame.

Then suddenly he remembered that Carr became Somerset, that the golden youth was to become that half-mad creature, father of Anne, who with painted, un-washed cheeks had cackled at him at Chiswick. Frankie must have married the fellow : then what of her husband, Essex ? . . . Of course ! he remembered something about a divorce, and he raged because in his idealistic contempt for scandal he had never condescended to listen to the tale . . . That was something he must find out and it should not prove difficult. Records must have been kept. Yea, the details, the examination of witnesses, must have been written down. He'd to the lawyers and seek them, for records could not lie.

With sudden energy at the thought of something definite he could do, Will flung wide the curtains on the sunlit room, then he gaped to see Archie Armstrong stand in a golden doublet, breeches and hose, trying to squint at himself in a tiny round mirror.

" What, what the devil are you doing here ? " gasped Will.

" Whisht, lad ! " said Archie in an aggrieved voice, slipping the mirror into his sleeve. " Is that the fashion to talk to your samaritan and me with my arms and back yet aching from the weight they had to lug from the river yesterday, and you sick as a pig down my pretty clothes ? I had to borrow these to replace them. I found them in a chest in a large chamber . . ."

" Take them off ! " howled Will, his voice splitting with rage and horror. " Take them off this instant ! They're my father's ! "

" And an excellent choice he has, too," approved the jester, " although a wee bit subdued in colour for my complection. There be not enough tags and ribbons for a gentleman ; but they will do."

" Take them off ! " roared Will.

" And why should I be taking them off," said the jester with dignity, " when my own good garments have been ruined in your service so that even a twopenny-poet'd be shamed to be seen in such things ? "

" They're my father's, you can't . . . O ! " groaned Will, rolling on the bed and clasping his hot forehead. " I thought I'd lost you, curse you."

" Not me," said the jester. " D'ye think Archie'd abandon a comrade, and him sick as an owl, to be robbed in the streets with cut-purses and whores and beggars and all the cogging-crew around you ? But for my protection, laddie, you'd mayhap have had a knife in your bowels by now, and here's all the thanks I get for such good service ! Ingratitude ! Ah , it'd have come mightily expensive had you hired a guard as honest as I ; but I ask nothing in return save a cup of red wine for breakfast and a clean pair of hose. Yet you grudge me even that ! It'd serve you right if I left you as many a less soft-hearted fellow'd do."

" For God's sake, go ! " moaned Will.

" And me thinking hard till I cracked my eardrums all the long night, wondering how to help you ! What base ingratitude is this, and what will they say at court when I tell them of such miserable treatment of a drunkard's benefactor ! I do not like to think what your poor father would say when he comes to hear of it, and he a man of such virtue that he's even forgotten how to laugh ! And you in love with a ghost as you were telling me, haunted by that trollop Frankie Howard so that you cannot sleep of nights with dreaming of her flagitious fascinations and what she showed the world to prove herself a woman."

" I never said such things ! "

" Ah, you said more than that, laddie," said Archie in

a melancholy voice as he sat on a stool. "You told me that unless you proved her innocent of what she did you'd hang yourself in your own garters, so you did, and that live women were but carrion next to her dead meat, said you, for the dead could be more real than the living."

"No, no . . ."

"Do not fret yourself," smiled Archie. "I've a tender heart even though my nose be twisted and I wept to hear you talk in such fashion. A bonny lad like you in love with a bogle when there're so many plump things of honest flesh to slap and pinch gadding on real legs over the earth ! That's not right, said I, 'tis not fair to the ladies ; no, said I, Archie, we must mend this lad who's mayhap wolfed some witch's cockle-bread and known not what he guzzled. For that undoubtedly is what you've done. Something on which Frankie spat a spell you've eaten and I must cure you of her aphro-disiacal poisons. But, thought I, what can I do when the lad calls me liar in my own teeth ? He'll not heed me, thought I, on a stack of Bibles. While I was stripping off your clothes—and good, expensive stuffs they're made of, laddie : sad to spoil them with such behaviour as yours yestereen ; nor would I have the servants touch you but locked out a she-cat who wanted to put you to bed, and she old enough to know she'd not be wanted, for servants be thieves, even the best of them—well, as I was rolling you into bed I thought that I must help you in some wise, and you calling me a liar and crying for Frankie to come to your aid : me a liar ! when there's no more truthful man in England, nor even in Scotland ! For truth is meat to a jester, 'tis what he's paid to say that men might laugh at it and believe the lies they like better. But I forgive you, for you were drunk and you're young and in love with a ghost that has no legs. But I'll rid you of that ghost, I'll show you what kind of a she-devil Frankie was . . ."

" You ? . . . I could never trust you ! "

" That," said the jester, jutting out his paunch, " is the most ungrateful thing that ever I heard ! But I am thick-skinned to insults and misunderstandings, that being my trade, as I say, to speak truth that none might believe it. Like honest women, honest men are ever hated in this sinful world that rewards the wicked and makes an earl of a lickspittle and a duchess of a whore. So we'll speak no more on it. But I am on my mettle, laddie, and this morning I was talking to your house-keeper and I told her that you had commanded a banquet for next week——"

" You . . . you what ! "

" Now, now, be not angry with your friend, sweet lad. You'll kiss me and reward me when I tell you why. This is no real banquet, although we'll stuff our wombs, God willing, expensively on food and wine of the best : it will be a bobtag gathering and you will sit at one end of the board and I at the other and we will have your guests to talk."

" What guests ? "

" I've not decided on all of them yet. There is Mrs. Forman if I can find her : she's the wizard's widow ; and a lad I met at the Tower who was there in Overbury's time ; and there's a servant of Overbury's, a poor loon starving in Gunpowder Alley who writes what he calls poetry ; and there's a lawyer who'd sell his soul if he had one and who worked for Cokie at the time and should know secrets ; and there's a whore from Frankie's household. Yea, she's an honest whore now, taken to the game on Fleet Street, having had so liberal an education in that house ; and there's a leech who was apprenticed to old Lobell of Lime Street, him that married the sister of Dr. Mayerne, the king's apothecary, and he must know the truth of it . . . From amongst such villains you should hear what happened and I'll be master of the table by right of my motley. I'll have each

speak in turn, and thus the whole tale with no conceal-
ment will unfold before you. And you'll have no need
to call poor Archie a liar in his own gob, for I'll not
speak save to keep order and to make them act respect-
fully."

" I will not have it," groaned Will.

" It was the truth you asked after and now you say
that you'll not have it ! Of course, it will come a little
expensive : they'll need rewards for opening their gobs
and for the time lost when they might have been turning
a dishonest penny elsewhere . . . But if you do not want
the truth . . ."

" I must know that it is the truth ! "

" Amongst them all, you'll hear it. And why should
they lie to your honour ? "

Did he wish to hear it ? Or did he prefer to remain
in the darkness of his love for this dead woman, trying
to believe her honest, like a man with a wife he fears to
doubt and shuts her mouth with a kiss lest she break
his faith with proofs of adultery ? That was the coward's
unhappy way ; and what was this ghost to him but the
mother of Anne ? Being drunk last night, apparently he
had babbled of loving her above live women. That was
wine's exaggeration : he had meant to say that he
loved her as symbol of Anne, not for her sake alone, she
being dead, lipless, fleshless, a skull he could never take
in his hands . . . Yet even in this morning-light with the
hard bright eyes of Archie watching him, Will still had
the feeling that she was close. It was as though he felt
her presence with a sense not human : with extra-touch,
extra-smell, extra-sight, extra-hearing, by some means
too subtle for men's sealed understanding. Almost could
he hear the rustle of her golden hair purring like a cat
and could smell the acrid sweetness of her skin. He
could see her watching him with tenderness, with love
and pity, yea, with pity, as though she suffered with him
in the impossible longing to clasp her body of air.

"I want the truth," he groaned. "Gather your rascals . . . But first take off those clothes!"

"And run naked through the street!" cried Archie. "Nay, nay, I'd not believe that of you. You but jest and that is naughty of you. To jest upon a coatless jester. But you would be getting up and I must be off . . . I'll summon Mrs. Buskin and see you at bed-time . . ."

Before Will could leap from under the sheets to catch him, Archie had strutted in his golden costume from the room, and Will could only pray that his father might not notice that it had disappeared. But he forgot Archie in the sickness of his stomach and head when he stood up and he had to cling to the bedpost lest he fall with the sudden giddiness that spun the room around him. Then he blinked, ashamed, when the housekeeper, Betty Buskin, tiptoed in to look at him.

From babyhood had he known Betty, a gaunt, elderly woman with pale blue eyes, up-slanting as though she dragged on her greying hair and skewered it too tightly. And at every step she took her lacing squeaked, while she clattered on wooden chopines as though forever scrubbing floors.

"And are you not ashamed of yourself, my lord?" she demanded, smiling tight-lipped into his green face, "and me with more work than I can do with you opening the house to play high jinks in with that Scotch devil who knows not how to address a lady, and with none to help me but that slut Zenocrate that has to be spoken to thrice before she hears once? I hope your belly wambles, my lord, for there's little else you deserve, making a Paris Garden out of My House. I suppose you think you can hide here from your good father and mother and play the rogue in London, vomitting over my clean stairs and yammering about whores or ghosts or both. I'll not have that greasy fellow in My House again, d'ye understand me, sir? If you'd play cockleorum

you'll play it elsewhere and him having the audacity
to tell me to make ready a feast and wearing your noble
dad's best yellow doublet and breeches as if he'd gone
and paid for them. ' My good woman,' says he to me,
the insolent lidderon ! ' Good woman?' quoth I, ' I'm
not your good woman nor your good wife, the Lord be
thanked and pity on her poor soul,' quoth I, ' and if
you'd good woman me I'll show you how good I can be
with a broomstick on your prat, leading my good master
to the kennel and bringing him home all bemoiled and
bespattered as though a pig had rolled on him,' quoth
I ; but he'd not listen, he was afeared. Says he, you
would have a feast and no expenses spared, says he, the
guests being quality . . . "

"Bett, Bett, please ! " Will begged her, hands to his
head as he sank on to a stool. "I'm not well," he
moaned, " and your voice is like a bodkin through my
skull. That fellow is King Charles's jester, a most
important gentleman . . . "

"Gentleman ! " She shrieked with furious laughter.
" And him with a face like a pudding and a voice like
a bee and never a penny-piece in my hand as any gentleman would offer after sleeping a night under My Roof
and dirtying My sheets ! If that be a gentleman, may
the Lord be praised I am no lady . . . Ah ! my sweet
lord, in your innocence don't be deceived by such folk,
jesters or jokers or what have you, for what would your
sweet mother to say to have you vomiting and moaning
of ghosties and being sick as a child? This is no life
for a lad like you. Get you back to Woburn and I'll
never say a word of what you've done."

"I can't." Sadly, Will shook his head, "I have set
on an adventure, Bett, from which only a coward would
shy. Would you have me a coward?"

"A coward, indeed ! " she scoffed ; "a coward to
tell a miserly Scotchman that you hate his ugly face
and would kick his tail? Leave that to me, sweet

sir, 'twill be more than a pleasure for me to tweak his nose."

"You don't understand. Listen, Bett, you have been second-mother to me, nurse to me, and teacher, too. Pray, listen. I am in love."

"I thought it must be some such moon-madness for you to act in that filthy fashion ; but what has that Scotch louse to do with love ? She can be no honest lady if he's your go-between."

"He's not my go-between. I only met him yesterday at Whitehall. He is to help me to discover a secret. You, too, can help me, Bett. You must whisper this to nobody, understand ? Promise me. Swear by God and your mother's memory that what I say will reach no further than your ears. Will you ? "

"Why ? " said she, goggle-eyed. "Is it murder ? "

"I know not yet. Murder, adultery, witchcraft, bigamy : all mayhap, or none."

"May God protect you, my sweet lord ! " she wailed.

"But will you swear ? "

"God save me, but I will, my lord. By my father's bones and my hope of heaven, I'll repeat naught of what you tell me. Who is the woman ? "

"The Earl of Somerset's daughter, the Lady Anne Carr," he said, watching her closely.

He saw her stiffen and heard the spit sizzle between her teeth as she took a deep breath.

"No, my lord," she whimpered.

"Yea," he cried fiercely. "She is my own true love, my only love. We have loved since babyhood ; and now that I would claim her, all shrink away, you shrink away. Nay ! my own mother did not shrink away although I saw mislike in her eyes. She alone did not condemn me for what I cannot help and would not if I could. There is this dark mystery I would pierce and the jester will help me do it. He's bringing to this feast all those who know her parents' story. Now do you understand ? I would unriddle this mystery. Then I will claim Anne."

" There is no mystery," said Betty in a low voice. " The woman was a whore and that's the end to it ; and may God save you from her child ! "

" I am going to marry Anne," he said truculently, " no matter what you or anybody says. No matter even what my father says ; even though he disinherit me and curse me, I will marry her. If you know only vile rumours about her mother, bite your tongue, Bett, for I'll not listen. What do you know about her ? "

" What all the world knows : that she was a whore and an adultress and, even worse, a murderess."

" How do you know these things ? "

" Her ill-fame was on all men's tongues and she confessed the fact. Had she not been a Howard she'd have gone with her sister-in-sin, Nan Turner, and have swung at Tyburn as she deserved. You must never marry a child of hers."

" Rumours, Bett, only rumours. You never knew the woman."

" I saw her, cow-eyed and looking innocent but with a cruel smile. Many a time I saw her showing her bigs to tempt the men. She should have been whipped at Guildhall for the nasty-minded men to watch her stripped and thrashed to the buff. She should have been piped to the thew that we honest women might have pelted the cat's smile off her big mouth and lashed her likerous tail to stop it wriggling. Ah ! the brothel would be too clean a place for the likes of her. And yet you'd marry that she-cow's daughter ! "

" I *am* going to marry her daughter," he said. " But come, Bett, you've told me nothing whatever about her : only about yourself, unlidding what envy you women show at mention of the lady's name. She must have been very beautiful to have caused such hatred."

"Ay, she was beautiful enough, or so men thought, but she was a cat that with its breath can poison a sleeping person ; and like a cat, she had claws and liked to use men like mice. But there's a God in heaven as her ill-life proved, and she suffered for it in the end, may heaven be praised ! she suffered for it and I hope she repented at the last."

"Still you've told me nothing, nothing ! " he cried. "You wag only of what you've heard or suspected. What with your own eyes and ears do you know of her wickedness ? "

"I'll bring you a book," she said, "the story of her trial. Read that. Then ask me why I think she's evil."

It was a tattered book she brought, having been often read and certain pages were dirtier than others. Smiling, yet with dread in his heart, Will took it and put it on the table.

"Read it ! " she cried passionately. "You must read it all."

"I'll read it," he said, "later. In bed."

"Then may God be with you," she sighed, "for you'll not sleep this night."

Will tried to laugh and when she had left him he took up the book gingerly, half-wanting to throw it into the fire, half-longing to read it. Slowly the leaves unfolded and in heavy letters showed—*The Trial of Richard Weston at the Guildhall of London, for the Murder of Sir Thomas Overbury*, 9 *October, A.D.* 1615. Ah ! Will thought : this has nothing to do with Frances. It was some fellow Weston did the killing. Over fell the pages. *The Trial*, he read, *of Anne Turner, Widow, at the King's Bench, the* 7th *of November for the Murder of Sir Thomas Overbury, A.D.* 1615. Another of them ! Anne Turner. Dimly, he recalled Betty mentioning a Mrs. Turner, but he could not recall exactly what she had said. *The Trial of Sir Jervis*

Elwes, knight, announced the book as the pages folded apart, *Lieutenant of the Tower, at the Guildhall of London, the 16th November, for the Murder of Sir Thomas Overbury, A.D.* 1615. Another in the plot : Sir Jervis Elwes ! *The Trial of James Franklin, at the King's Bench,* said the book, *the 27th November, for the Murder of Sir Thomas Overbury, A.D.* 1615. Over fell the pages, limp with age, ragged-edged, greasy, stained with tallow and wine- and ale-rings. *The Trial,* he read, *of the Lady Frances Countess of Somerset, the 24th of May, for the Murder of Sir Thomas Overbury, A.D.* 1616.

With trembling hands Will shut the covers fast and stood back guiltily, chin up as though he wanted somebody unseen in that chamber not to know what he had read. Slowly on his heel he turned, twisting the book until he had made a funnel of it and could slide it inside his doublet against his fast-beating heart.

" It's not true ! " he cried, and he shivered when echo sighed from the walls : " True."

" No ! " he cried ; and " no," said echo.

He was alone. Yet he could smell the fragrance of a woman, not of grave-clothes, but of healthy skin and living hair. Almost like the touch of feathers felt her fingers on his hand as if to thank him for putting aside that evil book. What if she had been charged and tried ? Innocent men and women had been hanged ere this ; and jealous hatred of beauty was still a beast in human hearts. Innocence cannot always be proved. One cannot open one's heart to show its purity ; one can only cry : *Innocent, innocent, innocent !* and few will listen, each desiring to hear evil, hating youth and love and beauty and longing to destroy it, to crucify Venus as they had crucified God when he had walked amongst them.

Yet cold against his heart pressed the book and Will knew that he would have to read it through. No ! he swore, he would not ! even while he drew it out again. He'd wait till after this supper of Archie's, he said ; when he had heard what those suborned creatures said, he would discover what this old book had to contradict or substantiate their statements. Nevertheless, one glance he thought to give. Just one . . .

The Trial of Robert Carr, said the book in crooked type, *Earl of Somerset, May* 25, *for the Murder of Sir Thomas Overbury, A.D.* 1616.

Not there : no ! at the beginning. He would read Weston first. Only Weston, nothing further . . .

He trimmed the candle with his fingernails and drew it closer, then shaded his eyes and sat down and began to read :

" The Commissioners were, the Lord Mayor, Hayes ; the Lord Chief Justice of England, Coke ; Justice Crook ; Justice Doderidge ; Justice Haughton ; Serjeant Crew ; and Sir Henry Montague, Recorder.

" The court being set, the king's special commission was read, the lord chief justice gave the charge ; the effect whereof was,

" First, to express the king's pious inclinations . . ."

" What have you here ? " cried Archie, and Will started back, trembling, as the jester's shadow fell across the page. " What ! you have dug up the trials, have you ? Bah ! this is not the skeleton of the truth ! That'll tell you naught, only what the court wished to hear. Know you that when Carr was placed at the bar in Westminster Hall, on either side of him stood a man with a cloak ? And why, think you ? To hoodwink him lest he blab too much ; yea, and to hoodwink justice, too ! That was good King Jamie's way, may God bless his late majesty." Archie took the book and wrinkled his nose as though it stank while he riffled the pages. " Bacon was the royal hound," he said, " snuffing after what his royal master ordered, yapping and biting and barking, too, whichever way the king whipped him, the

fawning hound who had wagged before Carr many a
time to bribe his way to office. Now he had him at his
merciless mercy. Not only Bacon and the king, but
there was Buckingham as well . . . What will these
pages tell you of that, eh? This is what the king wanted
the people to read and therefore 'tis but the margin of
truth, a gloss to keep them from inquiring further."
He rolled the book and slipped it within his golden
doublet. "Lies," he said, "or half-truths. Else do
you think the king would let it be printed?"

"Give me that book!" cried Will, shaking with
anger. "I am reading it."

As though to caution a mischievous child, the jester
waggled a plump finger in front of his nose. "Now,
now, laddie," said he, "you must wait a wee bit longer.
I'll give it back to you, but do you think I'll have my
preparations set at naught? Not I, sir! Hear the truth
from the lips of those who acted in it; afterwards, read
these lies the king wished to have known. Betwixt the
two, you'll discover the truth, or as near as man can
coast to it when a woman's the pivot of the plot."

"I want to read it now!"

"Come, sir! I have taken mighty trouble today;
expensive trouble, too, has it been, but I doubt not your
honour's noble heart'll not see my purse lighten because
of that."

"You stole my purse yesterday. I had twenty
pounds in it."

"Twenty pounds, laddie, less what you spent," said
the jester imperturbably. "That was the most expensive
wine we drank, right good muscadine, but you would
give the jolly wench that served us—for all that I went
on my knees like a father to stop you—gold pieces to
slip under her tongue for every kiss she gave you."

"I did not! Never!"

"Ay, laddie, but you did. And she had a big gob,
that wench, and was most voracious of gold. Terrible

waste it was, as I warned you, to pay any woman in advance, but you'd not heed me. In you would toss your coins to see her click on them that you might lip her afterwards and seek to take them back with your tongue——"

"You're lying! I'd never do such things!"

"But, laddie, you did, I saw you doing it. But have no fear, brave boy, I'll not talk of it. Why! I'd not have mentioned it now had you not cast doubts upon my honesty and like a careful steward I must give accounting. Empty was the purse when we landed and I had to pay the waterman from my own pouch; but I'll not press for that. Let it be forgotten. 'Tis but a small matter between friends. But I need more gold. See! here are your guests. The wizard's widow and her new husband: she wants little payment beyond a full belly, and that I promised to give her, and of more than food I gave fair warning, she being yet toothsome, though ageing. A well-weathered and often-exercised female, I doubt not, by her gat-toothed grin and the way she blinked her eyes at me. Many peculiar tricks must she have learned from that wizard who could conjure Cleopatra when he felt lonely. I asked her how went her familiars nowanights and whether she could give me a potion to turn that wench in the tavern's bowels to mercy, and she put her foul breath into my ear-hole. 'Tickle her,' quoth she, 'tickle her with one hand and slip your purse down her bosom with the other, and any woman's open to the asking then,' quoth she, 'even Me,' quoth she, the foul naughty witch. But off I skipped before she could poison me with one of her stinking love-philtres. Small wonder, thought I, that the wizard delivered his soul to the devil on the Thames at noon, having such a she-devil at home."

"To the devil with her indeed!" cried Will. "Whom else have you asked?"

"The apothecary. He must be paid, but he'll come

cheap, being a fool. And the poet. He needs new
doublet and hose, not being fit to come to a gentleman's
table, as I told him, my fingers up my nose ; but I'll
buy them cheap at Rag Fair. They'll not come
expensive. Then there's the trullibub who worked for
Frankie. She swore that she could earn a pound a
night, the liar, when her feet weren't hurting. Ach,
even in a coal-hole she's not worth a penny, but women
have such pride in their flesh if not their souls, even when
they're old and mottled like brawn. So we must give
her a shilling, at the least, for her time spent here.
Then there's the lawyer. Him, like the devil, I could
not argue down. A pound the dog must have to oil his
tongue. The soldier from the Tower asked nothing, the
silly fellow. 'I have a bottle and a whore for you,'
said I, thinking I might as well have the wench work for
her shilling ; and he clapped me on the back as though
I were the laundry in need of a beetle and he swore by
cock that he'd be here. And that is the lot of them.
From their foul gobs you'll discover more truth than
you'd get from fifty books, and I'll be there to watch
and trip them should they lie. I'll act the hinge, my
lad, telling what I know, for I know Everything, leading
one from the other to make a whole. I have it all writ
down. The harlot will open, which is appropriate, she
having been in Frankie's household from the first and
knowing her mistress inside as well as out. Then the
apothecary and Mrs. Forman will speak—although
married again, she'll be called by no name but her first
husband's, because it is good for trade, said she, as she
deals slyly yet in love-potions and reading the future
for silly wenches who want to know why their lads won't
marry them after they've had all they want. Then the
soldier from the Tower ; then the lawyer and apothecary
. . . We'll have the whole tale unwound in a night !
Then you'll not call me a liar again."

"But the book ! my book ! "

"You will have your book," said Archie, "afterwards. Mayhap, we might read it that night, a piece here and a piece there to fill the gaps and to jog our memories."

"You are the most damnable, interfering, unwanted beast that ever I have met!" cried Will. "Get out and be damned to you!"

"That," grinned the jester, "is what my mother said before I was born."

CHAPTER VI

A Maid's Divorce?

In this, his father's town-house, Will found himself a stranger. Archie had taken command and even Betty joined in his conspiracy to ignore the young master, much to Will's surprise when he found the pair chuckling together in the kitchen, the serving-wench, Zenocrate, a fat dark wench of thirteen to fifteen gazing plate-eyed at them while she stirred a pot over the fire. At his entrance, Archie and Betty looked at him with raised brows as though he were the servant intruding on his betters while Archie hitched up his long violet taffeta cloak tasselled and laced with gold and lined with velvet, pulling down the hood to the point of his nose. It was, Will noticed, one of his father's favourite cloaks, but so weakened had grown his will under the jester's bland assumption of mastery that he made no protest. He merely said testily :

" For the love of God be careful of that cloak, fellow. 'Tis my father's best-loved one."

" Think you I am a babe to dabble my garments ? " growled Archie indignantly. " 'Tis pesky cold and would you have me catch a rheum and mayhap my death when I am about your business ? What a miserable lad you are, always worrying about money and grudging to give anything, even warmth, to your old comrade ! Mistress," he added, turning to Betty, and laying a long finger against his broken nose, " I can rely on you ? "

" To the very bottom of me ! " cried Betty.

" What damned conspiracy is this ? " demanded Will.

" Hey, lad," shrilled Betty, " I'm no conspirator I'll have you know but I work for the good of your soul with this noble friend of yours. If you're bewitched 'tis our task to unwitch you. We've been arranging for this banquet, what to have, whom should serve, for I'll have none that know you or your family at such a gathering. And I'd not soil my own hands with waiting on such a rope-ripe crew as Mr. Armstrong's been collecting for your elucation. But I'm going to be present. I'll not have such doings in My House unless I'm there to watch to see they pouch no spoons. This wench'll serve us and none other. I'll not have the men up there to listen to bawdy."

" She's a child. Aren't you afraid for her soul ? "

" Soul ! " snorted Betty. " She is a fool so what's she to do with a soul ? A poor daft creature like her has not the sense nor the looks to be wicked. Have you, Zenny ? Speak, child."

" My mother taught me my prayers," said Zenocrate sullenly.

" Then go you to them and be saying them without a stop when you serve this gallows' crew. I'll plug your ears with wax and I'll be watching if you listen to one lewd word, and I'll pinch you every time I think you dare understand what the men say to you. And don't you go outside in the dark with any of them."

" What men ? " asked Zenocrate, her eyes brightening.

" Pish," said Betty. " What men ? Any men. Those radishes who, when the wine's in them, sweat roguery and care not how a wench looks so long as she can lie down. Ah, she's a poor daft creature," she groaned, " and only from charity and a generous heart did I take her in, she being my own dead sister's child."

" I mind not the daftness," said Archie, stroking his thin beard while he measured the wench's girth with his eyes. " That can be welcome in a female. 'Tis the broadness of her and the size of her nose that mars her fortune."

" My nose ? " sniffed Zenocrate, feeling for the

minute red nob between her red cheeks. " What ails
my nose ? "

" 'Tis no nose," said Archie, " but a cherry the birds
have pecked. Yet weep not, my child ! man is
generous and Archie was never one not to pity a lass
when he can find no other bed. Mayhap one night the
Angel Gabriel will visit you in the mien of a jester.
Greater miracles have happened ere now."

" If I catch you snouting near that child," cried Betty,
working her arms like a bird about to fly, " there'll be
no jesting for either of you. She is my own dead sister's
bastard with none to love her but me and I'll not have
her debauched by a miserable Scotch crow old enough
to be her granddad. Him that ruins her marries her if
I have to drag him to the altar with the tongs on his
nose."

" Marry her ! " cried the jester, shuddering, " nay !
you'd not spoil sport with a ceremony, would you, dame ?
I'm no marrying man and God forbid she be a marrying
wench for her husband's sake. What harm in a kiss
even though the door be bolted ? 'Tis your lewd mind,
dame, that thinks only of naughtiness. I have nothing
but pity for all females, a father's tenderness. No harm
in it if I put my arm, like this, about her. And like this,
lickspittle her little gob . . ."

" Off with you ! " shrilled Betty, gripping his cloak-
hem and dragging him away from the wench concealed
within its folds. " I see I shall have to lock her up with
the spoons. Is nothing sacred from this locust you
brought into My House, Master Will, that even such a
drazel that I thought'd be safe in a monkery should
be mauled as though she were a pudding ! . . . Now,
sirrah, get you out ! " she cried, " or I'll pour the soup
down your neck ! "

" Not on my father's cloak ! " cried Will.

But with a low bow, his nose almost touching the stone
floor, the jester turned and pranced from the kitchen,

leaving Zenocrate gaping with round eyes and open mouth after him while yet she stirred the pot.

" Pish, he is but a child and only does it to annoy me," tittered Betty to Will's astonishment. Knowing her as being always prim-lipped and God-fearing, at least in talk, he had expected her to rail at so coarse and indiscriminate a lecher, but, nay! She grinned and was far from angry. " You look strangely at me, master," she giggled, " and wonder, no doubt, why I didn't beat him for his punkateering ; but those that talk bold and misbehave in front of others oft act cowardly in the dark. 'Tis only his way to fret me, I know, for even he'd not have mechal thoughts on that fat child."

" But yesterday you hated him and swore that he must leave."

" Yesterday was yesterday," she said, looking sly-eyed away from him while a blush darkened her wrinkled cheeks. " I didn't know him then to be so great a gentleman and the friend of kings ; and the tales he tells ! You don't know whether to run away or to hit him. If I didn't know him for a liar I'd believe him a lord ; and he has such sweet coaxing ways with him when you'd not expect them and such a knowledge of what a lady likes."

" Bett, Bett, I fear you love the dog ! "

" Me ! " she squeaked, throwing her apron over her head, " at my age, master ! You jest ! "

" She was in the fowlhouse with him hours and hours," said Zenocrate, " and the door locked on them both and fowls squawking, for hours and hours she was."

" And why not ? " cried Betty, tossing down the apron to glare at her niece. " We were getting eggs and he was showing me how to kill the creatures. One twist of the neck, like that, and never a twitter out of them. And me having to chase them with an axe when I'm hungry. And what were you doing, watching me, you slut ? Had you no work to do ? "

" I was thinking," said Zenocrate.

" And what were you thinking of, you fool ? "

" Of what you were doing in the fowlhouse," said Zenocrate.

" The wench is a moonling ! " cried Betty. " Take no heed of her talk, Master Will. We were not five minutes amongst the fowls and he just acting the gentleman, showing me how to throttle them and pluck them quick . . . Did you read that book I gave you ? "

It was now Will's turn to flush and look aside. " Yea," he lied.

" And," cried Betty in triumph, " what do you think of your dilling's mother now, eh ? "

" My resolution remains unaltered," said Will. " What care I what is writ in books or what her mother did ? "

" Pish," muttered Betty, " everybody's mad but me, methinks. If you've read that book, then you can read this other. But while the other was the truth, this one is lies, I warn you." From out of her gown's bosom she produced a ragged pamphlet and tossed it to him. " Now begone," she growled, " there's reading sufficient to send you asleep."

Glad to escape, hugging the pamphlet as though he feared Archie might suddenly appear and snatch it from him, Will ran from the kitchen and up the stairs to his own bedchamber. Safely inside it, he locked the door, and, sitting by the fire, he stirred the coals and opened the yellowing pages to read the title :

Proceedings between the Lady Frances Howard, Countess of Essex, and Robert Earl of Essex, her Husband, before the King's Delegates, in a Cause of Divorce, A.D. 1613.

" Twenty-one years ago," he murmured : " before I was born ; " and for some reason, that made him sad.

Eagerly he began to read but soon he wearied. He had hoped to find at least some of the secret here revealed but the legal jargon made the tale amorphous and he became as impatient as a man eyeing the clock when his loved one is late. But at least he had discovered that Frances had been thirteen when she married Essex. Not such a child, after all, girls of twelve being permitted to marry and often bearing children at that age. Nevertheless, she would surely have been too young to appreciate the importance of the act and to understand how she was wiping out any possible future freedom by taking this man's ring ? Her body, like her mind, would have been unformed, possibly ; with merely a pinch of breasts and not that full bosom which later was to drive men mad with longing had she walked towards the priest, her yellow hair unbound to symbolise her maidenhood, and the lad, a little her elder, at her side who was to be made her husband. At the masque that followed, he had heard, the men had dressed in crimson and the women in white, passion with purity. Twenty-one years ago : a small lifetime, and she never realising what tragedy was to open before her soon.

"That since the pretended marriage," he read, " at least by the space of whole and continuate three years after the said Robert had fully attained the age of eighteen years, as time and place did serve, after the fashion of other married folk, the said Frances Howard in hope of lawful issue, and desirous to be made a mother, lived together with the said Robert at bed and board, and lay both naked and alone in the same bed, as married folk use : and desirous to be made a mother, from time to time, again and again yielded herself to his power, and as much as lay in her offered herself and her body to be known." . . .

There was such pain behind Will's eyes, as though fingers squeezed the back of his nose, that he had to put down the pamphlet ; and he found that his legs were trembling. Those words from the dead, legal words, had yet fire in them to burn into his mind.

"Frankie," he whispered ; but she did not, perhaps could not, answer, although he knew that she was at his side as he looked at the shadows dancing from the fire, half-expecting to see a woman's shadow move open-armed amongst them. But silent, dead, remained the room, save for the crackling of the coals ; and the shadows flickering over the rushes, up the panelled walls and across the ceiling, were only shadows of the furniture and of himself crouched like a bird over the book.

Back to that book he turned after squeezing tight his eyes to squeeze away the image of Frances in her marriage-bed, yielding and longing for the motherhood denied her. Thus had it been, said the pamphlet, and the earl too had longed to make actual his desires. Unhappy pair, groaned Will, and he wept. Unhappy pair struck by enchantment into chastity.

" . . . she refused not," said the book, " but used the best means she could : notwithstanding all this, the said earl could never carnally know her . . . Yet before the pretended marriage, and since, the said earl hath had, and hath power and ability of body to deal with other women, and to know them carnally . . . Furthermore, the said Lady Frances hath been, and is fit and able to have copulation with a man, and such a one as may be carnally known . . . And furthermore, the said earl, long before this suit commenced, hath very often, and at sundry times, confessed in great earnest, that although he did his best endeavour, yet he never could . . . And lastly in regard of womanish modesty, the Lady Frances hath concealed all the former matters, and had a purpose ever to conceal them, if she had not been forced, through false rumours of disobedience to the said earl, to reveal them——. She requireth, since this pretended matrimony is but in fact, and not in right, it may be pronounced, declared, and adjudged as none, and of none effect ; and she may be quit and free from all knots and bonds of the same, by your sentence and authority."

Light-headed, grinning, with exultation, Will in his eagerness merely glanced amongst the lines, too excited to read carefully. Here, before a court of ecclesiastical law, judged by bishops and the Archbishop of Canterbury himself—men who, for their souls' sake, would countenance no lying—poor Frances had had to blush and stammer out her intimate tale. Yet from this had slander wrung its malice ! Who would dare denounce such holy men as liars ! They must have known her innocence. Therefore could he snap his fingers at Archie, Betty, and even at his father.

The Earl of Essex first gave evidence, Will read, and he had sworn that he had been fourteen at the time of his marriage and was now twenty-two and that he had attempted, he swore, to act the husband to his wife but had always failed. For a full year " at divers times," he swore, he had " attempted ; that the other two years, when he was willing, she showed herself sometimes willing, but other times refused, and he lay in bed most commonly with her, but felt no motions or provocations."

Tragic was the uncurtaining of that bed of over twenty years ago to Will : the young earl and his golden bride, all eagerness, to fail ! Had she been at fault, had she denied him, would not the earl have accused her of it ? True, he hinted at some such thing but he did not speak openly, while he swore that he could act the man with other women. But never with her. And he believed, he told the court, that his wife was not a woman fit for true love, " because he had not found it." Which to be blamed ? She swore that he was at fault, and he swore she was no woman. How could the truth be settled between such opposites ? The clergy had argued the question and other points that had perplexed them, then Frances's deposition had been read to them. She had been unable to face those grave good men and that was no mark against her. Modesty would have restrained her from speaking of such secret matters and therefore she had signed a confession and had not given evidence. Her statement was similar to her husband's, only more forthright, she insisting that the marriage had never been consummated although she had yielded herself willingly in the hope of bearing children.

Then came the witnesses, merely names to Will: Frances's cousin, Katherine Fines, daughter of Thomas, Lord Clinton, a girl of eighteen, had deposed that the earl and his countess, to her knowledge, had lived as man and wife together, she seeing them in their bed-chamber and "the earl go into the said chamber undressed and ready for bed; and she verily believes," declared the book, that "they did lie together in the same bed those two nights, for that she knows there was but one bed in the said chamber."

Next, Elizabeth Raye, daughter of William Raye, of Woodstock in Oxfordshire, deposed that she had known Frances above twelve months and that she, too, had seen her in bed with the earl. Following her came Frances Britten, widow, to swear that she was fifty-five and had known both parties from their infancy and had seen them dine and sup together like man and wife. At Lady Frances's lodgings at Hampton Court and Whitehall she had often found them in bed and one morning when she had entered their bedchamber, being called in by Frances's sister, Kathcrine Howard, the "Lady Frances stepped out of her bed, and left the earl there: That this was on St. Valentine's Day, for that Lady Katherine told the earl that there was a valentine for him. Cannot depose further, saving that when this deponent was at Hampton Court, as is before mentioned, after the earl and Lady Frances were risen, the lady missing a pendant ruby that usually hung at the ring in her ear, desired this deponent to look for it in the bed. That thereupon she and the lady's chambermaid turned

down the bedclothes, and there they saw the places
where the said earl and lady had lain, and that there
was such a distance between the two places, and such a
hill between them, that this deponent is persuaded they
did not touch one another that night."

A hill, a pile of pillows perhaps, to wall them apart
lest their skin chafe together ; and her ruby-earring, a
tear of blood, lost in the milkwhite emptiness of no-love
that had separated them through those unhappy nights.
Ah ! shame on parents' greed which bound younglings
together in a lifetime's misery, dooming them to sterile
nights of tears and repinings ! By God, Will swore,
never would he consent to similar shame. Should he
prove weak and marry either Elizabeth Cecil or Dorothy
Sidney, as his father demanded, who knew that he might
not meet a like situation, the door closed on laughing
friends and their lewd jokes who had rolled them into
bed, mayhap to hear his wife weeping at his side, her
heart already being another's, as his would always be
Anne's ? Never could he do it : never. This trial was
warning enough of the dangers he might expect. Of
that wretched couple, Essex, it would seem, had been
the greater sufferer, desiring the beautiful wife he could
never love. How many marriages fed on such hatreds ?
How many bedchambers could tell of bitterness, of
reproaches, curses, the wife ravished while beating him
off, or of the husband, leaden-hearted, turning to take
the quivering body into his arms while he flinched at
her touch ?

Poor Frances ! Will moaned : and poor Essex,
too . . .

" The deposition," he read, forcing back tears, " of
Katherine Dandenell, one of the Lady Frances's domestic
servants, aged about sixteen years . . ." She had seen
them often abed together, she said, at Awdley End in
Essex, at the earl's house at Chorley, at the Lady
Walsingham's, at the Tiltyard, at the Countess of

Leicester's at Drayton, at Salisbury House, and at Durham House . . . " The Deposition of Anne Jaconim, one of the domestic servants of Lady Frances, aged about twenty-four years" . . . She, too, at such and such places had seen them naked abed together. Thomas Bamford, yeoman, swore the same ; as did George Powell, William Power and Benjamin Orwell. Then came Frankie's father, the great Earl of Suffolk and the Lord High Chamberlain of the Royal Household. Would such as he swear falsely even for his daughter's sake ? He confirmed all that the previous witnesses had sworn : his child had been no wife to her husband nor had her husband been true husband to her. Thus also his Lady, Frankie's mother, the Right Honourable Katherine, Countess of Suffolk.

The case was proved, exulted Will, yet the Archbishop of Canterbury had suffered an uneasy conscience. Long in this pamphlet he talked about scripture and marriage amongst Christians " as instituted by God Himself in paradise, honoured by the presence of the Saviour Himself, declared by St. Paul to be a sign of the spiritual conjunction between Christ and the church . . ." On, on, meandered the old man, mumbling into Latin, quoting this, that and the other. And King James's answer was then read to soothe that prickly conscience. This royal letter continued for page after page until Will's eyes wearied, stumbling amongst the broken letters and ill-spelling, and he nodded by the fire, wondering where Frances lay hidden under these heavy words, until at last she sprang to life again within a cloud of modesty.

Was she a virgin yet married ? argued the court and, Will read, a jury of matrons " went from the presence of the commissioners into the next room where the countess was, who was left alone with the said ladies. After some convenient time they returned, and delivered in their report under their hands ; all persons being

removed except the register, that so the ladies and midwives might more freely deliver their secret reasons, etc.
which were not fit to be inserted into the record ; and
this is in sum their report :

"1. That they believe the Lady Frances fitted with
abilities to have carnal copulation, and apt to have
children. 2. That she is a virgin uncorrupted."

Will read no further, merely glancing at the last dog-
eared page to confirm that the marriage had been
annulled, so merry was his heart at this discovery. Here
was proof against the jester's slander. A jury of ladies
and midwives could not have been all bribed or
suborned in some fashion, yet they had examined
Frances and had sworn her to be yet a maid. Stronger
their evidence, evidence of wise women who had
inspected the girl and could not have been deceived by
a wanton's pretence of virginity, than all the slanders of
creatures like Archie Armstrong or of servants like Betty
Buskin who knew only what they had been told.
Always eager to believe the worst of others, they had
ignored what was here sworn on oath. Frances could
never have been Prince Henry's mistress ; she could
not have been Carr's mistress. A maid she had
remained and as a maid had she married a second time,
a note at the end of the pamphlet briefly stating that
" Soon after this sentence, the countess was married to
the Viscount Rochester, lately made Earl of Somerset."

As gay as though he were a married man who, after
distrusting his wife, had suddenly lighted on proof of her
innocence, Will laughed as he concealed the pamphlet.
He'd not speak of it yet. He'd let them talk, he'd let
Archie produce his liars, his crows to peck for carrion ;
then after they had spat their poison, calmly he would
bring this forward and ask them to read the verdict. It
was strange, he thought, that Betty could have let him
have the book ; but of course, she had dismissed it for a
pack of lies ; and perhaps she had given him the wrong

book. She had been confused at the time after Zenocrate's exposure of her and Archie having been alone with the fowls and therefore had not realised what she was doing. And for her to talk of Frankie ! She and Archie ! She with her chatter of virtue locking herself in alone with that rooster ! Yet she dared condemn Frankie who before a full gathering of England's churchmen, her young body submitted to the searching fingers of strange women, had been proclaimed innocent, a maid if yet a wife !

Ha ha ! grinned Will : it would be merry to see their faces after they had barked at her memory and he produced this ! . . . Yet, he flinched to remember, there had been that other trial, and accusations of poisoning in the Tower . . . But he'd not yet think of that. Doubtless when he dug under the malice, he would find her proved innocent again.

For the first time in many weeks that night Will sang while he undressed and went to bed ; and for the first time in many nights, he slept at once, deeply and undisturbed, like a contented lover in his mistress's arms.

CHAPTER VII

The Gathering of the Crows

WHEN at last came that day which he both dreaded and desired, Will dressed to suit his mood, funereally. Like an Italian, he wore black from velvet shoon to neck, only the turned-down lace at his wrists and the stiff lace collar being white. Doublet, breeches, hose : all were black save for the coral buttons and the sword at his girdle. Thus, like animated death, he stalked, tugging his thin beard, into the tapestry-hung Terrace Room which ran the full length of the northern wing, opening, as its name showed, on to the tiered terrace and walled garden. The day was cold when the friends and enemies of Frances were to meet, and therefore these doors were shut while on the table, laid for a banquet, candles stood ready for lighting when the shadows gathered. Food was prepared on salvers : cold meats with olives and capers and anchovies and neats' tongues and pickled oysters with glasses ready for the bottles of wine to be opened.

" I have eaten nothing, and that rarely, for two whole days," said Archie, " that I might prove myself a worthy guest, my lord."

Will swung round on his heel, hand on his sword, startled and angry, not having heard the jester tiptoe into the room behind him.

" Why must you be always creeping," he cried, " spying and listening ? "

" Spying, my lord ? What is there to be spied here save food ? And as for listening : how else do you think I know so many secrets ? "

" And that dress, why ? "

" It is my court-costume," said the jester complacently, " which I wear but twice or thrice a year lest it soil. I honour you with it, my lord ; " and he shook his stick on which hung coloured bladders, its top carved to the likeness of his own round visage. In motley was he garbed, striped red and yellow, and he had a horned cap on his head, bells on either horn tinkling at each move he made. " This becomes me well," he said, " and shows my leg wellnigh from hip to toe, and 'tis an excellent limb of grace and beauty, shaped for a jig or a kick or for lolling over a lady's lap that she may tremble at its shape. I like not this fashion today of shapeless breeches to turn a man's middle to a tub. They hide too much and are not fair to ladies. Would the days of codpieces and bull's chests might return for Archie to be recognised even with his head in a barrel. But, sweet sir, look not so sourly on your comrade. I dress thus to delight you and your guests, for I am master of the revels this day and who but a fool like me would sit as the king of misrule amongst such cutthroats ? But have no fear, I've locked all the doors and hidden aught of value. See, my master : I will sit here at the head—or the foot, no matter—and you will sit there, at the foot or the head. Beside me on my right elbow I seat the harlot that I might watch her lest she swallow the spoon with her food ; next to her have I placed the soldier of the Tower, having promised her to him for the price of his tale. On my left elbow will I have Mrs. Forman, the she-wizard, and next to her will sit her melancholy spouse, the other side from me. Beside him, our Mistress Betty Buskin. On the opposite side, here, next to the soldier will I have our poet that he might learn a sonnet or two from their lewd thrushing ; and after him, the lawyer. Forgive me, my lord, that I seat such a fellow beside you, but you are neither of you merry neighbours and should keep mum together best."

" There is an empty chair on my right," said Will.

" Ay," said the jester with a sly glance. " Marry !
sweet sir, do you not carry a ghost with you ? Oft when
you thought yourself alone I've heard you converse with
some lemure ; yet she can be no true woman, even if
dead, for never once have I heard her answer back.
That is your ghostie's chair. Come," said he, bowing
low and drawing away the empty chair as though for
someone to be seated, " my Lady Rochester, here is your
place even though you no longer have a belly for your
enjoyments."

" Fool ! " cried Will, trembling and stamping his
foot, " your insolence goes beyond bearing. You might
think this supper an opportunity to get hog-drunk and
act lewdly with the women——"

" Not I, not with these women ! " sniffed Archie.
" Wait, my lord, until you see them."

" ——but this is to me a serious occasion," said Will,
ignoring the interruption. " I'll have no mockery of it,
d'ye understand ? Today, if you have promised truly,
I'll hear what really happened in those long-ago times."
He smiled. " I am expectant of lies," he said.

" That shows wisdom," nodded the jester. " Never
expect the truth, my lad, and you might hear it, though
'tis rarely pleasant . . . But our guests should soon be
here. Zenocrate ! " he shouted, " stand by the door,
wench, and see that they steal nothing ! "

" I have a big stick behind my back," came Zenocrate's
ghost-voice from a distance, " with a rusty nail in it."

" Good wench, good wench," chuckled Archie.
" Who said she was a fool ? She'd be an apt pupil,
poor lass, and the unpretty ones are always grateful to
a fellow when he notices them. The old woman is
jealous of her youth, and by cock, I'll give her cause for
jealousy before I leave this house."

" You're not to debauch my servant ! " cried Will.
" And she a half-wit."

" Me ! " cried the jester with exaggerated horror, all

his bells clattering as though aghast. " I debauch no one, sir. I but go to the wenches in the nighttime and leave the rest to their low cunning ; and she's no half-wit, I tell you : she's but a woman . . . Ah ! here is somebody, at last ! "

Rubbing his hands, he stood, head cocked to one side at the sound of the front-door opening and a woman's voice shrilly raised in imitation of a haughty lady's.

" 'Tis sweet Mrs. Forman, the whore," said he. " Beware, my son, she being a wizard's widow . . . Ah, Madam Cleopatra," said he, bowing with a clash of bells, " welcome to our poor abode, beauteous lady. This is my good friend, the Earl of Hertford . . . and pest on it ! I know not your new married name."

" Call me Nan," said the little painted woman, showing her broken teeth in a smile and rolling round blue childish eyes. " And this is my new husband. Call him Mr. Nan," said she. " He answers to it."

Mr. Nan, a hunched young fellow with a hangdog lower lip and a creased brow, slunk in behind his wife's black velvet skirts, glowering from Archie to Will with dark suspicion ; but he did not speak. Whatever manhood he might once have owned had been clearly chattered and beaten out of him by his wife who looked his elder not only in years but in cunning and vitality. Wrinkled she was, yet she was also red-checked and clear-eyed and girlish in her manner, a woman who could never grow old in spirit and would never die, it seemed, save by an accident or a murder.

" Ah, my lord," she said, ogling Will while she sank into a curtsey that made her kneecaps creak, " once I had lords by the dozens waiting on me when my sweet husband, the doctor, was on earth ; indeed, more than half the royal court was in and out of our house at Lambeth. And most embarrassing it was at times, concealing wives from husbands, and husbands from

wives when they came at the same time and for the same
purpose. And the doctor always so busy bottling
philtres and suchlike and casting horoscopes and
conversing with demons—friendly demons, you understand, for he'd never have the others in the house
lest they make me blush—but those times, heigh ho !
are gone and the only lords I see now are painted outside
taverns. But I've never forgotten I was a lady once and
was treated like one by the greatest gentlemen in the
land. Sit down ! " said she, turning sharply on her
husband, " and don't talk."

" Here," said Archie, drawing back the chair he had
designed for Mr. Nan, and sullenly Mr. Nan sat on it.
Then seizing a sugared plum, he swallowed it with a glare
of defiance.

" That's right, my love," said Nan, " make yourself
sick. And where am I to sit ? "

" On my left hand," whispered Archie, " that we may
rub sparks from our knees, sweet enchantress. Sit you
here. The other guests are coming . . . Ah ! 'tis the
warrior ! " he cried as a giant in a leather doublet
stumbled into the room and stood grinning and blinking
until his glance lightened on Mrs. Forman, whereupon
his eyes widened while she simpered.

" Nay, nay ! " cried the jester, seizing his arm.

" Is that not her ? " demanded the soldier in a noisy
whisper.

" Your wench has not come yet, sirrah ! That is a
lady and not what you think ; and there sits her husband,
fool ! What think you this is ?—one of our vile taverns
where all's for sale ? This is a gentleman's home and
you must behave like a gentleman if you can. And
don't drink too much too quickly. Sit you there . . .
Hark ! I know that oily step ! 'Tis the lawyer, I wager
a pound to an onion. He slinks after secrets. Yea,
I knew it ! Enter, Mr. Lawyer. The company awaits
you . . . And you too, Mr. Poet. Have you starved

thoroughly? are the juices hot in your belly for a fattening meal? I warrant we'll have to roll you home after we've stuffed you . . . At last, at last! my rosebud! sweet Kate Dandenell . . . "

" What name ? " cried Will.

" Kate Dandenell," said the lean woman with over-painted cheeks and lips and mottled skin who gave him a likerous glance under lowered lids, her ragged green dress trailing on the rushes. " I cannot remember you, sir," she said. " But then, I can't remember them all," she sighed and shrugged.

" We have not met," said Will hastily. " It was the name : that was all ; I have heard your name some-where." Then he remembered the witness in the pamphlet, the servant of sixteen who had sworn before the commissioners that she had seen her lord and lady often abed. This woman then could not be forty at the most, yet she looked fifty at the least, and he flinched from her professional glances while Archie led her to her chair and introduced her to the soldier.

" One more to come," said Archie, sidling up to him again. " The rascal's late on purpose to make his entrance more impressive."

" You said that empty chair——— "

" I said that but to test you," laughed the jester. " I wanted to watch what you would do. If Frankie's ghost be here—and I pray that it is and would it could speak and sit on my lap—it needs no chair . . . Nay, there is a leech to come, although he's little to tell, but I thought it best to have him."

" Are all here? Are all here? " chirruped Betty, clattering in on her pattens. " Nay, there's one to come. Wench, wench, after the last guest's arrived, bolt the door, d'ye mind? then come and serve us . . . Ah, what a company ! " said she, sniffing as she gazed from face to face : the lean poet with his chin sunk on his chest beside the lawyer whose quick glance darted amongst the foodstuffs while he licked his lips ; the huge red-faced soldier leaning over the skinny harlot who simpered up at him ; the wizard's widow primly watching the pair from under her painted eyelids, and her glum husband munching a leg of chicken. "God forgive us," groaned Betty. "What would your sainted father say ! "

" I like them no more than you," growled Will, " and I'll be happy when this foolery is over. Would God I'd never seen that man ! "

" That is un-Christian of you ! " said Betty primly. " He does it for your good, Master William, and although at times he may talk lewdly and have peculiar ways, he's a proper man and there's little harm in him, no more than a woman can manage if she's her wits about her. But he must not go near my Zenocrate."

" Zenocrate ? " whispered the poet, looking up with glazed eyes. " Did I hear the sacred name of divine Zenocrate ? "

" A heathen name," said Betty, nodding her head and frowning, " to cap an idiot wench, but my sister liked the players, and small good it did her, for all she got from it were the pains of labour and a cold in the head watching them in the inn-yard. It was one of these players that taught her what she shouldn't have learned at her age and the child was called after him, I believe, or after somebody in one of his plays . . . Ah, she is . . . "

" O," said the poet, rising in his chair and gaping at the door,

> " Behold me here, divine Zenocrate,
> Raving, impatient, desperate, and mad,
> Breaking my steeled lance . . . "

" O," said he again in a lower tone, almost a whimper, as Zenocrate slouched in before the tall physician in his sombre gown and the gold-headed stick in his hand.

" Did I hear somebody calling me ? " she asked.

"A maggot-pated loon," growled Betty, pinching her as she passed, "who said he'd gone mad with a lance, the foul creature, to talk thus before a meal. Keep far from him if you respect yourself. I'll not be having your blood spilt, my girl, by lunatics. Now get you to the kitchen and bring up the birds."

"Attention!" roared Archie, striking the table with his bauble so that the bladders bounced before him. "All are now present. Be seated, revered leech. Come, my lord, seat yourself; and you, good Mistress Buskin. This is the sacred hour of eating and therefore I proclaim Silence save for molars grinding and bird-bones crackling. First, let us praise God for what we're about to guzzle and pray we keep the good things down sufficiently long to satisfy our bellies. Then with stomachs drum-tight and wits aglow with wine, we will discourse upon the subject that draws us here together. Until then, fall to, toss-pots and greedy gluttons, snatch, crack, bolt and guzzle. Come, friends!"

Will sat back, the bare thought of food making him ill while he watched his guests eat as though they feared the viands would be snatched from under their noses; and he prayed Frances's forgiveness that in her name such creatures should have gathered under his father's roof. Whatever they might say of her he could never believe. Such animals could only lie: the wizard's widow with her broken-spirited lout of a husband; the harlot and the stupid soldier; the lawyer with his greasy elbows and worn coat; the tattered, sharp-featured poet; and the leech in oft-mended robe, the gold of his stick being plainly brass at a second look. No, these came from the kennel, malice made animate, with not one honest person amongst them save perhaps the poet who nibbled his food, dazedly rolling his eyes after Zenocrate as though he could not believe her real, this tub with the name of Marlowe's queen. Will could hear him murmuring lines from *Tamburlaine*, the name Zenocrate chiming now and then ; and he pitied the fellow.

" The Muse takes strange shapes at times," he said.

The poet gazed at him and shook his head. " 'Tis blasphemy," he whimpered, " 'tis blasphemy."

" But she's a kind heart if a little simple, and she works well."

" Not my Zenocrate," groaned the poet, watching the living Zenocrate, until, growing conscious of his regard, she blushed and dropped the plates and threw her apron over her head to smother her giggles until Betty pinched her back into decorum.

" I hear," said the lawyer, in a dry voice like the rustling of old papers, " that you are interested, my lord, in that ancient case of murder anent Sir Thomas Overbury. I have here," he said, producing a bundle from under his coat, " many pamphlets and my own records, I having been present in court from beginning to end. Now this . . . No ! that is of no interest."

" Pray," said Will, " give it to me," and he seized the pamphlet, having noticed Essex's name printed in thick letters on its front page.

" My lord," cried Archie, " what have you there ? "

" A pamphlet," smiled Will, pushing back his chair. " Ladies and gentlemen," said he, " will you excuse me for a brief while ? I would read this, with your permission. Let me not hold you from your pleasures. Mrs. Buskin will attend you ; and Mr. Armstrong, I am certain, will make a more worthy host to such as you than ever I could be.

" What is that pamphlet, my lord ? " squeaked Archie.

" *Some Memorials*," read Will, " *touching the Nullity between the Earl of Essex and his Lady, pronounced September 25, 1613, at Lambeth (and the Difficulties endured in the Same), by George, Archbishop of Canterbury.*"

" Ah, you may read that," said the jester, picking a bone from his teeth.

" Thank you, sir," said Will with mock gravity ; then he hurried off, glad of an opportunity to be quit of that repulsive company, feeling that he was able to breathe again only when he was alone in his room with the door bolted. The fire was out and it was cold, but he did not heed the chill as he drew the stool near the window and, flattening the pamphlet on his knees, began to read.

It made tedious reading he soon discovered, yet on he kept, hoping always to find some reference to Frances that would vindicate her. The archbishop had written that he had been deeply troubled when made a commissioner on her divorce. It had irked his conscience and he had discussed the matter with the Earl of Essex only to find him " much reserved in talk, but only avowing the ability of himself for generation ; and that he was resolved never to lay any blemish on himself that way." More than ever dissatisfied, the archbishop had then tried to pass his conscience on to others, stopping the lord chamberlain, Frances's father, in a gallery going towards St. James's Park and explaining his perplexities. " The lord chamberlain," wrote the archbishop, " said that perhaps the father's sin was punished upon the son ; that it was truth, that the earl had no ink in his pen ; that himself had confessed, that he could not know a woman, and that before divers noblemen, and some of them his own friends . . ." Yet, unsatisfied, everywhere had the archbishop ferreted for the truth ; and again had he spoken to Essex.

Will sucked the breath between his teeth for now, from the earl's lips, must surely come the truth ? " He gave me the reason for his having no motions to know his lady carnally," wrote the archbishop, " and of his thinking that he never should. ' When I came out of France, I loved her ; I do not so now, neither ever shall I.' When he was to answer to the article, that she was Virgo Incorrupta ; he smiled, and said, ' She saith so, and she is so for me.' "

A double-speech. Will suddenly disliked this Earl of Essex that he could thus mock at the mystery. But now, ah ! here came Frances herself to speak. To the seven purgators she had stepped to take the oath and before such good churchmen assuredly she'd have muffled that milky bosom lest she dazzle justice, and have hooded those bright eyes that she might not blind them in a look ? But then this wretched archbishop had refused to accept her evidence unless it were first written down because, forsooth, he " found it too bare and slight to enforce anything." What else could he expect from a woman alone amongst men telling of bedchamber-doings ? Would he have had talk like some hedgerow-jill with a wet back from lying on the grass ?

On dragged the case and the archbishop's perplexities, his sending for this man and that man, his squirmings and tortuous attempts to evade giving the decision his king demanded. Even when the king wrote expostulating with him about the continual delays, the silly fellow could not make up his mind. Threats could not stir him, either from king or lord, until he heard that Frances's father, " was every way a kind father to his children ; but in this of his daughter, he was so passionate till it had an end, that he lay as on a grid-iron, broiling till the matter was accomplished." Then said the archbishop : " It shall not be delayed by me." Yet delay it he did for many more pages of crooked type, the king roaring at him and cursing the necessity of younglings having to marry " before they be acquainted one with one another. He told us the inconvenience of it," wrote the archbishop, " how he knew in Scotland a father who married his only child to man against her will ; that she withstood it ; yet her father forced her to marry him ; that being gone home with her husband, after a very few days she run away from him : that her father jerked her, and sent her home again : that not long after, she poisoned her husband, and was burnt for it, while the king was in Scotland. After his majesty's going out, I followed him, and told him, I evidently perceived, that it was in the Earl of Essex, ' Vitium Animi non Corporis.' His majesty swore he thought so. There passed some other speech from the king to me, touching his own lying with the queen the first night that he married her. But at the last, I kissed his hand and departed."

Tedious and prolix though the pamphlet was, it taught Will one thing : how great had been the scandal of that divorce, how the king and his ministers and the favourite who ruled the nation had all tried to bend the archbishop from his scruples to their will. Little else could have been talked of at the time, both within the court and outside it, some damning the lady as a hot drazel and others calling her an unhappy child beaten to a hateful marriage with a lad who was no man. Only Essex now could ever tell the truth. Will had not met him and had heard no ill of him and believed that he had married again, yet he hated him as a man hates a successful rival. Even though the fellow had not possessed Frances, he had lain in the same bed with her, he had seen her in tantalising undress, he had breathed all night within the same bedcurtains as she, he had felt her warmth through sheets and blankets and had heard her sigh and stir close by him . . . and that it seemed to Will should be sufficient bliss, even though it were also agony, for any man. Yea, even that barren bed was preferable to his empty bed . . . The idea shocked him and he looked up guiltily, ashamed that he who had lived in chastity, avoiding not only women but the mere thought of immodest things, should now torment himself with such images of long ago and become jealous and desirous of a ghost. Yet it was no betrayal of Anne, he assured himself, to love her mother, that mother having become Anne who in spirit and flesh was the dream made carnate, her mother's very self, and only in her arms would he embrace, not only her, but Frances, too.

Yea, Frances, too . . .

Trembling at that thought, Will turned again to the pamphlet and frowned while he struggled through the broken type, following the archbishop over his mazy courses. " On the Thursday at ten of the clock, we met in Lambeth-hall where my lady's counsel took on them to answer some scruples objected by Dr. Ferrand . . ." Futile seemed these many theological and legal arguments to Will when the king was plainly set on the divorce. All that the archbishop achieved by his wriggling was to make the affair notorious until Frances must have become the mocking-stock of every rogue and harlot in the realm ; and Will winced to think of the kind of jests that would have been said about her, the puns and rhymes made on her name, the lewd stories invented and the quirks and quips, the winking and lip-smacking and the shrilly virtuous clamour of women who concealed their sin and did not carry it to be argued in the open by churchmen quoting scripture for a precedent, there being no precedent to be found for this case in English law. That was what worried the archbishop, a famed persecutor of papists, puritans and ritualists, and which stiffened him even against the king's persuasions and the black-browed enmity of Frankie's relatives. Friends and old books he consulted in vain, and when the king sent him a treatise written by some Scotsman he was displeased, he wrote, believing " it the work of some hungry fellow, who lacked twenty shillings to buy food for his belly."

From the distant room where his guests were dining, Will heard shrieking and laughter and he smiled grimly, pleased to think that they were becoming drunk which meant that they would be garrulous when he returned. As garrulous perhaps as this faint-hearted archbishop in the pamphlet, no doubt, but, he hoped, not half so tedious.

To the conclusion of the narrative he read, then turned the page to find even duller matter on *Some Observable Things, since September 25, 1613, when the Sentence was given in the Cause of the Earl of Essex, Continued unto the Day of the Marriage, December 26, 1613.*

" The sentence being for the nullity," he read, " the minds of men in their several places were wonderfully distracted, and everyone spake according to their fancies. But for the most part there was a detestation of the thing, and a great dislike of those that gave sentence, which was expressed by all courses that men durst adventure upon. On the other side, there was a strange applauding and commending of those who withstood the separation . . ." Nor was the archbishop forgiven by the king for some time. At the end, brave if deluded man, he with four others had voted against the nullity so that when next he visited James he found himself " strangely looked on," while those who had obeyed the royal will were honoured, the Bishop of Winchester's son being made a knight so that ever afterwards was he known as Sir Nullity Bilson because of it. Disgraced, the archbishop yet bore all meekly, even when the king wrote sharply to him about his disobedience, and the granting of church-livings was taken from his hands. At last, however, after many pages that hurt Will's eyes to read, the poor man gave way and was present at Frances's marriage to Somerset.

Over the page again and the narrative started afresh with the speech the archbishop had intended to make when it came to his turn to vote on the nullity but which apparently he had not made. Here it reposed in broken letters, ponderous, involved, the archbishop being worried because he had found only one precedent, the case of a certain John Bury who had taken to " wife one Philippa Monjoy, his first wife, Willimot Gifford, being then alive." Later, Philippa deserted him and married a Mr. Langeden, all of which gaddings-about seemed to Will to have little to do with the case except that Philippa accused Bury of impotence. But Will cared not a rush for Philippa, John, Willimot or Langeden : his search was after Frances through these pages, and he realised how right the jester had been when he said that he'd learn nothing here ; and at last, irritably, he threw the pamphlet aside, not troubling to peruse the king's letter to the archbishop with which it concluded. The truth was not to be dug from the convolutions of even an archbishop's conscience : he would have to go to the bottom of a very foul well to find it, down into the depths of a jester's memory and amongst the recollections of a harlot, a wizard's wife, a soldier, a lawyer, a leech and a poet.

Sighing, he stood to his feet, reluctant to return to the banquet, to close the door on this quiet room fragrant with Frances's invisible presence and to talk with rogues to the shame of her memory.

" Forgive me," he whispered, holding out his arms. " Whatever they might say about you, I know your heart, Frances, a true woman's heart, because I love your daughter."

And he felt—he swore it—he felt lips brush his ; and his heart quickened at the pressure of a body he could not hold lifted tight against his as though a woman stood tiptoe to reach his mouth, straining out of her ghostly world to re-enter the living and to become again a woman, passionate and proud and beautiful, rewarding her knight who fought for her good fame.

CHAPTER VIII

A Husband would a Lover be

ALL save Betty, the jester and Zenocrate were drunk, or near drunk, when Will re-entered the dining-hall ; and the jester, too, might well have been drunk, his belly seemingly being made of leather or metal, so faintly did the deepest potations appear to unsettle him. At the head of the table he sat, his small eyes pin-pointed with malicious delight, a glass of red wine in one hand, his coloured bladders in the other and the bells tittering on the points of his cap when he laughed. Beside him, Anne, the wizard's widow, sat erect and tight-lipped, staring from under her eyelids at her nose's point that she might not see that the soldier opposite had one hand down the harlot's flat bosom while he kissed her throat. Mr. Nan looked even more surly than before and drank with a desperate air as though the wine were poisoned and he was glad of it ; the leech and the lawyer, because of their grave professions, attempted to appear sober and succeeded only in looking both sleepy and foolish ; while the poet, sunk in his chair, formed women's shapes with the wine spilt before him, murmuring verses to himself, now and then moaning when he looked up to see the mountainous Zenocrate moving behind the chairs, taking away used dishes and replacing them with clean ones or floundering off for further wine, as though even yet he could not believe that so doughy and double-chinned and double-breasted and double-bellied and -bottomed a wench could bear the name of Tamburlaine's queen.

"Welcome, my lord," cried Archie, bouncing his bladders on the table. "We have been long awaiting you, and all is ready. I have here before me a list of narratives, and, as in a play, each character will speak, one now, one later, each at my command, telling what he or she knows of this or that until, piece by piece, the tale will be fitted together. If I remember right, on that precious day of our meeting we had reached the return of the lady's husband from abroad. Now that, for once I confess to it, is a tale I know only by hearsay, not having been attached to her household—save by proxy a few nights, viz. one of her wenches—and many were the lewd rumours running on legs to court of a stiff-backed wife and a baffled husband. For this reason I would have Mistress Dandenell to open, she having been present ; were you not, sugar-lips ? ''

" I've been everywhere, to hell and back again," said the harlot, shuffling out of the soldier's embrace and taking a deep draught of wine. " This," said she, " is as jolly a banquet as I have had these many years : 'tis old times back again. Would we could be drunk forever and there were no mornings to wake up on." Smiling to show her blackening teeth, she looked at the company, her pale eyes seeming rubbed, their glance settling nowhere. " Yea," she said with a bitter laugh, turning to Mrs. Forman, " you may well stare at me, dame, you remember me ; and after all I'm honest at the game and do not cheat. I'm not one to buy a stallion to break its spirit, as you've broken the spirit of that poor creature at your side."

" You are speaking of my husband, woman ! " cried Mrs. Forman.

" I know, poor soul," sighed Kate.

" Come, come, ladies," cried Archie, beating the air with his bladders, " let's have neither compliments nor clawing. Sweet Kate, I've asked you to begin. You knew the Countess of Somerset ? "

" Too well," said Kate, twisting her mouth.

" And her first husband, the Earl of Essex . . . ? "

" Poor soul," she said. " He was a proper man, for
all the lies she told about him. I knew the truth of
that beyond all questioning. I have seen him get out of
bed in the morning, and the bolster between them all the
night, and he with his nightgown up near his shoulders.
I know the truth of it. I was a tit then, but sixteen or
seventeen, but already was I woman, having served
my lady, and I thought it sport to mock at a gentleman
to ruin his manly reputation so that for years to come
the women tittered at him and turned their backs,
leaving him a married man without a wife and none to
warm his bed . . . "

" We know all that," said Archie. " Bridle your
tongue, lass, but tell us instead of the day when the
earl came home and would have bussed his lady, like any
honest husband."

" Unhappy man," sighed Kate. " Hubadub he came
in his riding-boots, too impatient to see her to kick them
off, running into her chamber where she sat with me and
other of her women. It was sad, but I was young and
the young are hard-hearted about all save themselves.
Behind my fist I laughed to see how stiff she held herself
and hung dead in his arms when he bussed her. He
was shy, he blushed and almost tip-toed to her, his spurs
clinking, and he touched her as though he feared she'd
bruise. Bruise ! she who'd not flinch from fierce
encounters, but arched to meet them ! you could have
flogged her had she loved you and she'd have shown no
more than a rosy glow of satisfaction. That was my
lady . . . She let her husband hold her a moment
and put his mouth to hers : no more ; then she pushed
him off and rubbed her lips and said : ' Pho, pho,
you stink, my lord, you sweat ! ' He knew not what
to say at that, seeing her rub her lips with her hand,
and then she turned her back on him. She was
trembling. I noticed that. So was he, but for a different
reason.

" He looked about him, puzzled, then he looked down at his riding-clothes as though he feared he'd fouled them, while he blushed behind his beard. Ah ! shame was it to hurt so good and simple a lad ! for gentle he was and loving but slow-speaking. Had my lady been like any ordinary woman she could have lived in comfort, taking her lovers with the earl never knowing, he not being of the suspicious kind, but rather a predestined cuckold any wife would be grateful to own. But not my lady, eh, not her ! She was so proud she thought none her equal and would not put up with the irksome necessities that most wives have to bear. She was too vain, intolerant and selfish. The poor fool loved her, she being beautiful and plump. Yea, she was beautiful. I loved her, too, and was happy by the hours to brush her golden hair to make sparks and to touch her skin, and when she was lonely some nights and would call me to her from my truckle-bed at her bedfoot and take me in behind her curtains to talk and bear her company against the cold . . . then was it very heaven for me, to be with her . . . "

She sighed, her eyes shadowed purple, then she took up her glass again and drank greedily, glaring defiance at the company, as though she would drown that memory of the girl who had been in her mistress's bed.

" I was a fool," she growled, " and being young, I worshipped her. I thought that I'd be young forever and she, too ; and now she's dead and I'm . . . You know what I am. It's no trade I like but everyone must have a living and I was taught no other. I must thank her for that. She set me here as surely as if she'd whipped me at the cart's tail, pox take the bitch ! No ! I love her still, I meant it not ; and yet her evil living—— "

" No ! " cried Will, then he blushed to see them all turn and look at him.

" Poor gentleman," said Kate, " you are like most men and think a pretty woman must be pretty inside, too. I know. I remember my own youth and the good gentlemen I scoffed at because I thought them foolish when all their foolery was in loving me. We learn too late, alas ; we want what is difficult to get, women often loving more from hate and fear of other women than any liking for men. Such was my mistress and I followed her ways. She wanted the prince because no woman could have him ; and she took him and broke his precious heart ; then she wanted the earl because he was the king's dilling and she took him and ruined him. I thought her the rarest creature who could not fail whatever she essayed, and I aped her ways, thinking I also could take what man I liked and spit at those who failed to stir me or had not gifts enough. That is why I am what I am. The lads soon learned that the only way into my placket was with gold or some trumpery jewel. And when I took from them—and I took everything and anything—I laughed at them and, when I could, I wriggled from my promise, laughing and laughing at my cleverness. Thus, step by step, I came to Fleet Street, and where I'll end I know not. Why should they have married me when they could buy me? Then in time none wished to marry me and, desperate for comfort and a child and man to love and keep me, I saw how I had wrecked my life and future, like my mistress; then it was too late ; and I had grown so used to likerous living that I could not stop it had I wished.

"For that must I thank my lady. Her pride, her wilfulness, her pettish ways with men whom she would lure for the delight of mocking them, bred in me contempt for them also that they could suffer and pay so much for so little a thing."

"To Satan with you and your little thing !" cried the jester. "What of your mistress when her husband came home ?"

"She spat at him," said Kate in a dull voice, sinking back into her chair. "Oh, the wicked, harsh, un-

seemly things she said ! The names she called him !
And to his face, too ! She had a tongue that liked
bawdy and the filthiest words when she had a mind to
them. She curled them all about her husband and he,
poor silly lad, bewildered, cried to her that he loved
her and asked what ailed her. 'You,' said she with
such bitter loathing that he blanched. 'Why, why?
why?' he kept on crying, scatter-witted. He had been
sick with longing for her, he said, poor soul : he had
thought of nothing but her while he was away and had
kept himself chaste amidst all temptations that he might
be worthy of her, and this was his homecoming ! 'Why?
why?' he wailed. 'To come back like this,' said he,
' happy and eager, and to be given not so much as a
kind glance she'd throw a dog, that was bitter indeed,'
he said ; and asked what it was he had done. Had
someone lied about him ? What ? But she turned away,
her shoulders back. Quivering she was and her lips
tight-set until he touched her. Under the ruff he
touched her naked shoulder and she screamed and
called him vile names and slapped his cheek. 'Twas
sad to see and sad to hear the words she used. I think
she was a little mad that day, being frightened of what
he might do and how she might lose her love. Even
we wenches were startled, never having heard her speak
so shrilly, although we knew her tempers and on occasions
had been beaten by her when she was vexed or
thwarted or her beloved had failed to keep a tryst. But
after such beatings, she would weep and fondle us and
bring us gifts, being so sad for our bruising and scratches
that we too would weep and love her all the more. But
this was different. Never had I seen her in such panic-
fury which trembled from her toes and made her eyes
burn like silver fire.

"Her angers were soon over. They made her sick.
I have seen her vomit after such a fit. But although not
often did she fly into such a fit again, she could not bear

her husband and would not bed with him. At times she would try to speak pleasantly and he, like a little dog, would wag with joy, but once he'd touched her if only with his finger, ah ! then 'twas different ! You'd have thought he'd scalded her the way she'd flinch and squeak, crying, ' Don't do that to me ! You men are beasts and want but one thing from a woman ! let me alone ! ' But for all his meekness, he was no weakling, only ignorant of women. He should have tied her up and beaten her, yea, then she might have respected him and, out of fear, love might have grown. Most husbands would have used the whip with the bedpost ready and cords at hand, but never the earl who thought in his simplicity to woo her by kindness ; and she despised him for it.

" At times his passion overmastered him and he tried to take her, but then she'd scratch back and scream and he would let go, fearing he'd hurt her. Usually however, he crawled to her, imploring her to like him a little and be kind. And seeing him at her feet, she despised him utterly. Nor was he the only one that suffered. As though she were diseased with her insufferable torment and horror of his touch, her eyes grew hollow and her skin lost its glow, the flesh turning dull, greenish, and her eyes having no sparkle, as in an illness. Yet he with iron resolution was gentle as a maid with her. As a maid, say I ! Nay, as gentle as a man can be, for maids are rarely gentle, being wayward and ruthless, unless they love. And all her love was for her golden Somerset, who was then, you must remember, but the Viscount Rochester : but I will call him Somerset to save confusion. Him only did she love with a terrible passion that consumed her night and day ; for her poor husband she knew only loathing. And such loathing ! The looks she gave him would have curled a snail. Yet he was a proper young man who not only for his own good qualities merited any woman's love but he loved her with an extraordinary affection, having a gentle, mild and courteous disposition, especially towards women, the foolish lamb. He could not believe the truth, he would not believe it, she being so adorable that it was difficult to realise what blackness dwelt the other side of her mouth. Her face might have challenged nature of too much hypocrisy for harbouring so wicked a heart under so sweet, so bewitching a countenance.

" He knew, of course, naught of her evil living with the prince and Somerset, and none would dare tell him, fearing her displeasure, and he thought that it was but unnatural modesty that ruled her. Yea, despite the filthy language she would use and the names she dubbed him, he could not realise that she knew the meaning of such words and on one occasion he spoke reprovingly to us women for having taught her such naughty things to say. We knew not where to look while he lectured, and the dear fellow told us how ill things fed on ill things and how little by little we could fall from grace, bad talk leading to bad deeds, and so on ; and when he'd left us we rolled on the rushes to kick up our skirts and we talked the foulest bawdy that we might prove to ourselves how very abandoned we were, as though that way we spited him and did not lose our souls.

" Ah, God ! if I had my life to live again !

" She smoked his meaning and, instead of abuse, acted the maid fearful of ravishing. That was a part that pleased his honest, pious mind. Then was he more gentle with her than ever, if that be possible. He even permitted her to remain at court. That made her kind towards him, she being assuaged in her passions with secret meetings with her lover, and no wife can be so gentle as she who's cheating her husband, being sleepy with satisfaction of ill-doing and therefore compassionate towards the dolt she cuckolds. Gradually, however— mayhap he heard whispers—the earl began to change. Yet I misdoubt if any would have dared speak of her wantonness to him, knowing how my lady and her lover could take revenge. Mayhap, strong-willed and virtuous as he was, a great Bible-reader and lover of long sermons that would have nodded most of us to sleep, he no longer could bear to have her near him and not possess her like a husband should. Which is understandable, he being young and vigorous—yea, vigorous ! and a fig to her lies of impotency : not that he was a lecher : never ! he had no woman save his wife at that time, and her he never had ; but as I have told you already, going to and fro into their bedchamber after—this was later—he forced her into his bed, I have seen him step out and, forgetting my presence, pull up his shirt ; then I knew her for a liar. Yea, a great liar she was and after the divorce was settled everybody should have cried Shame ! on her for the lies she told to make out he was splayed to his great shame and loss of women's company. Had the ladies at court known the truth on it, they'd have trod her to death ; yet I, ah me ! I loved her and thought her both wise and beautiful.

"But his tenderness began to leave him and he grew fretful and in great pain with his longing for this beauty given him by God and man, his ring on her finger, which he was not allowed to touch or even breathe on. He grew angry as he should have been angry from the first. I heard him shout once when she was petulant and slapped the hand that would have stroked her, I heard him shout that if she'd not come to him willingly, she'd come willy-nilly and he'd force her. My throat swelled to hear him and I trembled for her, yet he looked splendid in his rage, the veins showing on his forehead and his eyes alight : and all for love of that wee girl ! Wonderful is the power of love, indeed, and girls are foolish who abuse it, as I abused it and am therefore here, damned, for my sins."

She drank and spilled the wine down her goose-fleshed throat, so shaking was her hand ; and all looked away, not wishing to see her in her misery. Will stared at the table, shading his eyes with his palm that he might escape the jester's and Betty's mockery, and he told himself that this harlot was lying, her trade being a lie, a mockery of love : why therefore should he trust her tongue which the jester had probably bought ? Yet he knew, struggle from the admission though he tried, that she had told the truth. One could not doubt it, hearing that husky voice splintering now and then on furious regrets : Frankie had behaved in that fashion, with- holding herself from her first husband ; yet did not the evil in this lie only in what the harlot had imagined ? Mayhap Frankie had been pure and disgusted by the crudities of sex. He had heard of such women, wives who stiffened with dislike in their husbands' arms and others who preferred another woman's more gentle fondling . . . Had Frankie been like that ?

" She was rotten to the heart, to the finger-ends, to the very bottom of her," said Kate viciously, the glass tinkling against her teeth ; " yet as I say, I loved her and fools of men adored her and would have spent all their fortunes to have one night in her arms. But my lady was not like that. Her love was all for one man, and it closed her oyster-tight against all others, even against her own husband. That will I say in her defence. She was no wanton, if a whore : she loved and thought the world well lost for love. That was why she was cruel to other men.

" Her husband went to her father who was the Earl of Suffolk, as you know, a great man and the lord high chamberlain, and the earl her husband asked him to use his authority to rule his daughter. This he confessed when he came home one night and my mistress cried out as though she were wounded by this treachery. ' No, no ! ' she sobbed, ' you'd not have me sent away, would you, my sweet lord ? ' Yes, he said, he was taking her away. He had her father's authority for it, he told her.

But she could not believe it until her father himself came heavy-footed and commanded her obedience as a wife. She must go with her husband, he told her, lest the scandal rage so high that not only she but all his family might be ruined by it. ' And mayhap,' he said, cocking his cunning old head to one side, ' others also might be ruined, for should his majesty hear of it, he might tumble one who is very dear to him . . . and to you,' he said.

" Then, while she wept at her unhappy lot in a tumble of sheets and bit the pillows, God, or the devil, came to her aid. The poor carl was struck down with fever and sweated near to death. Although it did not kill him, that illness bred in my lady's mind a fearful fantasy. I'd not believe it at first but soon I learned the truth, being often her go between. And wicked and wanton though I was, I shuddered from it, yet in time I thought nothing of it. Such is our nature, and so is it in many things, important and unimportant. Our first disgust goes and we can accept and even learn to relish things which at first revolt us. Love is like that, too. Few of us like our first taste of it, it is hurtful and we cry Enough ! and weep ; and yet again we venture, and again, until delight out-soars all hurt and that which we thought a black sin which God'd never forgive we think no more of than the drinking of a cup of ale. Thus does the devil snare us, habituating us to forbidden feeding. I doubt not that even a murderer thinks little of a corpse after his first killing. The human heart can turn to leather quickly. And this abomination from which I shrank, my skin lifting from my flesh, soon I thought little of and laughed at it and thought it brave doing. But as I say, at first I'd not believe it.

" She was ever at his bedside, not that she tended him, not she ! but to watch to see how near to death he sweated while continually she asked the physicians how ill he was, and was there hope ? she'd ask—but she'd not say whether for hope of death or life. Then the

leech, smiling and bowed, told her that he would live
and she sobbed and wrung her hands. I saw her grip
the bedcurtains lest she fall and such hatred was in her
eyes that it curled my innards, used though I was to her
ways and knowing her thoughts. Then she took up his
glass of medicine and smelled it and turned and looked
at me. Our eyes met and in hers plain I read their
meaning. Her husband's death, his death in that glass.

"'Are poisons difficult to get?' she asked me.

"'No! no!' I cried to her. She shrugged and with
her tight cat's smile looked long into my eyes and put
her arms about me and whispered wet in my ear : 'He
almost went last night,' she said, 'what sin in aiding
nature? Had he not been so strong a man he'd have
died of it. The doctor told me so. And that shows
that God intended it, only his body was too stout.'
Even then I'd not believe her, even when she asked if I
understood the use of certain herbs or whether I knew a
leech skilled in moonlight-specifics. And I thank God
that I could say that I knew no such man. But I was
numb and fearful and told myself she jested. Alas, she
did not jest."

With her round bleached eyes, Kate gazed expressionless from face to face of her listeners ; and even the
amorous soldier at her side kept his hands on the table,
caught by the tale into forgetting lechery. The others
stared at her in silence : the jester grinning and idly
tossing his bladders; Mrs. Forman demurely gazing
down with lowered eyelids and a tight smile curving her
full painted lips ; her husband beside her crouched on
his chair, scowling, alert yet scornful, as one who knew
all women to be liars and listened under protest ; the
leech measuring with his eyes the wine in his glass as if
he wondered whether the dead Frances had drawn it
and poisoned it ; the lawyer with underlip pressed out,
in his glance the amusement of a man inured to
wickedness ; the poet, ashen-cheeked, glaring at the

stretched gown of Zenocrate who stood in the shadows, stiff with horror ; and Betty smiling at Will who crumbled bread between his fingers and, teeth clenched, glared at the table, sullen and rigid with disbelief.

" Go on, lass," urged Archie. " You tell a titillating tale. No doubt you need to in your trade when clients ask for money back or the watch come stalking."

" I have long hours alone," sighed Kate, " long tramping hours and standing in wet alleys and hiding from the watch. I have much time for thinking and I hate to think, for back I go over my life, regretful if not penitent. I see myself a child happy with my mother ; I see myself a youngling, wistful yet fearful of life, fretful with aches I half-understand, while shrinking from lad's fingers ; I remember my schooling—what there was of it—and my impatience with the horn-book ; then my entry into that academy of vice, my lady's household. And after that, a bold front, hot lips and a cold heart, bubbling men and thinking I'd have the power and the looks to cog them forever ; until now, the cobbles pressing through my shoes and strangers haggling with me in the dark, and the watch to chase me and the justices to strip me to the buff at Guildhall to be flogged while lewd men lounge to quiz my bigs shaking under the blows while I stamp and bite my tongue and squirm and swear I'll not scream until I scream and curse and am flogged the harder for my blasphemies. Yea, I see all this, tramping the night alone with memories of the girl I was, the woman I became and the creature into which I have sunk. Once a woman loses her honesty she cares not what's the villainy she does, for she blames others and rarely herself for her fall. But I am not so great a liar as that now. 'Twas different when I was younger and had hopes . . . Now I see the truth and blame myself, but more than myself do I blame that woman I took as mirror for my behaviour, gladly swimming into that sweet hell of

voluptuousness into which I have sunk to the bottom.
My soul's the devil's and even my body's not my own.
As near as I can, I avoid the French disease and try to
keep myself in brave apparel and I pay tribute to a
bawd, having need for protection as honest people pay
for the watch, being subject to the whistle of any desperate
ruffian with coins in his pouch."

"Pish, pishery!" cried Archie, striking his bladders
at the wench's back, "we come not here to weep on a
strumpet's derry-go-down. Get back to your lady. It
is her history, not yours, we want to hear."

"But mine is hers in little," said the woman, "only
she was more fortunate. She died. But I'll go back
to her and that sick-chamber which I'll never forget and
can smell its sickly odours to this day. Then it was that
the devil took my lady ; but how she found those to
her kidney I cannot tell for certain."

"I can tell that," said the jester. "I can give it
one name : dear Mrs. Turner with her yellow starch."

"I knew her well," said the wizard's widow, and
smiled.

CHAPTER IX

The Wizard's Daughter

"Who did not know Anne Turner," laughed the jester, " to their own ill fortune ?   Good master, we have now another name and one that you must mark well.   Anne Turner's.   She was a small, big-bosomed lady with yellow hair and a brisk manner, and very delectable to look at.   I said to look at : dangerous was it to try a closer meeting.   I knew her well.   The widow of a doctor of physic she was, and she'd learned many of her tricks, abortions and such, from study of his books, but her heart held more wickedness than any doctor's tome could teach her.   To all the ladies at court she was Sweet Turner and she had the entrance to their bedchambers, poor gulled husbands never thinking ill of a woman, while women be as busy together fomenting wickedness and each pricks on the other with wanton instigations until they are all champing to out-do their friends in venery.   A bawd for love of the game was this Nan Turner, a very woman indeed whose mind spun only on lechery.   It was to be seen in her gait, in her bold blue eyes, in the puffed bosom and honeyed voice. She could have cajoled Diana out of her moon to a double-bed at a price.   O, she had her price.   A price for everything and she knew strange pleasures and where to find them.   Men resorted to her when they wished to plunder some lady and sent her to corrupt the woman, to oil her with words in readiness for sin. Lucrece would have opened her window to Tarquin had Mrs. Turner lain with her first.   No one was safe on whom she cast her eyes.   Children she taught naughtiness for the mere delight of stealing their innocence ; young boys and girls would she skilfully fondle till she'd itched them ready for mischief. She could find whatever filthiness was asked her. Yet with big innocent eyes could she look when husbands found her with their wives, and she had rosy cheeks and dewy lips. A pox on her ! I loved her once . . . But that's a different tale. In and out of bedchambers was she ever gadding with her short little steps, click-clack, as though she walked with her legs together, the liar, clipperty-clip, with love-notes down her bosom and love-potions up her sleeve to pour into some deluded fellow's glass to spur him to love, or drugs to keep a husband fast in sleep. And shameless, devilish, I have heard were some of the rites she performed in mockery of Venus, sacrificing birds and beasts on the altar of nude women's bellies . . . Ah ! it was a bad world, that world of King Jamie's and he as great a hunter of witchcraft that ever burnt an old hag. All the court buzzed with talk of sorcery, and girls and matrons, too, resorted to wizards for nasty charms and philtres and horoscopes . . . Did they not, my wizard's rib ? "

" Indeed, they did," said Mrs. Forman. " My husband had a constant trade in charms and horoscopes and waxen images and suchlike. I had naught to do with it myself, of course, so I can't be blamed if it was sinful or beyond the law. He was a wise man, though, having studied at Cambridge University. He could call up spirits when he needed them and I have seen him with his wand stand in his circle . . . But nay ! I must not blab holy secrets. Did not my sweet husband beg to be buried deep for our blessed sakes ? And I'd not call him back, not I, dear loving spouse though he was to me and as powerful as a bullock. Ah, he was a wise man."

"Yea," said Archie, "he was one who in most questions, particularly theft, was judicious and fortunate."

" The stars made him so," said his widow, " and he was a master of sickness, too, being a doctor of physic and astronomy, having learned at Jesus College, Cambridge. And he was cunning also in resolving questions about matrimony. That was why the ladies liked him."

" He was a devilish creature," shuddered Kate.

" A charlatan," croaked the physician. " We summoned him once before our learned society for practising without a degree. Four times we jailed him and we fined him once. That was why he went to Cambridge. After that, we could do naught against him."

" 'Tis all but fantasy," smiled the lawyer. " Such a rogue works on sick minds or on silly women. He gives a harmless potion to some greensick maid and she makes her fellow drink it, then tells him what it is, and he, believing himself poisoned by love, dotes on her because he thinks he must."

" Indeed not ! " cried Mrs. Forman shrilly. " I could tell you many a tale of a stubborn man who changed overnight, after taking but a few drops of my late husband's preparations, into so raging a lover that he terrified the lady who'd given it to him ; and of ladies who fleered from a gallant only to fall on their backs screaming with love after a taste. One sip was sufficient to melt the hardest heart. Often have I heard this Mrs. Turner you speak of tell how she loved a gentleman. Sir Arthur Mainwaring it was. There's proof of his skill. Names and all I'm giving for this once to stop you sneering in your ignorance. So hot was she for him that she could not sleep with longing and he cold as a stone to her until my blessed husband employed his cunning for her sake and Sir Arthur so raged for her company that he dug his spurs into his horse and galloped through a fearsome storm and a black night just to get at her. There's proof for you."

" Fantasy," smirked the lawyer, smiling with closed eyes, " fantasy, my good woman."

" What had this wicked charlatan to do with Lady Essex ? " cried Will, white-faced, glaring at Archie.

" Ha ha ! that is a tale to be told," smiled the jester.
" The web is woven. The sick husband. The thought
of poison to free her in the adultress's mind. The
wizard at Lambeth. And the bawd Turner gadding
with her quick steps in and out of court, ready for
Frankie's using. There is the skein with murder at the
heart of it. It was Mrs. Turner who led your mistress
to the warlock, was it not, Kate ? "

" Yea," said the harlot, waking suddenly from an
unhappy dream and gaping at the company. " It was
that intriguing creature that ruined my lady, and me
with her. Had it not been for her all might never have
happened. I have cursed my lady but she was not truly
evil. She was wilful and easily led by her own desires.
That wicked thought by her lord's bedside might have
led nowhere had not this Mrs. Turner been close and all
the court ladies caressing her because of her medicines
that could kill the unborn, and her venerial potions to
inspire a backward lover or to make a sterile woman
conceive. She was this monster Forman's emissary,
luring men and ladies to Lambeth to waste their gold on
drugs and parchment spells and little waxen images to
melt before the fire or to have pins pressed in them to
kill men or women slowly in agony. I am told that
Mrs. Turner had once been wealthy, and certainly she
was a lady bred, but that she had ruined her husband, a
doctor, melting his fortune in the oven of her lusts.
Ruined, she used her cunning as a bawd and lovers met
at her house or she would compromise a married lady
until the unhappy creature paid what she could to keep
her quiet and had to help her in her wickedness.
Having spies everywhere, soon she learned many secrets
and had letters stolen that she might be given money for
their return. Innumerable were her tricks and she it
was who killed whatever honesty was left in my unhappy
lady and opened her to ruin.

" Under her protection, my lady and the Earl of

Somerset—or Rochester as he then was—would meet and my lady would weep because her husband, growing well again, would carry her into the country. I heard her lover swear that if she went and left him he'd not see her again, for he'd never share her, he said, even with her own spouse ; but she swore that no matter what happened, she would stay true to him and her husband would never have her. And always was Mrs. Turner near to watch over them and to incite them to amorousness, although my lady needed little spurring. He was the laggard, as if he feared her passion. I doubt not that already she gave him philtres in his wine to keep him true to her. As she was also giving her husband powders, ah me ! but for a different purpose.

" The good earl, strong again, had not forgotten his resolve to tame her. Finding his wife ever at court instead of at his side and seeing no possibility of reducing her to reason without estranging her from the relish and delights she sucked in there, he made his condition again known to her father. That old man, troubled by his daughter's disobedience lest the king hear of it, and embittered too with his wearisome and continual chidings to wean her from those sweets she doted on, forced her into the country. But how harsh was that parting, her being rent from the place where she had grown and flourished, and from her darling Robin ! Yet she left her engines and imps behind her : the old doctor and his confederate, Mrs. Turner. Mad was my lady, weeping and storming, blazoning all her miseries, kicking and ready to die at loss of her beloved. Chartley was a hundred miles from her happiness and to her the distance was an eternity. Yet she had to go with her husband, that being the law.

" Even then, knowing her bold and resolute mind though I did, I'd not believe she'd carry out her hellish design, her husband being so loving, if often stern and commanding ; but she was set on it, as you will hear.

Sullen and darkly she entered his country manor, although it was the pleasantest time of summer, and she shut herself in her chamber, not suffering a beam of light to peep into her dark thoughts. If she stirred out of her chamber, it was in the dead of night when sleep possessed all others but those about her. I was one of those. I watched her walk, a living ghost, and wring her pale hands and curse and weep and pray. In this implacable and discontented humour she continued many months, always murmuring against her husband and showing him not the faintest civility or respect. The good man suffered patiently, being loth to discover his shameful misery to the world ; but having a man's courage, he would sometimes break into a little passion, seeing himself thus always slighted and neglected. Yet never could he win from her one kind word or glance. This was the strangest marriage that ever there had been, yet at the time I pitied her and never him. I thought her ill-used because she could not have her lover and must live with the lad she'd married.

" Sometimes they brawled, but only with words. The fool would not beat her and only thus might he have won her in the end, words meaning nothing to her who liked to scream back at him. But these quarrels were not often. The poor man had such an extraordinary affection for her—as well might any man, she being so golden, plump and beautiful—and his being an honest and religious love, ready rather to suffer in silence than to correct her outrageous manner, he would patiently admonish her to a better course of life, telling her that her honour was safe from the wicked temptations of the court, and he would remind her how all her fortune depended on his prosperity, and therefore in her cruelties she did more injury to herself than to him, he said. But he might as well have talked to a cat with a needle in its bottom as to her with her loathing of him and her craving for Somerset.

" He had shut the court away from her but not Mrs.
Turner. They corresponded, of course, but when she
came to Chartley, the earl saw no harm in this woman
who wove his happiness's destruction and rather
welcomed her that she might divert his lady out of her
sullens. Little did he know that she took letters for
Somerset away with her while bringing with her packets
and vials from the wizard. I was drawn into their
conspiracy, having with Mrs. Horne been my lady's
darling and confidante, and soon I shed my doubts and
fears, Mrs. Turner having a serpent's tongue that would
have charmed a hermit and such coaxing girlish ways
and merry laugh you could not believe that anything she
said or did was wicked. I became as evil and as excited
as they, desiring my poor master's death and finding a
voluptuous pleasure in seeing him eat and drink. But
first, not wishing to kill lest he be hanged for it, the
wizard hoped to imbecillate my lord. No linen came
near his body that was not first rinsed in his camphoric
compositions, and other faint and wasting ingredients ;
and all inward applications, drugs and potions, were
foisted on him by corrupted servants like myself, so that
in all he wore, in all he ate and drank, poisons were
mixed.

" Narrowly we watched him, impatient to see him
wither and totter to his bed, but he was a powerful
young man, honest in his living and much given to
riding and other exercises ; and we saw no change in
him to our great chagrin. As well as ever he had been,
he stayed, and my lady moaned her miserable case and
cried that God had forgotten her. In her despair,
weeping often in my arms, she would sob that she could
endure her miseries no longer and could never be happy
while that man lived. To this Dr. Forman would she
write, calling him her Sweet Father and pleading with
him to make speed to rid her of her incubus. But in
her hate of one she did not neglect her love for the

other or her affection for her Sweet Father as, I say, she called this wizard . . ."

" So did they all," simpered Mrs. Forman complacently, "high and lower, countess and tavern-wenches, young and old. They would kiss him on the lips and comb his beard and call him lovingly their own Sweet Father ; and he liked it, too, being a vain man."

" Her Sweet Father would she call him," continued Kate, glancing with loathing at her interrupter, " and would beg him to find out whether Somerset still loved her. Thus with love-philtres to one and poison to the other, she wriggled with impatience, crying that the whole world was against her and that even the heavens were not favourable. Yet still was my lord lusty and merry, drinking with his men, and all the answer she got from him when she asked how he fared was abuse because she would not play the wife.

" Her family, fearing the scandal, sent her brother to teach her how to behave and he was not one to bridle his tongue with a love-sick sister, but all he got from her were tears. Times there were when I wept to see so pretty a thing waste all away, and I could not understand the stubbornness of her love that made her so wilful. Alack, I had not her courage nor her true heart. And I told her, for peace sake, to let her lord have his way with her now and then ; it could do no harm, said I to her, her Robin need never know of it and it would make her lord content and then could we all have been merry. But she'd not do it. She slapped my face and pinched me for saying such things. ' Sweet Kate,' she sobbed, ' ask me not that. No matter how angry grow my father and mother, I'd rather died a thousand deaths than do it.' ' But 'tis so small a thing,' said I, ' and so soon over.' ' 'Tis not that,' said she, gripping my arms and glaring into my eyes. ' Nay,' says she, ' I would lose Robin's love : he warned me of it ; if ever I let my husband even think I loved him, I could go hang, he said. Besides, are you not woman enough to understand?—I could not look in his dear face again.'

" Yet she weakened. Not wholly but a little way. It was not so much the urging and raging of her family or the pleadings of her husband that did it, but the ache to see her Robin again. She agreed to bed with her husband that he might not be mocked at, but she must have pillows betwixt them, she said, on condition that he took her back to court ; and he, poor long-tried soul, was as weary as she of that hell in the country where they could not escape one another ; and so long as his reputation as a man did not suffer and people thought him her husband in act as well as name, he consented to it. After that time, they slept in the same bed, but far apart, the pillow between them, and all rejoiced to think that the good man had tamed his shrew.

" Back to court they went and it was wonderful to see her change. Visibly, before my eyes, she seemed to fatten and grow rosy and she laughed. Sweet it was to hear her laugh again, so like a child she sounded ; while the earl, unhappy creature, sat glum beside her. It was at her uncle's, the Earl of Northampton's house, that she again met her Robin ; and afterwards I attended her to strange houses, low places where people of her rank did not usually consort, to strange bedchambers smelling of others who had slept there before them. Stuffy, sour and unaired. Masked, we would go in hired coaches into some foul alley, my lady dressed in old garments and hiding in her hood. And often did we travel to Lambeth to see her Sweet Father."

" I remember," nodded Mrs. Forman. " Whiteskinned she was and big-eyed, bold as a beast, and her lips seemed always wet. My husband liked her well."

" Into his study would we go," continued Kate as though the other had not spoken, " with its queer charts on the wall and its astrolabe and its spy-glass and dried

beasties and little pots and bladders. Often was I shut
out while in secret they conferred. I know not what
wicked rites they did, but once I heard my lady cry
aloud and, when I would have entered, she pushed shut
the door, but I saw that she wore nothing and had
strange figures painted on her skin and that there was
blood in her hair. Peculiar yet not unpleasant smells
would steal from that den, making one feel dizzy and
vaguely amorous ; and sometimes would come the stink
of brimstone to turn one sick ; but what they did
together I never learned. One parchment, however,
that my lady showed me had names writ on it which
were, my lady told me proudly, all the names of the
Blessed Trinity that were mentioned in the scriptures ;
and there was another with crosses and letters betwixt the
crosses ; and a third with *Corpus* writ on it, and on that
parchment was fastened a little piece of dried skin from
a dead man. I recall one which my lady told me had
on it the devil's favourite names and it was, said she, a
very potent and terrible spell and, should her Robin
ever prove untrue to her or cease to love her, all those
devils with names writ on it would run to torment him.
She said that Mrs. Turner also had one lest Sir Arthur
Mainwaring weary of her. But most of what they did
I never learned."

She stared full at Mrs. Forman who stared back at
her. Then Mrs. Forman shrugged. " I've naught to
hide under a figleaf," said she, " and if I must pay for
my dinner with my tale, I'll tell you all I know. But
already in open court have I confessed everything and
I gave the judges the images and papers my sweet
husband left. So why should you look at me like
that, you brazen baggage ! I have naught to hide, my
business with my husband having been in bed and in
no magic circles. He made figures and papers to please
the ladies, but I knew naught of them. I gave them up
to justice."

"Yea," chuckled the lawyer. "When they were shown in court there was heard a crack from the scaffolds which caused great fear, tumult and confusion amongst the spectators and throughout the hall, everyone in terror lest the devil himself were present and was angry at having his workmanship shown by such as were not his scholars. And this terror continued a quarter of an hour after silence proclaimed. But the wood was old and the mob great to look on Mrs. Turner. She was small but fascinating, that is true, and hard to believe with her trim figure that she had had three children by Sir Arthur alone."

"That was my husband's doing," said Mrs. Forman. "That's how I stay young, too. O, he was a wise man and a loving one, and he would laugh at the ladies after they had gone. I remember well those figures, for I helped to make them. There was one moulded in lead for the Lady Essex, and another for Mrs. Turner likewise, of a man and a woman at the ancient dance, as bare as beasts. Pho! 'twas a nasty thing that I'd not have kept in the house, as I told my sweet master, and he, kissing me long and savourly, said, said he, undoing my ribbons, ' I need not such figures,' said he, ' when I have my poppet to dandle,' I being more beautiful in those days, and much younger. Oft would he say that men would have no need of his aphrodisiacal powders if they could have me, me being all aphrodisiacal and the very compounding of love's essences and as invigorating, he would say, as eringo or cantharides."

"Tush, tush," growled Archie. "What of these figures and conjurations, woman?"

"They were filthy," said she, wrinkling her nose and shuddering. "Some of lead and some of brass, and he also made pictures, and a black scarf full of white crosses. Ask me not the meaning of it : I know not. And there was one pretty figure I remember, in wax it was, very sumptuously apparelled in silks and satins ; as also another in the form of a naked lady spreading and laying forth her hair in a looking-glass. Such like things he made. And when Mrs. Turner or my countess would come, often would he lock himself in with them, sometimes three hours, sometimes four ; and I remember another thing he had : a ring that would open like a watch. And he had an alphabetical book in which he made his visitors write their names with their own handwriting."

"Yea," cackled the lawyer suddenly, " I wot well that book, for there was much mirth in court when it was reported that the first leaf Lord Justice Coke lighted on he found his own wife's name."

"Doubtless," nodded Mrs. Forman, " the highest to the lowest visited us : ladies— " and she curled her lip at Kate—"and their beggarly servants also were not above begging love-potions and cures for the itch."

"That book," said Kate darkly, staring back at her, " was made that he might hold his foolish visitors in awe should they complain, as well they might have complained, of his abusing them, as in truth he did naught else. Besides, it was believed with good reason that all his visitors did not come for conjuring and that the art of the bawd was more beneficial to him than necromancy, and that he was a better artist in the one than the other," she said, almost spitting into Mrs. Forman's face, " that you might know how real was his skill, he himself was a cuckold. Yea, madam, deny it if you can ! I've heard you many a time when charged with it, say with your own lips you did it to try his cunning ; but it fared with him as with most astrologers that can't foresee their own destiny."

Mrs. Forman simpered and looked at her hands. " He said that he knew Everything," she giggled, " and what woman of spirit would not try him out on that ? And I proved him a liar, too, often ; for I was a pretty young wench, and he was old."

"He was a rogue but a foolish rogue," said the physician. "He had wit enough only to cheat ladies and other females by pretending skill in telling their fortunes, as to whether they should bury their husbands and what second husbands they should have, and whether they should enjoy their loves, or whether maids should get husbands, or enjoy their servants themselves without co-rivals. A very dog he was of a charlatan."

"You're jealous," shrugged Mrs. Forman. "All the Society of Physicians were jealous of him. He told me so."

"He was the one who'd cause to be jealous had he examined your tail," snarled Kate. "I've heard the tale—is it true, ma'am?—that you so woman-tired him with your chatter that you drove him to his death and he ran to hell to escape you. Were you not in your garden-house having supper when you asked him, if he was so clever, could he tell whether man or wife should die first, and asked him whether you should bury him or no? 'Oh,' said he, being weary of your prattle, 'you'll bury me but you'll repent of it.' Then said you, never satisfied but ever chitter-chattering : 'How long will that be?' to which he made answer, 'I shall die before next Thursday night be over.' The next day, goes the tale, being Monday, all was well ; Tuesday came and he was not sick ; Wednesday came and still he was well. Then you, his impertinent wife, did twit him in the teeth with what he had said on Sunday. Thursday came, and dinner being ended, he was well and went down to the waterside and took a pair of oars to go to some buildings he was in hand with at Puddle Dock, and being in the middle of the Thames, he presently fell down, and once said, 'An impost ! an impost !' and so died ; whereupon a most sad storm of wind immediately followed. Thus had you harried and tormented the poor creature that he was glad to have the devil take him."

Smiling, Mrs. Forman fluttered her plump hands over the table. "Mayhap," she said, "mayhap he died that way, foretelling his own end ; I'll not contradict it, being a good wife who'd not hurt her dead husband's reputation. Yet he never liked to leave me long, his little pigsnye, he called me, and his moppet. And rather than go out or row on the river, he'd loll about my neck and say that I was Cleopatra's self except that I had a prettier nose. So wise he was, and I do miss him with a heart-break."

"We have heard enough about this conjuring cuckold," growled the jester imperiously. "Nan, back to your tale. Your mistress got her potions, her aphrodisiacs for her lover and the poisons for her husband, her lewd figures and her conjurations. What effect had they ?"

Nan wrinkled her nose. "I know not," she said. "On her husband, little or none ; on her lover . . . who can say ? He met her constantly and yet he feared her demands on him, I am certain, Reluctant he was at first, embarrassed by her furies and her embracements, yet he could not cast her off ; and her husband thrived. Nevertheless, she continued to pay great sums to her Sweet Father and to Mrs. Turner and the others she employed ; and all she got in return were promises and magic baubles. Once came to her, I remember, an enchanted nutmeg and a letter, one to be given to her Robin in a drink and the other to be kept next her heart. And there was the waxen image of her husband she kept in a cupboard. Into this she and Mrs. Turner would press thorns plucked from a tree that bore no leaves that the earl might be pierced to the heart and suffer torments of pain. Then her Sweet Father died, lashed by his wife's tongue to his death. And distracted was my poor mistress that he should go like that before he had granted her desires, but Mrs. Turner caressed her and consoled her, swearing to find her a more cunning man until, like a child, she sobbed herself to sleep. As bad as her words was Mrs. Turner, bringing other rogues whom my lady in her open heart trusted. There was a Dr. Savories and one named Gresham who soon were busy with potions and powders and such devil-gear.

"Whether—who can say?—it was the last spells of Dr. Forman or whether this Savories were more cunning, certain it is that from now my Lord Somerset grew passionately fond of my lady. He had contracted her distemper and could not have enough of her. Mad were they together, insatiable, lipping and fondling as though they could never weary, and when not embracing, they were gaping and gazing on one another, his one-time backwardness forgotten in his passion for her. Had she not been a married lady, sweet it would have been to see them at their play; but always was there the risk of spies, spies being everywhere, or of her husband bursting in on them. And plain now was it even for the blind to mark that they were lost and lived but for each other."

"My darling husband was so cunning," murmured Mrs. Forman.

"Whether it was magic or natural adoration, I have no means of knowing," cried Nan, "but it was natural adoration, I believe, each being the mirror of the other in perfection, no man his equal and no woman reaching near to her in beauty. New places of meeting were continually being arranged as they could no longer visit Lambeth, not trusting Mrs. Forman's babble, but mostly they went to Mrs. Turner's house at Hammersmith. My lady now had obtained all her desires, save her lord's death, her Robin being snared in her net and she the most admired of women at the court. Now was she happy, or would have been happy had she not been married, and she became more imperious, more hard to please, ever demanding this and that, then tossing it aside when it was given her. Her Robin no longer struggled to escape ; or rather, I should say, the more he had struggled, the faster had he been caught until liked a tired lion in a net he thought it best to lie down and surrender. Places of more frequent and private meetings were concluded between them, persons fitting for their purpose, myself of course amongst them, being made to help."

" She had bound him in enchantments," said the poet suddenly, sitting up with flushed face and staring eyes. " I was Tom Overbury's friend and he confided in me, for I helped him as his secretary. Ah, tragic was it to see the unhappy Viscount Rochester—for such was the Earl of Somerset then—run to his doom. I and sad Overbury saw the good parts consume within him under the fire of that witch, and we wept to watch so noble a man, like another Antony, being destroyed in this little Cleopatra. Affairs of state he forgot or neglected, all his thoughts being on ribbons and toys, on new fashions and fal-de-lals. He and his whore must be forever prinking themselves with yellow bands, dusted hair, or curled, clipped or frizzed hair, with slicked skins and open breasts beyond accustomed modesty, with many other inordinate attires worn by each of them to show the world their horrid lunacy and to increase their own dishonest appetites. Pho ! it was vile, it was vile ! Surfeiting thus on pleasures caused him to fall into all manner of forgetfulness, letting everything go to wreck, becoming careless in attendance, neglecting state affairs, ignorant of his own worth, subjecting himself wholly to the lustful appetite of an evil woman and accounting no time well spent nor hour deemed so happy as when dalliance passed between them, either in words or writing. Thus did he lay himself open to the evil thoughts of them that hated him, since the eyes of all men are on such as are eminent ; and as black on white is soonest discovered, so evil conditions and lasciviousnesses are soonest seen in such persons."

" Lack a day ! " moaned the jester, " he rants like a priest."

" I loved Tom Overbury," said the poet. And as though he were weary, he passed his hand over his forehead before he sat down again.

" 'Tis true," sighed Kate, " that her lord grew wild in his passion, which strengthened the more he fed on it and her ; and that they might meet without enemies to watch, my lady bought Sir Roger Aston's house at Hounslow, ten miles or so out of London and a quick gallop from Whitehall, and there they lived luxuriously on wines and sugar-cakes and kisses ; and my lady was ever careful to distil into his glass the philtres that the wizards gave her to keep him passionate and tireless in her service. Yet there were days when she had to wait, watching the clock, distraught with uneasiness and longings, when he was detained by the king. On such occasions this Overbury would sometimes come, lean as malice, with messages from her lord and with hatred in his girl's voice."

" He had the right to hate her," shrilled the poet. " Yet he'd not meddle in the matter more than he could help at first. He left them alone in their vicious courses and rather appeared to be ignorant of what went on than to take note of it. Yet against his will, willy nilly, was he drawn into that amorous conspiracy and he champed against it."

" That was why she wished his death," said Kate.

" Death, death ! " cried Will. " You say she would have killed her husband, yet he thrived on what she fed him. Now you would give another murder added to bestiality, witchcraft with obscene images, goetic rites and stinking sacrifices, mammets to be stuck with thorns and melted by the fire, and venomous potions drunk . . . It is not true ! "

" It is all true," said the jester.

" And now more talk of murder," moaned Will.

" Yea, of murder," said the jester. " First, the husband ; afterwards, the friend ; but the husband had a bullock's strength and survived. Tom Overbury was not so fortunate."

" I'll not listen to these lies ! "

" Cruel and sharp is the surgeon's knife," said the jester. " . . . But we will pause to give your honour time to digest the truth. Ladies, gentlemen—if I may call you so on this occasion—let us be merry if we can. Who will sing and laugh with me ? "

But there were none who would sing or laugh, the gaiety having fled their hearts, while they looked from the corners of their eyes at Will at the head of the table with his face in his hands.

CHAPTER X

The Netting of Overbury

BEAUTY dissected, her bosom bared, her heart laid open,
and all her secrets shown. Will refused to believe what
he had heard although he knew it for the truth.
Frances had done those diabolical things. Yet always
for love had she done them : and that surely was some
extenuation ? All for a love so great that, far from
being the harlot that men said, she had risked scandal,
beatings, insults, rather than bed with a man she
disliked, her rightful husband. In that alone could
Will find some small thing to honour her. But in
nothing else. Her love had not been human in its
frenzy. She had consulted Satan's agents. She had
dosed her husband with poisons and her lover with
aphrodisiacs ; she had submitted to goetic rites in that
den of Forman's ; she had stuck pins and thorns into
images of those she hated and had worshipped her own
and her lover's images moulded to ruttish shapes. All
these things, risking life and soul, had she done for love
of a red-headed fool. That the poison had not acted on
Essex did not excuse the deed ; and mayhap the rascally
wizard, not wanting to become entangled in a murder-
plot, had sold her harmless drugs. His other drugs,
however, those for Somerset, apparently had worked.
Now could Will understand the haggard look on that
old man's face—nor could he have been so old in years
as he had thought—the look of the damned glaring out
of his eyes. He, the helpless, the doomed one, trapped
in enchantments, drawn against his will into passion by
the smoke of magic potions steaming under his heart,
could be pitied. He had not been a man but a mammet,

165

a lover conjured by Frances herself to fit her own desires, as will-less as the sylph some succubus might build from air to feed her nights. Will could pity Somerset and, try though he might, he could not hate Frances whatever the villainy she had committed. She, too, mayhap had swallowed some drug, some nymphomaniacal elixir, and had been possessed by a ravenous spirit spurring her to inexhaustible lechery.

" They were bewitched," he groaned.

" He was bewitched : I grant you that," said the poet, " but all the enchantments lay in her bright eyes and a snow-white bosom. Thus did the wanton twine him to her, tangling him in her hot golden hair. Witchcraft, yea, but a witchcraft known to all women and enacted every day ; and fortunate are we silly men that few are the ladies wicked and beautiful enough to use such power over us for our destruction."

" Why ! " cried Will, " do you think she was happy in it ? "

" Yea," snarled the poet. " Women are always happiest when they can master a man. As Father Chaucer said, all their desire lies in sovereignty. She had the man she desired her slave, the most beautiful, the most gracious and powerful and handsomely dressed man in the country. Therefore, like any woman, was she happy, exulting in his ruin while driving him to seek his sweet friend Overbury's death."

" You have no right to say that ! "

" Every right, forgive me, my lord. I was Tom's friend. I saw it all. She hated Tom because she feared him, knowing that he was her lover's master. For all that the pretty lout was praised, his skill in diplomacy and such must be laid at his ghost's feet. Tom was that ghost schooling the boor, teaching him, a child, what he must say or do or write, just as it had been his sugared pen that had entrapped the Lady Essex and drawn her to loving Rochester. Mayhap she had

discovered the truth of that, finding her poet no longer
a poet when he was away from his ghost ; if so, it must
have added to her hate, thinking how Overbury must
grin at knowing her for a fool cheated with another
man's words. Few women could forgive that trick,
having been gulled, shown as a simpleton. Then when
my master would not heed her allurements, flouting her,
her hatred could not be contained. Ah, for such a
woman, a Messalina, to have the power to kill a poet !
For Overbury was a poet and a great scholar, yet he
served his friend for little money and no fame. And he
was growing weary of it."

"He talked too much," grumbled the jester. "He
had a scorpion's tongue and a Scotsman's pride, although
he was no Scot. He was like a lustful woman, never
satisfied but orgulous and avid after favours. He
wanted men to fawn on him, he wished to be the trusted
friend of kings, he wanted power. For all his book-
wisdom, the man was a fool and oft I told him so ; but
he'd not heed me, not he ! On to his own destruction
he ran his venomous tongue and his insolence, boasting
when drunk of how he had made Carr and how he could
unmake him. Carr heard and Carr was tired of his
demands and boasting."

"That little bitch drove hatred betwixt them ! "
cried the poet.

"Yea," said the jester, "she distrusted him as any
wise woman distrusts her husband's familiar. But
Overbury himself whetted the weapon for her use. He
swaggered and he patronised his patron, he treated Carr
like a boy. Even that, Carr would have accepted,
being a good-natured fool at heart ; but Overbury
insulted Frankie and that he would not have."

"For his own good he warned him against the
whore," shrilled the poet. "He tried to unhood him
that he might see the wanton for what she was. Often
they quarrelled on it, Overbury, sweet fellow, striving to

167

wean him from his lunacy and, like a poisoned rat that
seeks a hole in which to die, Somerset fled from him to
dandle in his lady's arms that she might bind him
tighter hers in thraldom and whisper hatred of the man
she feared. Then when Overbury learned that the
love-struck fool would have her divorced that he might
marry her, he raged and pleaded and implored his
friend not to commit this final madness. It would lose
him the king's love, he warned him ; but in his vanity,
thinking he had the king forever his slave, Somerset
laughed at him. He did not know, as many suspected,
that already was the king weary of his arrogance and,
with fickle heart, was seeking another favourite to replace
him. Glad would his majesty have been to be quit of
Somerset, even for a woman, and when he heard talk of
the divorce, misliking Essex for his boorish ways, he set
himself to it as did her family with him. And Overbury,
seeing so plain the tragedy ahead, tried to stop his
friend from tumbling into hell ; and was himself
destroyed because of it."

"You are a poet," murmured the jester, "and you
see these things poetically ; but I am a Scotsman with
my eye at a keyhole and my nose to a stink. I saw
Overbury a puppy that thought itself a mastiff ; a spoilt
child stamping its feet because it wants the world its
slave. Cunning and dangerous he was, and spiteful if
witty ; but there is no man so cunning and dangerous as
a woman hurt in her vanity who fears to lose her lover.
And Overbury was a fool. He had his lord's head
under his girdle, as he thought, and believed that he
could bully him out of love with menaces of discoveries
of state secrets and such-like. Is that not so ? "

"He . . . threatened : yea," muttered the poet ;
"but he intended no harm, only good that he might
save his friend."

"With a big stick ? " jeered the jester. "Come,
fellow, you know as well as I that he was puffed with

vain-glory and ambition and therefore loth to have any partner in his favours with Carr ; and especially not any of the house of Howard against whom he had always professed hatred and shown opposition. Many a day he made his brag that he had won Carr the lady's love through his letters and his industry. Think you that either Carr or Frankie liked such talk ? The fellow was corrupt and naught and, worse, a fool."

" Nay," wailed the poet, sweating, " you knew him not as I did, how merry he could be over his wine, and generous as well, when the mood took him. But he could not sit idle and see his friend consumed by a succubus, and he told him so. One night I remember when with another servant, Henry Payton, I waited up for him. We were in a chamber nigh the gallery at Whitehall and we saw Rochester—as Somerset then was —meet our master. ' How now,' quoth Rochester with a guilty look, ' are you up yet ? ' ' Nay,' said my master bitterly, ' what do you here at this time of night ? Will you never leave the company of that base woman ? ' Then they broke into quarrelling and presently I heard my master cry : ' Well, my lord, if you do marry that filthy, base woman you will utterly ruin your honour and yourself ; you shall never do it by my advice and con- sent,' quoth he, ' and if you do, you had best look to stand fast.' Then, red in the face with shame and fury, my Lord Rochester shouted, being bewitched by the countess's love : ' My own legs are straight and strong enough to bear me up,' he cried, ' but, in faith, I will be even with you for this ; ' and so parted from him in a great rage."

" What did I say ? " shrugged the jester. " For all his wit, the fellow was a fool. He could not stem the divorce when all the Howards pressed for it and it amused the king. On went that divorce and even the Archbishop of Canterbury himself could not stop it."

" I read of that," muttered Will : " Let's hear no more of it."

" As you desire, my lord," said the jester, bowing,
" yet it was almost stopped and had not the countess's
family moved quickly to stamp the scandal out she'd
have been ruined before her time. You must know the
truth of that, Kate, of the witch that was snared. Her
name now I forget."

" Mary Woods was she called," said Kate. " But I
knew not the heart of the trouble, so numerous were the
wise women and conjuring men my lady consulted.
This Mary Woods was a bent old crapulous creature
with hairs on her hooked nose and no teeth in her head.
She used to frighten me. She had the evil eye. She
told me so ; and sure, if ever eyes were evil they were.
Bright and black as a bird's they were, in red wet rims
that had no lashes. Muttering and mumbling to herself,
she'd race along, aided by her stick, faster than most
men could walk, and she had claws for fingers and they
all scaly and horrid to touch. She had, or said she had,
a familiar spirit whom she would give her blood to suck.
Spotted she was as though from bug-bites where the
devil had sucked her and she had extra-teats for his
feeding—she showed them to me—one under her armpit,
one on her groin and one under the buttocks, that the
creature might drink when it was athirst. Yet my
darling lady would fondle this woman and make much
of her and call her her Sweet Mother and I would
shudder to see her kiss her with her fresh lips and dandle
her : it was like beauty with a toad, innocence caressing
a lizard and not knowing it to be venomous. Cunning
Mary was this woman named and she was notoriously
evil and lived by getting money from women on pretence
of giving them husbands or babies, whichever the fools
desired. The law had caught her once, I was told,
and the wonder is she was not hanged, but her devil
shielded her, no doubt. They charged her with
administering deadly drugs, but she swore that she'd
refused to give some wife the poison she had begged that

she might be quit of her husband ; but the truth of that I know not, only that she was freed.

"My lady would give her many things and she would steal what she could when no one watched, but the trouble broke when my lady, in sudden rage at her thefts, sent her pursuivant, Dick Grimstone, after her to get back a ring set with diamonds and some money she'd thoughtlessly given the crone to take charge of, as she was in haste herself to go to court. But Dick, never knowing his mistress's secrets, instead of taking back the ring and money, charged the woman with the theft of them. 'We are undone ! ' cried my lady when she heard, and she tottered and almost fell. And true it was, nearly ruined were we by that rash act of Dick's. My lady swore that she'd rather have lost ring and all than have the matter public ; but she was too late. Cunning Mary'd not give them up and silly Dickon carried the hag to court ; and there, out of spite, the woman swore that my lady had promised her a thousand pounds if she'd procure poison to kill her husband, the Earl of Essex, asking particularly for a dose that'd not act within three or four days but would gradually eat his life out like a candle's.

"The divorce had been prepared and all was ready when these tidings were tattled and although my lady hushed the scandal as well as she could and had the woman let loose, the whispering had begun. Poison. It was a dangerous word and for a time even the divorce was dropped ; but only for a time. Soon, when rumours began to die, my lady became as brisk again as ever and as determined to marry her love, and Somerset was as eager as she that they might no longer have to meet in nasty secrecy. Only Overbury stood between them, saying malicious things about my lady and writing libels. There was one poem, *The Wife*, which sent her into her bed with vexation."

"It was an excellent poem," said the poet, "and

most virtuous. It vexed your lady, I doubt not, because it was so virtuous. He asked of a perfect wife neither birth or beauty, while your lady had both ; and as for her portion, ' neither will I shun,' wrote he, ' nor my aim it make.' What he desired, he said in these lines, if I remember them rightly :

> Let it be good ; when these with virtues go,
> They (in themselves indifferent) virtues prove,
> For good, like fire, turns all things to be so.
> God's image in her soul, O let me place
> My love upon ! not Adam's in her face.

He asked no learning of the lady, for learning, said he, with wit, made women frail, and domestic duties did become them best. That he thought it no ill work for a virtuous lady, I know because he sent it to the Countess of Rutland, the daughter of that brave thrush, Sir Philip Sidney, whom he hoped to marry, and he had Ben Jonson read it to her. She delighted in it, but not the evil countess. To her it was a mirror of all she was not. ' He comes too near,' he sang, ' who comes to be denied.' Such lines were vitriol to her who had denied many if not Rochester. Yea, it was not only a beautiful poem, it was a noble one, which no good woman could mislike ; and it sold after his death, ah dear ! edition upon edition."

" I saw no harm in it myself," said Kate, " but my lady railed because she said it was against her. It had been written, she said, to make her Robin want to marry a maiden with no wit outside a kitchen, and therefore was it, by implication, an insult, extolling all in a wife that herself was not. It was from then that my lady became seriously determined on Overbury's death, having but toyed with the idea before . . . Yea, my lord ! though for some reason it pains you to hear it," she said, turning to Will who sat, white to the lips, gripping the arms of his chair. " I must speak truth. Little by little had she been drawn into wickedness, led

by Mrs. Turner step by step, from love-potions to
poisons and necromancy, so that by now she thought
little even of murder, having tried to kill her husband.
Besides, she was afraid, and people in fear strike out
lest they be struck. Always, too easily had she got
whatever she desired. No man, nor woman neither,
could withstand her coaxing, save this Overbury ; for
she had childlike winning ways belying the cruelty in
her heart. Many a time have I seen her pout and
wriggle her hips, swinging the farthingale, while raising
her plucked brows and seeming ready to cry : then
always, whatever she hankered after was weakly granted
to keep her happy. In everything, since babyhood, she
had had her wilful way, nothing whatever denied her,
as though her beauty made her divine and must be ever
pampered and appeased. Thus after a time, finding all
thrust into her greedy hands, was it not natural that she
should grow orgulous, imperious, and would suffer
denial of nothing from a sugarmeat to a lover, thinking
she could do no wrong and could suffer no harm ? All
men bowed in adoration before her ; even women
surrendered to her superior loveliness and granted her
domination over them, unable even to be jealous of
such beauty which raised her above all, beyond whatever
that could be found in paint-pots. On her had God
spent all His cunning. She had, as I say, no need to
colour her skin or to dye her hair or to paint the veins
on her bosom. All of her was perfect. That was what
destroyed her, pandering to her pride, making her
peevish, demanding, driving her wild with screaming
and kicking and pounding of pillows when thwarted by
the littlest thing. Who can condemn her for it ? Not
it. Her beauty was to blame and the worship it
commanded.

" That was one reason why she hated Overbury.
She feared him. Even the king who shrank from most
women, smiled on her ; Overbury alone, in his disdain,

remained untouched by her magic. He alone in all that court shrugged from her arts, looking from under his eyelids into her lifted bosom as though he'd blow his nose on it. And he'd titter as though he'd found some blemish on her which only he could see ; and of all things we women fear, even the loveliest among us, we fear ridicule. That can so easily make us foolish and rob us of pride, making us feel naked and mis-shapen in company even when we know we look our brightest in our newest gown. Then let somebody snigger and whisper, glancing with a smile towards us, and we crumple inside and, in panic, wonder what spots be on our cheeks or whether we show too much of what should be concealed. Overbury could make my lady feel that way. And she had other reasons for hating him. He knew too much.

" My Lord of Somerset was open-hearted, guileless. His rapid rise to greatness had not truly spoiled him and he trusted men and women. Long had he loved Sir Thomas Overbury. They were David and Jonathan until my lady came."

" Yea, yea," said the poet, " right loving were they together. All men spoke of it. My Lord Rochester and his ghost. Deep was the trust between them. My master had an agile mind and my lord Rochester would tell him his secrets, handing him—I have seen it often— sealed despatches from ministers and ambassadors, leaving everything for him to manage. My master ruled the kingdom. Was it not natural that he should desire to have his genius recognised ? He and Rochester had a code that they might write to one another and nobody knew what they wrote. Never was there such a love as betwixt those two until the woman came, vicious, insatiable and cruel and jealous."

" She was not cruel, never ! " cried Kate. " You did not understand her. In many ways she was a child not realising how others could be hurt. Being given everything, like a child, she was enraged when something was denied her ; for unlike others, she had never learned to want and not to get. Until she met Overbury and recognised the hatred and the menace in his eyes. That must have startled her : to find somebody, a man of all things, who was not quickened by her beauty. It was something unprecedented, beyond her comprehension ; therefore it had to be destroyed. She tried at first to woo him, languishing before him when he rode to Hammersmith to excuse her lord when he was detained at court, exposing to him all her little arts, her shrugs and sighs and underlidded glances, her helpless airs, having her golden hair curling over her shoulders, her bosom almost bare, her farthingale cast off that, in her pleated shift, he might note the length of leg and curving of her shape ; but all in vain. He merely smiled at her and postured as though to show of his shape and his legs for her to envy. And she would redden and sulk and bite her curls.

" She had her spies at court and knew all that he puffed on her reputation and of an anagram he had wrought out of her name, re-shaping the letters of Frances Howard to make *Carr finds a whore*. Yet still she hoped to win him until he wrote that poem, *The Wife*, upholding to a sniggering world the ideal wife which she was not. More than japes and insults, that poem stung her, drove her to such frenzies I feared she'd suffocate. This portrait of a meek lady, virtuous, kitchen-loving, near whom, so virtuous was she, no man had ever even coasted, set her teeth on edge with hate and jealousy. Mayhap she feared her lover might find deficiencies in her over-knowledge and voluptuousness and hanker after some such watery timid maid. She was outraged. She knew the love there was between this fellow and her lord, she knew the rascal's power and acid tongue ; and she feared perhaps lest that poem unseal her lover's eyes.

" You must understand that Viscount Rochester knew naught of her magical doings ; he knew naught of the potions on which she'd fed her husband or the venerial potions she gave him in his wine to bind him hers. In her life she acted many persons. So do we all, women particularly, performing such and such a character to such and such a person, being maiden, harlot, wife, mother, child, roguish or lewd or innocent, whichever role the lovers like to see. Towards her husband my lady was a vixen ; towards her lover she was modest. He never heard her swear or prattle naughtily. He thought that, save towards him, she was all virtue and blushed easily. But Overbury was not deceived, he knew the truth. Him alone she could not bubble however arch and babyish she looked, this ghost who had wooed and won her for another's bedding. Growing intolerable in his pride, he cared not what he said nor to whom he said it, delighting in his power to wound and seeing others cringe to him. But being lost in love, my Lord of Somerset was deaf to his malice, disbelieving his scandalous tales and thinking my mistress a very Lucrece who had not used the knife because she loved him above modesty. How he ignored the memory of the prince, I do not know ; but you who have been lovers must remember how, in the agony of that time, you smothered truth and blinked away from the reality, arguing black to pink, twisting some treachery until you could make of it something almost noble. Such liars are we all at such times. This my lady realised and she feared that some day he would remember the prince. Some day his eyes would open and he would see that she was only flesh and not divinely made. Even the sweetest foods grow sickly, even passion has its ebb : not hers, she felt ; hers grew the stronger, the more insatiable the more it banqueted ; but men are often fickle and his love had never equalled hers. Mayhap that was what bound her to him, this fear of losing him, he not being at heart an ardent lover, loving himself too dearly, but fired by her fire and lured by her adroit caressings and the drugs she fed him. Therefore Overbury had to die."

"Alas!" groaned the poet, "such wit to be slain because a wanton feared to lose her bully-boy!"

"There was another, even stronger reason," said Kate. "The king was favourable towards her as towards a dog that made him laugh, and he was a man who prided himself on his wisdom and religion. No matter how red his sins—and red they were—he believed himself a saint cherished in heaven, and had he discovered her magical doings, such horror had he of witchcraft— he wrote a blast against it once, he might have had her hanged. At least he'd have forbidden her the court, which was as bad as hanging to her, and have caused her Robin to abhor her. And her divorce was slowly coming to its fulfilment. That might well be stopped should his majesty sniff the truth and find that she had lied and was no maid but had refused her husband's love. Strict was he in justice, although he made the laws himself and thought that he alone could break them. And Overbury knew almost everything about her. From the first had he been in the plot and, had he spoken, he could have revealed her meetings with her lover. The king would never have forgiven that. He'd have forced her back into her husband's hateful bed. Therefore again had Overbury to die, and she sought a sword with which to slay him.

"Much hated was he, an upstart crow delighting to peck at his betters. Many longed yet feared to kill him, knowing how loved he was by Rochester and so powerful in the state, but there was one gentleman of the queen's household who made no secret of his enmity, the queen also loathing the fellow and therefore fondling those who, like this gentleman, spoke ill of the dog. He was Sir David Woods, a boisterous and atheistical soldier, a braggart and a bully. Both Somerset and Overbury had worked against him in some way. I know not the rights of it, but he swore that he'd been robbed of over two thousand pounds which should have been his. My lady called this fellow to her. She waited until the king and queen and her Robin were all at Rochester that she might not be disturbed ; then, dressed in all her beauty, in private she had him brought before her.

" Half-lying, half-seated, she was by the fire, her hair brushed and combed until each thread glittered, her bosom embusked high to press up those roseate buds with nipples half-concealed beneath a frill of lace. No man could see her and not wish to love her. Low, as though she were Venus herself, Sir David bowed before her and I saw his lips twitch and his eyes gleam before such beauty. She was honest with him, wasting few words. There was a man she said who had annoyed her, one who went piffling on her name, a braggart, said she, bred from some dungheap who should be taught his place. She spoke the name, Sir Thomas Overbury, low, slowly dwelling with loathing on each syllable. ' I would give,' said she, ' a thousand pounds to the man who, by way of a duel or otherwise, should slay me this snake. Not only that,' said she, ' but such a man would find himself honoured, and he who is now your greatest enemy, Sir David, would become your greatest friend.'

" There was no need for her to speak that name. Sir David knew that she meant Rochester for whose favour all men struggled ; but having been Overbury's enemy, Sir Thomas had become Rochester's enemy as well. Tempting therefore was my lady's offer, the gold and the favourite's love, but Sir David, though a braggart, was a cautious man. He had lived too long at court not to know that few secrets remain secrets there for long and that a man who sells his sword might find himself betrayed, jailed and mayhap hanged.

" ' If my Lord Rochester,' said he, watching my lady carefully, ' will give me his hand, or pass his word, that if I do this thing I shall escape and have his pardon, I will do it.'

" That, of course, was impossible. Her Robin must never know of her plot against his friend lest his love turn to loathing. Angry with Overbury he might be but he'd not have forgiven his being killed at her command, and he would then have seen her clearly, unhooded of love, as a woman pitiless, a murderess. She would think on it, she told Sir David, and later give her answer. And think on it she did, fretting her darling brows and biting her pink fingernails, after Sir David had departed ; but there seemed no way whereby she could use her Robin's name that would convince the fellow into doing the deed. Yet she could not relinquish the plot and late that night she sought out Sir David again to try once more to coax him to the murder, telling him that it was impossible for her to give the guarantee he asked but, said she, she would be his friend forever and would grant all favours possible to him ; upon her life, she swore it, if he would only do that deed.

" But Sir David shook his head. ' I am willing,' he told her, ' to bastinado Sir Thomas ; but for killing him, I am loth to be carried to Tyburn in return for any lady's pleasure.'

" Thus was she thwarted of revenge and it sickened her into one of her spasms of frenzy so that she rent her garments, broke her necklaces, wrenched out her hair and stamped upon the floor, beating and spitting at us, her women, when we dared approach her. But having determined on her enemy's death, she'd not be put from it by Sir David's natural caution and she turned to her old friend, the poison-box, wondering whether she could suborn the rogue's cook or lackey. But she need not have worried. In his insolence, Overbury at court was kicking his own grave, each day becoming more intolerable to my Lord Rochester, and they quarrelled constantly."

" Constantly ! " sighed the poet. " My master tried all things to save his friend from that wicked woman, by argument and coaxing and by threats, and all failed before her witchcraft. At my table, pretending to be writing, I would sit, heavy-hearted that a man so beautiful and so great as Viscount Rochester should have become a wanton's toy. It grieved my master to the heart and all his skill of persuasion he used to make his friend see the light. He reminded him that his swift rise had earned him many enemies, men enviously waiting a chance to pluck him down, therefore was it needful, he would say, for him to step cautiously, offending none, that those honours be not smirched with scandal. From such pleadings would he turn to up-braidings, being unable to control his anger before the other's sulky stubbornness, and he even threatened to leave his service, declining, he said, to serve a man who, despite his honours, rewards and expectations, would cast everything away for a woman noted both for her impiety and immodesty which would pull upon him the hatred and evil contempt of great personages. But frowning, biting his beard, the viscount would not heed him. O, my poor master ! I would feel tears under my lids that any man could be so stupid as the viscount as to destroy himself for a Messalina, a Poppea, a Phryne, a Jezebel, a Salome, a harlot, a thing of naught but evil humours in a fair envelope.

" Weeping, my master asked him to consider this woman, her behaviour since youth, her irreverent conversation, and all the dishonour that was now attendant on her. People already talked, he said, and thought it unnatural for a man to make a wife of one who had already been his mistress. It was plain warning, said he, that she would treat her second husband as she had her first once she had tired of him.

'Already are you accused of incivility,' said my poor
master, ' of levity and even of effeminacy and are judged
by many to be unworthy of the honours the king has
bestowed on you, and,' pleaded my sweet master,
' should these surmises be fulfilled by this marriage with
so notorious a woman, the evil that were now but
suspected would be exaggerated and laid at your charge.'
. . . ' Honour,' I once heard him cry, the veins swelling
on his noble brow, ' honour,' he cried, ' is not attended
with voluptuousness, nor are the ruins of a rotten
branch to be cherished upon a new-planted tree ! '
Then as the earl—he was but a viscount then, of course
—grew maddened by such plain talk, I feared they'd
come to blows as like two cats they spat at one another
until my master, shaking and sweating, demanded the
payments due to him, saying that he desired to be left
to his own fortunes as he could not longer endure these
inordinate jangles . . . But he'd never have deserted
his precious lord. Anger it was that spoke, and not his
heart."

"He could not surrender power, you mean," said the
jester. "A monstrously conceited fellow was this Overbury with ever a stink under his nostrils. Him leave
his patron ! Not he ! Does the parasite desert the beast
on which it leeches ? Pah ! I'd have cudgelled him
myself had I worn a sword ; many a time would I have
done it."

" He was misliked," muttered the poet, " but only by
those who did not know him as I knew him. He loved
his patron. That is why he could not leave him."

" He loved power and gold," said the jester, " and
that is why he could not leave him ; but he had trodden
too far now in his insolencies. Even Carr was turning
from him and needed but the lick of his mistress's tongue
and a honeyed word or two from her relations, the
Howards, to be quit of the fellow ; yet I misdoubt if he
ever wished him murdered. There was no cruelty in

Carr, just heartlessness. He wanted only to be rid of a ghost who, like an ill conscience, dogged him with up-braidings. None of us here can tell what arts were used, how Frankie and her relatives, the Earl of Northampton in particular—he who was in the secret pay of Spain—worked on him, but work on him they did. Often I saw Northampton leaning on the fellow's shoulder, whispering in his ear, warning him no doubt that Overbury was his enemy and, folk said, his master, fretting his vanity with his fears. It is not difficult to guess the purport of those conversations and I was not surprised when it was bruited that Overbury was to be despatched as ambassador to France and the Low Countries."

"He'd not go!" cried the poet. "He knew it for a plot to get him out of the country that his books might be examined and all his work undone, somebody sitting in his place and stealing all his secrets. Therefore he scorned the post when my Lord Pembroke and Lord Chancellor Ellesmere came from the king and told him of it. He said he was regretful but must refuse his majesty's gracious proposal."

"Mad," murmured the jester, "mad with arrogance and folly, thus to insult the king!"

"He was courteous to them," said the poet. "He explained that he had not the gift of tongues and would be useless on an embassy. Besides, he said, he was an ill man, being so exceedingly troubled with the spleen that if he had a long letter to write he was fain to give it over. Therefore it would be impossible for him to send reports and to attend to such business as would fall to him should he accept the offer. My Lord Pembroke warned him that he must not refuse. He said that his majesty intended the post for his good and preferment and that he would be very ill-advised not to accept. But Nay! said my master, he could not take it. 'I will not leave my country for any preferment in the world,' he told them ; and he added other haughty speeches, knowing that the harlot had worked this matter to be rid of him ; but what he said was very ill-taken, he never having been one to guard his tongue."

"Therefore did he deserve the Tower," said the jester. "King Jamie danced like a bee when he heard it, I thought he'd break what few teeth he had left, the way he champed his jaws with the spit slathering over his beard. His tongue being too big for his mouth, which was big enough for a cow, he talked as he ate and drank, in a most uncomely fashion, enough to turn a weakling's belly. Now he drooled and stuttered when he was told of Overbury's impertinence. 'To the Tower with the dog,' he squeaked. 'O, miserable king,' he groaned, and for once he was in the right of it, so miserable an object did he look. 'O, miserable king,' quoth he, 'that I cannot obtain so much of a gentleman and one of my servants as to accept an honourable employment from me.' So into the Tower went the perfumed coxcomb and all the court was gay again . . .

"Oft have I wondered," he said after a pause while he tugged at his nose, "how deep in that plot was Carr. Was it all worked by Frankie through her relatives or did Carr work with her ? At the time 'twas thought Overbury's ruin would mean his master's, too ; but Jamie soon showed with his kissing and fondling that it was not so. There was one tale that Carr had told Overbury to reject the embassy because he had better employment for him at home, and that was why he acted so foolishly. But who can tell ?"

No one could tell. Even the poet remained silent, staring into his wine-glass.

CHAPTER XI

The Ghost in the Tower

" THEN let that pass," shrugged the jester. " 'Tis a small matter. With or without Carr's design—although I think he had a hand in it—Overbury was locked into the Tower and Frankie was determined he'd not come out again save in his coffin. Kate can tell us best of that : eh, my bellibone ? "

" She was determined on it, ay," said Kate. " I went with her to Hammersmith. Excited she was, and trembling as though with ague, and she could not sit still in the coach ; and when we got there, she threw herself into that evil Turner's arms and hugged her and wept. Never had she been so defamed in all her life ! she cried. None but Overbury, she wailed, that negro, that scum of men, that devil incarnate, would have dared be so saucy as to call her with an impudent face a base woman, aye, and worse names, to her own sweet lord. Then did I see a strange thing which perplexed me rather. My lady wept, and I have often seen her weep, but now she wept and choked and hiccupped on her weeping, and Mrs. Turner wept with her. It was wonderful to see the pair of them howling like a couple of slapped babes, clasped in one another's arms, tears pouring down their cheeks while they cried out together on that miserable wretch who had been so barbarous with my good lady's name. To see and hear them you'd have thought they were the most virtuous of ladies who'd been suddenly confronted with undeserving scandal. And I think they believed that, too. I believed it for a time. I bawled with them. The three of us howling and blubbering and calling Overbury a heartless wretch that he could say bad things about my mistress ; then when we had had our frantic humours out, we sat down over a bottle of wine to discuss how best to murder him.

"I remember Mrs. Turner saying, smoothing my lady's curls and kissing her as though she were a child to be petted, wiping her cheeks and giving her her muckinder to blow her nose on, I remember her saying that the fellow did not deserve to live. 'Ay,' said she, 'that he doesn't ; and a pity it is that he should continue to defame so honourable a lady, one so well descended, to the utter disparaging of your house, my love ; but rather than that he should continue his wicked ways, I,' said she, 'shall be his death's man myself.'

"Thus Mrs Turner boasted but when they had settled on details they found this killing of a man was not so easy a matter as smacking flies. Within the Tower Overbury seemed further from their malice than he had at court, and more difficult for them to reach. There the assassin could not steal upon him with a dagger. Poison it would have to be, they decided. But whom could they trust to administer it ? Their wizard Gresham had followed Dr. Forman to the grave. When he knew that he was dying, he gathered together in his Thames Street house all his spells and charms, his letters and leaden and waxen figures, and such other baubles of his black trade, and, wrapping them in a scarf, he gave them to an apothecary's assistant, one Tom Weston, to have them buried in the earth that they might work no further evil. Thus had they lost another of their foul confederates."

"Gresham was a rogue," said the physician. "I knew him well. After he died he left behind him a man and a wench, one to be hanged for a witch and the other for a thief soon afterwards."

"I know not of that," shrugged Kate, "but only that he was dead and that his death distressed my lady and Mrs. Turner who wept again at their unhappy lot. But this Tom Weston, the apothecary's assistant, had served Mrs. Turner's husband when he had been alive and a doctor. Therefore she knew him well. A meagre fellow he was, with a bloodless face and a grizzled beard, and he had served my lady at times, carrying messages between her and her beloved. Him therefore they chose to ferret them out another doctor who could compound a poison to slay a man, not quickly to rouse suspicions, but gradually that it might seem natural. This rogue they found in a Yorkshireman, one Dr. Thomas Franklin of Doctors' Commons, an ugly fellow of common stature with a red beard of which he was monstrous proud and red hair on his head, one curl of which he called his elf-lock and had it hanging down his back. A professed atheist he was, drenched with disease in both bones and marrow, and it was said that he had once poisoned his own wife.

"Having now their poison-compounder and their emissary in Weston, the ladies next conspired to have the Lieutenant of the Tower removed. This they did through Rochester's influence, although he knew not the cause of it, having one they thought they might trust, Sir Jervis Elwes, given the place. But how deep in the plot was Rochester none can tell for certain, although I believe he was innocent. So besotted with love of my lady was he that he could suspect no wickedness in such a one with her innocent big eyes.

"The next move was to get Weston into the Tower and this my lady managed through Sir Thomas Monson, he being Master of the Armoury and glad to please a lady, and she asked him to give a letter recommending the fellow to the lieutenant that he might wait on Overbury. Thus was all arranged and Mrs. Turner bought from Dr. Franklin in the back-parlour of his house a bottle of aquafortis. Fearing to be cheated, recalling how my Lord Essex had recovered from countless doses of Dr. Forman's sending, she and my lady gave some of this to their cat to drink. Poor beastie ! Soon it languished and pitifully whimpered for the space of two days and afterwards died. This was no good to them, said they, this was too violent, too quick and too painful. Overbury would vomit it out and others might suspect the truth to see him in his agony.

"To her house my lady summoned the doctor, he having access even to her bedchamber, though she was in bed, and he came in his dingy cloak and gold-topped stick, his tawny beard dangling to his chest and curled over his shoulder. 'Doctor,' says my lady, 'aquafortis is too violent in water. What think you of white arsenic ?' He shook his hoary head. 'Too violent, too,' quoth he. 'What say you,' asked my lady with sparkling eyes, 'of powder of diamonds ?' 'I know not the nature of that,' grumbled the leech, biting his moustache at having to confess ignorance, 'never having had sufficient money,' said he, 'to try so precious a thing. But doubtless, being a reflection of the sun, it should prove hot and deadly,' quoth he. 'I have used it,' said he, 'in the mouth of liars and of men and women subject to anger, and it cured them instanter ; but useful is it also to those who are hungry and would fast.' 'You are a fool,' said my lady and she gave him some gold pieces wherewith to purchase some of that powder for her. These he took with great love and, being now in my lady's secrets, was so bold as to ask why she wished Sir Thomas poisoned. My lady looked startled and flushed a little, not wishing to blab the truth, so she said that he had been prying into her estates and had become dangerous to her family ; and with that, she dismissed him."

"Close your pretty gob a moment, lass," said the jester. "Now is the turn for your gallant to open the Tower for us. You were there, were you not, fellow ? you saw the prisoner Overbury and heard tales ?"

"Yea, yea," said the soldier, bouncing on his stool, proud and red-faced to have everybody look at him and listen to him, " but I knew not what at the time, wot you. Only later, when there were the trials and we were all questioned did I see the truth and know what great affairs I have had under my hand and me blind to it all. At first I thought no evil. Why should I ? And I was friends with Weston, or as friendly as one could be with a fellow who had a button to his purse, and he as white as death, no matter what he drank. She—I mean this Countess of Somerset—may have been a great lady but she was a greater fool to trust that snivelling dog. Right from the beginning does he blurt the truth had I been open to believing him, but I thought he talked pish-pashery and took no heed. One night to the tavern on Tower Hill where I sat, he came to me and he was shaking and there were tear-stains on his cheek and you could have wrung out his beard for the water in it. I thought him drunk and therefore called for drinks. And drunker yet did I think him after he had gabbed, for I could not make top nor bottom of his jabber. Later, of course, I understood. He had met Sir Jervis, our lieutenant, our master, he told me, when he was carrying Sir Thomas's supper up to him, having a glass in his other hand. ' I thought,' said he to me, ' that he knew the plot.' ' What plot ? ' said I. ' The Plot ' says he. ' How am I to know,' says he, ' which be friend and which be foe ? Why ! ' says he, ' when Sir Jervis halted me I thought he must know all ; so with a wink, like a fool I says to him, says I: "Shall I give it to him now, sir?" and I near dropped supper and glass when the lieutenant cries: "What, what? give him what?" and scarce knowing what I said or did, says I to him : "Why, sir," says I, "know you not what is to be done?" And he shook, the lieutenant,' this Weston tells me in the tavern, ' he shook and he sweated and he gripped the battlement

till I thought he would shake out of his shoes and all
the while he eyed me and demanded what I meant.
So I told him,' says Weston. ' Yes, I told him everything,' says Weston, ' all that my lady had instructed
me and how much to give and when, and "O, I am
undone !" cries the lieutenant, and he called down
God's judgment on me that I should do such a thing and
he talked of sin and hell and Satan until I sweated more
than he and blubbered and begged for mercy. "Go,
wretched fellow," says the lieutenant,' Weston tells me,
" 'Go, wretched fellow, and sin no more," and I fell on my
knees,' says Weston, ' and thanked God and him and
I told him that I had cause to bless God for such a
master who had withheld me from doing that act. Then
he raised me up and drank to me. But 'twas a terrible
dangerous moment.'

" Thus did this dough-faced Weston babble to me,
wriggling and weeping and wiping his face with his
beard and drinking quick, and me puzzled, thinking
him drunk and not understanding top nor bottom of his
talk. ' What's this ? ' says I to him : ' what be your
trouble ? why should the good lieutenant sweat and
pray and him drink to you ? This is a very Bedlam,'
said I in my ignorance, ' and the moon's not in the
west neither.' Then he gaped at me. ' Lord forgive
me,' says he, ' I talk too much.' And off he ran, leaving
me perpexilated.

" I was attendant on Sir Thomas, y'understand ? him
needing careful guarding. Though none knew the
wherefor of that, a lean weak body such as him that a
maid could poke her finger through, so ghostlike was he,
coughing and mousey-voiced. When first he came he
glared at us and was imperial in his demands, squeaking
that he was innocent and asking for a Bible that he
might swear on it to the whiteness of his soul. ' What
mean you to do with me,' he kept on squealing, trying
to look bold but with panic in his glaziers when he saw

the bars over the windows. ' Do with you ? ' says my
master, the lieutenant, with a merry laugh, ' we mean
to refine you,' says he, ' that your presence may appear
a little better.' And Sir Thomas rolled his glaziers and
trembled, but said no more as we closed about him with
our halberds and led him to his chamber. My master
talked with him while he walked, friendly-fashion, and
I heard him say that he—meaning the prisoner—would
be well-advised to give way to the match between the
Viscount Rochester and the countess, says he. Upon
which, Sir Thomas bubbled within and spat, growing
hot at the mention of those names and choking on his
words. 'Twas as though a wasp had stung him. ' If I be
the Countess of Essex's prisoner,' says he, with a wild
glint in his eye, ' then,' says he, ' I care as little to die
as she does to be cruel.' Strange words thought I to
say about a lady, and she a countess ; but then he was
a strange prisoner indeed and woeful sick most of the
time I guarded him."

"Sick unto death," said the jester grimly. "The
countess was sending him her loving philtres, was she
not, my bud ? "

"Yea," said Kate in a low voice, looking at her
broken fingernails. "She and Mrs. Turner. Little
Weston took them. He might promise the lieutenant
that he'd reform after the foolish truth he blabbed which
might have ruined us all had the lieutenant not feared
to meddle, yet he carried out my lady's wishes. Or he
said that he did. And he was well paid for it. He'd
report to my lady or to Mrs. Turner and they'd reward
him ; yet methought often that it was not so much of
the gold as hunger for my lady that he did it, such
longing, such dog-looking, was in his eyes when he
turned to her. But while Sir Thomas lived, said Mrs.
Turner, she'd give him naught so he had best be busy.
' You shall have your reward,' said she, ' when Sir
Thomas's dead, and not before ; ' and she gave him

further potions bought from Dr. Franklin. There was aquafortis and white arsenic and mercury and powder of diamonds, I recall, and lapis costitus and fat spiders and cantharides."

" Lord protect the poor gentleman ! " cried the physician, lifting his thin hands.

" All these and other poisons came from Dr. Franklin," continued Kate, " and, through Weston, they were given to Sir Thomas at several times. He never ate white salt but there was white arsenic in it. Once he desired pig, and Mrs. Turner put into it lapis costitus. At another time he had two partridges sent from the court, and water and onions being the sauce, Mrs. Turner put in cantharides instead of pepper to make it hot. So that there was scarce anything that he did eat but there was some poison mixed in it. For these poisons my lady sent the doctor his reward : she sent many times gold by Mrs. Turner. I know because I delivered the money to her."

" Some of these cookings were so villainous," said the soldier, " that the stink would make you puke. There were some tarts sent once and I saw them so black and foul and of such strange colours that my master the lieutenant did cause the cook to throw them away and to make other tarts and jellies in their place."

" And all the while," growled the poet, " the Viscount Rochester was writing to his ghost, his victim in the Tower. My sweet master showed me the letters and was blithe because of them, trusting in them and thinking he would soon be freed, the earl having promised to deliver him before long. Woe is me ! he meant his deliverance by death."

" My lord knew naught of it," said Kate, shaking her head. " My lady walked in fear lest he discover it. All her terror was of that, her Robin trusting her and believing her inside as white as her outside."

" Yet with his own hand he wrote to my master,"

insisted the poet, " and urged him to take a white powder he had sent, telling him that it would make him vomit but to fear not. He would, he wrote, make this sickness a means for his deliverance and to recover his health. And in simple faith, my master swallowed it and was sick."

" That was at your master's own request," said Kate. " I remember the viscount telling my lady of it and asking what he should do. Sir Thomas he said had begged of him an emetic that he might pretend illness that the king should pity him and remove him out of that prison ; and when he told my lady this, she laughed until she had to clutch her belly, to think the fool should beg for poisons when he ate and drank naught else ! She thought it a prime jest and often did I hear her and Mrs. Turner laugh and laugh and laugh at it until they wept for very jollity."

" Pitiless," groaned the poet, " is the heart of a bad woman. Yet," said he, glancing at Zenocrate's girth, " they can oft be as soft as they are cruel. Angels or devils, either. There is no understanding them, perchance because they do not know themselves but are as amorous straws blown on the winds of passion. Had this wanton lady but seen my unhappy master in the Tower, would she have melted ? I fear me not, but rather would she have exulted over his misery, his tears, his wasted form and sallow cheeks, the blotches on his face and the blisters on his back and belly. At first, such was her terror of discovery and her heartlessness, no visitors were permitted him, even his own family not being allowed to weep beside him in his cell, and never any letters or tokens delivered, that he might be severed from his friends for the bloody sacrifice ; but the lieutenant—God's blessing on him for it, even though he be broiling in hell this moment—the lieutenant was not so stone-hearted as his masters and he at times let me and other servants visit him and tend him. I went myself to this Somerset, who was then but Rochester, and begged of him to let me wait on my poor master, but he told me : Nay. ' Soon,' said he, ' your master will be released ; ' and with that promise must I be content and with the few occasions when, by the kindness of the lieutenant, I was allowed into his cell. Sick he was but I did not suspect poison, nor did he, having faith in his faithless friend.''

" The earl had naught to do with it, I tell you ! " cried Kate. " My lady was furious with him when, hearing that Sir Thomas lay ill, he sent Dr. Craig to him to undo what in secret she had wrought. With terror she waited lest the doctor smoked the truth, but apparently he had not, nothing being said of it. And that, Mr. Poet, be no lie. All was my lady's doing, hers and Mrs. Turner's ; the earl knew naught of it and wanted only to have his friend locked safely away until after the divorce lest he hinder it by talking of the countess's adultery. He wrote also to the king's physician, a Frenchman, Dr. Mayerne, and asked him to cure his friend ; and Dr. Mayerne regretted that he could do nothing from a distance, but he recommended Dr. Paul de la Bell, and he attended him, to my lady's distress and terror. And from his own table, my lord would sent him good wholesome foods. But my lady, too, was sending him foods ; only hers were not wholesome.''

" I watched him die,'' sobbed the poet ; " his hands grew scaly and cold and his voice hollow, and often would he moan and wring his hands, asking whether Rochester—as the earl then was—juggled with him or not. He wrote letters to him, still thinking him his friend—or rather, I wrote them while he lay in bed and told me what to say. Woeful were those letters, entreating Rochester that he free him from that dreadful place ; but on occasions he would threaten. One line do I remember : it made my hand tremble as I set it down. ' Drive me not to extremities,' he had me write, ' lest I say something that you and I both repent.' Also, in secret, he wrote the true history of their friendship, and he warned the earl what he was writing ; but that book has never been found, yet he swore it would be published were he not freed. I would like to have seen that book."

" I, too," cried the jester. " It would have made a notable scandal, he having a witty and venomous tongue ; but no doubt after his death it was burnt, alas ! "

" I know naught of it," said Kate, " but I know that my mistress underwent great fear when she heard of it and she begged her sweet lord to have it destroyed for her sake ; desperate was she growing, Sir Thomas still living, if most ill, after all the venom she had given him. Continually did she send to hear how he was and, wherever she went, messages followed her with tidings of his health ; and ever the same tale to drive her distracted : Sir Thomas was ill but not dangerously ill. She railed at Weston, cursing him and Dr. Franklin, saying that she'd have them whipped because she doubted not that they were too great cowards to do that deed and they were lying to her, she said. ' Would God I were a man,' she cried, ' and wore a sword ! We women have the stomach for such deeds but lack the power.' Weston muttered, wiping his nose on his beard, that he'd given Sir Thomas a thing that'd have killed twenty men. ' Yet it did not kill him,' says she, ' and he such a pitiful wretch, all bone and skin that the wind might blow away.'

" Doubting not that Dr. Franklin cheated her with harmless potions, she searched for others who might help, urging with monstrous passion her familiar, Mrs. Turner, to do something to rid her of this rogue. My lady it would have seemed was the one who had been poisoned. But with hate. She could not live, she cried, while that man lived ! And certain true that seemed, she being now a mad thing, trembling and weeping at a word and praying to God that she might die. Sick she was, but with lust after his death, like those creatures I have heard of which feed on people, growing fat while their victims' blood is sucked. For thin now she became and haggard-eyed and haunted-looking with lust after his ghost ; and she was troubled too by the long delay of the divorce which it seemed would never be concluded, the archbishop and others having thick consciences which even the king could not ease.

" Then from somewhere Mrs. Turner found a fit instrument, an apothecary's boy who stole his master's drugs. For twenty pounds the lad gave Sir Thomas a clyster and that was the end of him."

" I saw it given," said the soldier, " and dreamed no ill, nor did he, meekly squatting that it might be inserted and its contents squirted in. He squealed, 'tis true, and groaned most grievously ; but who would think of poison in that way ? Not I, even while he lay and vomited until he brought up blood ; and at five in the morning he gave a whimper and kicked his legs and lay stiff as a board."

" My lady trembled when she heard it," whispered Kate. " She shut her eyes and I feared she would swoon while up from her belly and over her breasts her body seemed to ripple. ' It has been long, long waiting, Kate,' she sighed ; and then : ' Now that the scab has gone I am clean,' she said, for always had she called Sir Thomas the Scab. And as though she were tired, she sat down and crossed her hands on her lap. Three days before her marriage was to be annulled, at last her enemy lay dead ; but ah, alas ! there were those other enemies into whose hands she had delivered herself ; and they were many. As though the scab's ghost had raised a rabble against her, they clamoured to be paid. Too many knew her secret. Weston, first. She gave him a hundred and eighty pounds and promised more ; and Dr. Franklin insisted on having a pension for life. Two hundred pounds a year was what he asked and he threatened her with a glance ; and another two hundred he demanded that he might give her future philtres to keep her lover's love until the end. His bill was very long and was made up of many items, down to two and sixpence per day for his boat-hire and ten shillings a week for his food. Mrs. Turner, too, had to have her life's settlement ; and Dr. Savories wanted money. He wrote to Mrs. Turner, threatening that unless she gave him more for having won her Sir Arthur Mainwaring's love he would betray her. Then there was the apothecary's boy, William : the only one who had earned his pay ; and you, too, Mrs. Forman : you wanted blood-money."

" It was a lawful debt," said Mrs. Forman, " and I was my husband's sole executrix. I had everything writ down and only wanted my just dues, of course."

" Like all the insects after blood," cried Kate bitterly. " I alone, being a fool and loving my mistress even now, asked nothing ; but her other maid that knew her secrets, Mrs. Horne, was paid well. And so was Mrs. Turner's toothless old servant, Margaret ; and Samuel Merston, a musician, who had acted the go-between ; and Mrs. Turner's man, Stephen . . . So many were they I can't recall them all. Wealthy was my lady but Madam Midas would have become penniless under such demands. She paid what she could and promised more, for she'd not think of the future, her heart being gay to know that soon she would wed and have her loved one all to herself, openly and forever ; for the commissioners had proclaimed her a maid again and she was quit of her husband."

" You have all talked much," said Will, taking the pamphlet from inside his doublet, " and I've not interrupted one of you. Each has spat venom on the memory of an unhappy lady who cannot reply, and the truth died with her. But some of that truth has remained. You swear, wench, that she was first whore to Prince Henry and then to Rochester ? "

" Yea," said Kate, " that she was, God pity her."

" Then pray explain to me," said Will with a quiet smile, " how were these ladies deceived, this jury of matrons and midwives who examined her during the divorce and swore that she was still a maid ? Do you expect me to believe that they were all her creatures, paid to lie about her ? "

" Nay, good gentleman," said Kate, giggling, " they were honest enough. They didn't lie. My lady saw to that. Under pretence of modesty, she begged to wear a veil during the examination and she caused a young wench of her own age and stature to stand the search in her place."

Will flinched, the pamphlet dropping from his hand, while the company lay back and laughed, thinking it a rare jest to have sent a maid in the wanton's place with a veil to cover her blushes. Shutting his eyes, Will leaned his face on his hands and wished he could also shut his ears to that ribald mirth that thundered about him ; and the tears welled from under his lids and trickled through his fingers.

Yet even now he swore that he could not believe it.

CHAPTER XII

The Ghost's Revenge

"FEW weddings were so splendid as my lady's," cried Kate, clapping her hands, her sallow cheeks reddening at the memory, " and for fourteen days the festivities continued——"

" I'll not hear of them ! " cried Will.

" But, good gentleman," said she, " it was all so beautiful and never had I seen my lady so rosy and adorable, looking indeed the purest of maids in her white gown for purity and her golden hair well-brushed and all unbound as though she were yet virginal—— "

" Tell me naught of it ! " shouted Will, " this blasphemous travesty, if what you've told me be the truth ! a wench bought to take her place in that examination, and she such a wanton . . . Never ! "

" Nay, good gentleman," clucked Kate, " fret not yourself about the dead. She was happy for a time. But only for a time. And the masques were many and splendid ; and in the city there was tilting and feasting ; and she like the queen of love herself, blushful and coyly holding her husband's hand. So brief was the breath of happiness that I would dwell on it."

" And I will not have it ! " cried Will. " Get you to after-marriage. If she was this monster that you say, how could she sleep at night with Overbury's ghost to haunt her ? How could she nestle into her husband's arms, knowing that his desire was counterfeit, the results of drugs and enchantments ? There are none who could be so vile, none ! "

" Ah, she suffered for it and was sick, poor lady," sighed Kate. " She knew no peace now that she had got all she wanted, all she had plotted and lied and killed to attain. No doctor could tell what ailed her although her doting husband brought the most expensive in the land. Over her flawless body they shook their heads but could not heal her, the ill being in her soul. All the gifts her husband gave and the love with which he tended her could never ease that sickness. For a time they lived in Sir Baptist Hick's house which her lord took at Kensington ; then they moved to Chesterford Park near Theobalds, and there they entertained the king for a night. But in order to be close to Dr. Burgess in whom he had the great faith, the earl—he was the Earl of Somerset now—took her to Isleworth. Yet still pale and sickly she remained, trembling at a sound and weeping easily, moved with causeless passions and a terror of losing her new husband. And all the while, giving her no peace, Mrs. Turner, Dr. Franklin, and the horde of others were pecking after her, their hands out, demanding and threatening, threatening and demanding, until she knew not where to turn for money, not daring to let her lord know of her pensioners.

" The greatest lady in all England now she was, next the queen, and the most unhappy. Where the king went, her Robin had to go ; and where her Robin went, she must follow. And little was the sleep she knew, not so much from remorse of her ill-doings but from dread of the future. Overbury had friends and relations and they were asking questions about his cruel death and hurried burial. Rumours of murder in the Tower were whispered and her name was linked with them ; and she heard. She could not escape, having her greedy pensioners to tell her everything to frighten her into digging up more gold. Always, threatening her, was that ghost, a scab no longer but a wound that might open her to death. I mind that day when in fearsome terror she fled to Mrs. Turner and wept and wailed on her bosom because someone had told her of tavern-talk of having the corpse dug from its grave and dissected. Such were her torments, while her husband suffered his own troubles, the king being weary of him."

"Buckingham had come to court," chuckled Archie. "He was but plain George Villiers then with scarcely a whole cloak to his back : an insinuating, insolent fellow, yet he had charm. Yea, when he wished to win you, he could coax you like a wench. But never me. I did not trust the fellow from the start, and Carr, as was natural, hated him. I told you that the dog was a loon. So long had he ruled the king that he thought he could do what he liked with the dribbler, and now he lacked Overbury to guide him. Yet he knew his dangers, there being few men more vigilant and more jealous than a favourite, especially towards the waning time. No woman looks so anxiously into her mirror as such men seek for blemishes. At first he despised Buckingham—let us call him by the name he has made notorious for selfishness and greed—and thereby showed his foolishness. But at last he had to recognise the upstart's cunning and in a stupid fashion thought to ruin him, having one of his servants spill a dish of soup in the youth's lap. As Carr had hoped, Buckingham hit the lad and that by law—giving a blow in the presence of the sovereign—meant that he should have his hand chopped off. Did the loon really think that the king would chop off so pretty a hand ?—and they were pretty hands, as Buckingham knew and displayed them, being as plump and white as any woman's. Nay ! he pardoned the youth at once and scolded the servant, and that was another fall for Carr.

"But 'tis not Carr's tale, 'tis his lady's we would hear, so I scurry over the rivalry while Buckingham gradually pushed forward and pushed Carr down. Yet that you, my friend, might understand his foolish temper, let me add that the lower in favour he went the more haughty and unbearable Carr became, even bullying the king and shouting at him, bursting into his private chamber at unreasonable hours to scold him, rattling all the time against his rival. We wagered who would win in the end, but soon none would take odds on Carr while all fawned on Buckingham as Carr's sun sank sullenly, if hotly. Yet the king, who disliked quarrels, liking to stab in secret with a word, being a perfect Judas, and seeing the many wolves slavering to fang down his old love, had written a general pardon for Carr, covering any crime he might by chance have done, including murder. Yea," grinned the jester, " including murder ! but whether there was a purpose in that only God and the king could tell, and one of them is dead. Nor was that pardon ever signed. The lord chancellor would have naught to do with so foolish a document and on his knees, weeping, he implored the king never to sign it, saying that it was a dangerous precedent and gave the earl the power to rob him of the crown jewels, and naught could be done to him afterwards. And the king did not sign it : nay : he took the paper with him but he didn't sign it, leaving Carr, the once-beloved, a star loose in its socket, ready to fall when the malice of Buckingham could take heart to strike.

"You did not know that king, my boy. I speak no treason, him being dead, but he was one who could fawn and kiss you while begging you to sip a poisoned glass. He liked to work in secret, tortuously, being proud of his duplicity which he called statecraft. Not for him to stand forth and say : ' I have shed my love and would take to me another favourite.' Weary of Carr as he was, of the loon's ill-temper and his shoutings and upbraidings, and his brawling with Buckingham, he masked his feelings, awaiting the chance he knew must come when with a good conscience he could toss him down. Little did Carr reck how vulnerable he was, his wife having about her a crew of poisoners, bawds and wizards sucking away not only her money

but her peace of mind, when at last she should have been
happy in her love and having her enemy dead. But
God gave her no peace. Beauty she yet possessed in
full, and youth ; but her heart was rotten and terrors
watched within her bedcurtains. One cannot be continually loving. Not all the aphrodisiacal potions
compounded by Satan's brood can keep the body strong,
however lustfully the spirit might rage. There must
have been times when, in her arms, Carr slept while
she lay awake, with the ghost of Overbury ten times more
dangerous to her dead than ever he had been when
living. Beauty or the beast, my lord ? You once
asked me what lay in the heart of Frankie. And I tell
you now : both beauty and the beast. Beastial she was
and beautiful."

" And pitiful," sighed Will.

" She had no pity on Tom Overbury ! " cried the poet.

" Nor on the Earl of Essex," said the jester.

" For none but herself," shrilled Mrs. Forman.
" I mind me I have seen her weep, but those were
crocodile tears shed because she could not have her way
in a hurry and my sweet husband for all his skill had
not slain her husband for her. Not he ! He was no
fool, my husband ! He wanted no risk of a hanging
and gave her harmless drugs for the venom she asked.
And she wept, but only because she could not murder
her husband easily. Was that pitiful, sir ? "

" She had no tears for Essex," growled the lawyer,
" when with her saucy face she lied about him and made
him the mocking-stock of the world, a cuckold and
impotent ; and he a man indeed ! "

" What she did," said Will, " she did for love."

" For lust," cried Betty, " and not for love ! "

" She could not bear to be denied a thing," said Kate.
" That was what drove her, rather than love or lust or
what you will. Had the earl wanted her from the
beginning, mayhap she would have fleered from him as

she fleered from many a man hungry for her beauty. Because he, too, was beautiful and difficult to snare, she had to have him as before she had to have the prince, to exult in her conquest, smiling at the other ladies who had failed before her. The earl was the one man of whom she was never certain. Even after she had married him she feared to lose him. He was no passionate fellow and was easily sated. Therefore she needed her vile drugs to keep him at fever-point and she used every wanton's trick to make him desire her ; and always was she afraid that he would yawn and talk of something else or would get up and leave her. Therefore, the drugs, the cockle-bread, the spells woven in the darkness of the wizards' houses, and the mammets made to parody God's act of loving. Doubtless, Mrs. Turner spurred her to it. That woman of a thousand lusts corrupted her, but she was already ripe to be corrupted. Yet Turner would have changed a nun into a whore with her bawdy talk and nimble fingers. I know, God save me ! for did she not ruin me with my mistress ! "

"Yet the wicked did not flourish," said Betty with relish, nodding her head and pursing her lips.

"That is true," said Kate. "My mistress had lit her own hell and she fried in it. She heard what was being whispered about her and Overbury's death. ' I am undone, undone ! ' many a time she sobbed, until even Mrs. Turner, hard as iron though she was in sinning, caught some of her terror and also began to sweat. It was the boy, the apothecary's boy, that opened them to ruin. Him had my lady paid well and had sent him out of the country, but he was young and conscience-ridden and he fell ill. Finding himself near to death, Overbury's ghost lying heavy on his chest, he blabbed the truth. He raved in his sickness of the clyster he had given. And in the way of ill news, quickly the tale reached England. Mr. Secretary heard it and repeated it to the king, yet naught was done, although my lady vomited with terror, the king, we prayed, thinking it but a tale."

"Not he," smiled the jester, "not King Jamie. He tucked it gleefully into the sewer of his mind and held out his tongue for proofs, merry to think that now he might have the opportunity to rid himself of Carr that he might enjoy his Buckingham in peace."

"My lady knew naught of that. Only she knew that the truth was out and, frantic with fear, she summoned Weston from the Tower. But she dared not have him in the house. In a tavern at Hogston she went to him, masked and cloaked and muffled, and she bade him be strong and silent, whispering to him in a private room. The shadows at last were over her ; at any moment that cat the king might pounce ; and I too shivered and hugged myself in my distress, having her guilt like a stone on my heart. 'If you be taken,' said my lady to Weston, and I saw the hairs rise on his head and the sweat trickle down his nose to hear her talk of his being taken. Like a little dog, he whimpered, and he, who was always pale, went white as snow. 'If you be taken,' she said, 'which God forbid ! I will protect you, I and my lord the earl. They'll never dare attack us in the open. But should you be asked, tell the truth of how you entered the service of the Tower ; but say naught else. And when you go back,' said she, 'speak to Sir Jervis and find how much he knows or how much he suspects. Tell Mrs. Turner what you learn, come not near me, and I'll see you when I can in London.' Yet for a time, the panic passed and naught was moved against my lady ; and she, having her Robin's child within her, began again to hope."

"That child," said Betty, "is the wench you'd marry, my lord."

With haggard eyes, Will looked at her, then he stared again down at the table. Conceived and carried while the shadows darkened about her mother's bed, Anne, the innocent victim of her parents' sin, was shortly to be born, unhappy child. The pity and love for her that rose within him brought tears to Will's eyes until he choked and longed to run off and take her in his arms that with tenderness he might console her for the lonely childhood she must have suffered.

" Yea, soon was their daughter to be born," said Kate, " and in that thought alone was my lady happy, being assured by her wizards and astrologers that it would be a son and would have a future greater than his father's, being a child of strength and beauty. Hers and Robin's. Her constant fear, the fear that had drawn her into all her villainies, that Robin might weary and seek elsewhere, began to weaken when she felt the skin tighten on her stomach. The child, she felt assured, would bind him to her by stronger ties even than her potions and embracements. Then could he never leave her. And strange it is that one so lovely and so worshipped should fear the loss of any man, but certainly she feared her Robin's lack of interest, he, as I have said, being no great lover and liking often his mirror above her eyes. More her abandon to him and the knowledge that he owned the most highly sought-after lady in all England made him delight in her company with the pride of ownership, smiling to see desire flicker in other men's eyes while he, the proprietor, put his arm about her shoulders.

" She realised that and therefore watched her mirror with anxiety. Should her beauty go she feared his love would go with it. And the looking-glass can be both a lady's good and evil genius, her partisan and her enemy. Into it she stares, devouring her own image, yet not blind to its defects. She might even speak to it, watching, fascinated, her lips move, and it will answer her ; and always—I know not why, but it is true— always it is the dark side of her that is seen at such times. It is her selfish, most spiteful, most ill-mannered and ruthless self that answers her. In that glass her villainy is hatched, her gentle self vanishes, and the cruel, hard part of her with marble eyes looks back and makes her vicious. Do not disturb a woman at such times lest you find a stranger and not her whom you love.

"Now, with the child under her heart, my lady watched herself with more assurance and became less harsh and more beautiful, it seemed to me. And my lord could never leave her. Ever running to her he was, bringing gifts, making her lie down and rest and not letting her walk one step lest she miscarry. Had their love not been nourished on dark arts there would be no happier pair in England ; but she was haunted and could never sleep. He, of course, knew nothing of what she had done to capture and hold him and therefore had no doubts of their great future, save for occasional twinges at the thought of Buckingham rising higher ; but she, unhappy woman, could not forget. Her pensioners gave her no chance to forget with their perpetual clamour, one no sooner paid than another thrusting out his hand. Too many knew her secrets and all were insatiable, bleeding her of every penny she could scrape together, and then not satisfied. And when at last the truth became known, in a queer fashion I believe she was glad, thinking she could outride the storm and be declared innocent to the world, not realising how the king had bided his time that he might be safely quit of her husband."

"That was Jamie's way," chuckled the jester. "He liked to watch his victim smile and believe himself safe. That gave him joy, to be able to chuckle to himself and think what powder-keg he sat on. When at last Mr. Secretary Winwood—a smooth, puritanical rascal whom Carr had raised—came with proofs, even I, who knew his heart, shivered at the smile the king sought to hide."

"Proofs ! " cried Will. "What proofs ? "

"It was that fool Sir Jervis Elwes who let out the secret," said Archie. "Mayhap he thought that by telling what he knew he might escape the hangman, so strong had grown the rumours of Overbury's death ; beside his guilt lay only in his silence. He had reproved the poisoner, Weston, and was innocent save that from fear he had held his tongue. Now, too late, he confessed how he had discovered Weston with the poison-phial and how Carr had been continually sending the prisoner dishes from his own table. Of course Sir Jervis swore that he'd not been privy to the conspiracy and had destroyed whatever had been sent to Overbury ; but he gave a name. He mentioned Mrs. Turner. Names were what King Jamie needed, and now he had two of them, apart from Sir Jervis's : Turner's and Weston's. To that woman-tired old hectoring scoundrel, Lord Chief Justice Coke, he called and bade him set his nose to it."

"When my lady heard, she swooned," said Kate.

"Coke was a skilled lawyer and most pertinacious after truth," said the lawyer.

"He was a liar," said the jester, "a treacherous friend, a bully, and the king's lickspittle who'd have boiled his own mother had Jamie bade him do it, and would have made the boiling legal, too. Indeed, he was a lawyer to the bile and spleen, and a father who, for a gracious smile from Buckingham, strapped his own darling daughter to the bedpost and flogged her raw till she consented to marry the man she feared and hated, Buckingham's idiot brother. His wife was the one who knew him best and she'd not lived with him nor speak to him save when she spat ; nor would she use his name, but called herself by her pre-married one and was known therefore as Lady Hatton and not Coke. This was the pettifogging hound the king unloosed to sniff at Frankie's fewmets that he might be rid of Carr, the favourite of whom he was weary now that Buckingham—his Steenie as he called him because he said, may

God save us ! the spintry looked like the saint !—had become his Ganymede.

" Cokie caught Weston and soon twisted the truth from that curd-faced loon. That brought further names, of course : the wizard's, ah ! and this was what the king was hoping to hear. The name of Frances Howard, at last ! Snared and doomed was she from that moment. All her jewels and her gold and her countless garments, her yellow hair and her plump bosom and coaxing ways, her supercilious smiling and her big eyes could not save her then."

" In fearful dread she was," said Kate, " yet of strange courage also at times. From one mood to the other would she hop, from dread to courage, weeping in mad terror one moment, gripping her belly as though to guard the babe, and the next, jetting it like a queen and saying with a shrug that, of course, nothing could ever be done against her, a Howard, and that the king so loved her husband he would see she came to no harm. ' Who'd believe a little rat like Weston,' said she, ' when my word stands against his ? O, I was a fool,' said she, ' not to have sent him out of the country or to have given him some of the scab's medicine ; but there are so many in it . . . Too many ! ' she wailed and dug her nails into her hair and shrieked as though she were mad and the axe was already cold on her neck."

" God's truth at last was being made known," chirruped the poet, " murder most foul was being brought to light. I and other of my sweet master's servants hurried with what we could to the chief justice. We told of how we had been kept from our master and of powders and such we had found being sent to him. All that we knew we told, and often more than we knew. What we suspected. And the lord chief justice wrote it all down, blowing out his cheeks."

" Industrious to the wonder of all men was the lord chief justice," said the lawyer. " As one of his clerks, little sleep was granted me. Deposition after deposition had I to take down. But as yet my master would not order the arrest of those whom he knew were the true murderers, the Earl and the Countess of Somerset. First, he wanted all the evidence against them collected that he might tie them in a net from which they could not bite or scratch their way. Such being the king's instructions. No witness was too menial for my master to neglect, but personally he examined each, questioning them until they sweated and wept and knew not what they said. He had the coroner who had sat on the corpse brought before him and the woman who had laid out the body."

"I told him," said the leech, "how when I saw the body it was worn to skin and bone and had ulcers and blisters wellnigh all over it, which was strange to see and most uncommon. Yellow blisters they were, with blotches, blains and boils."

"Carr'd not believe it when he heard," chuckled the jester. "He thought it but the malice of Buckingham and his other enemies, being still bewitched by the white wanton, and he could not believe that he had truly lost the king's love, having been his master for so long. The king would hide his treacherous thoughts and smile on him and fondle him as before, swearing that he had nothing to fear ; then he would run to Cokie and stir him to be busier at his task that he might be rid of this importunate favourite. Now was the game played in which Carr must be the loser, the cards being shuffled, cut and dealt between the king and Cokie, and the stake was Carr's life and his lady's, with their fortunes and her great relatives ; and in truth, the game was not played above-board. The day that Jamie went from Whitehall to Theobald's, and so to Royston, he summoned all his judges and, kneeling before them, he lamented the miserable condition of the kingdom that Italian customs of poisoning should be introduced. Rolling his rheumy eyes and slavering at the chops, he bade his judges go to it and to spare no one, to hunt the guilty, high or low, out of their holes. ' If I spare any of the guilty,' says he like a just and incorruptible king, ' God's curse light on me and my posterity for ever.' Carr was with him at that time at Royston and he must have shook to hear his master's pious curses. Ah, perfect was that king in the art of dissimulation or—as he preferred to call it—kingcraft.

" When Cokie summoned him to be examined, Carr would not go, but says king-craft Jamie to him : ' You must go, for if Coke sends for me I must go too.' Carr never parted from him with more seeming affection than at this time when the king knew he would never see him more. Had you seen that seeming affection, as I did, you would rather have believed he was in his rising than his setting. When Carr kissed his hand, the king clung about his neck, slabbering his cheeks, saying, ' For God's sake, when shall I see you again ? On my soul, I shall neither sleep nor eat until you come again.' Carr told him he'd be back on Monday, that day being Friday. ' For God's sake, let me,' said the king, ' shall I ? shall I ? ' Then lolled about his neck ; then ' For God's sake, give your lady this kiss for me.' In the same manner at the stair-head, at the middle of the stairs and at the stair's foot. But Carr was not in his coach when the king used these very words : ' I shall never see his face more.' "

" It was not fear that troubled my lord," shuddered Kate, " such trust had he in the king's affection, but horror at the facts revealed. Distraught, wild-eyed, he looked upon my lady and she fell with a moan on her knees and I feared she might miscarry. ' For love of you, my lord,' she cried, ' for love of you ! ' ' For love of hell,' said he. Had she not then been with child, his child, certain he would have beaten her and trampled her, so huge was his horror and loathing of her crimes. It was not his friend's murder—mayhap in his heart he had suspected the truth of it—but the tales of her witchcraft and dabbling in potions that appalled him. She had sold her soul to Satan, he cried, and he'd be doomed to hell along with her. She wept and begged his mercy : it would have moved a stone to see her, her hair tumbling over her face, and to hear her blubber as though she could not stop, almost retching with sobs ; but not my lord. His love had turned to hate and he pushed her off when she would have embraced his legs. 'Tell me the truth,' he cried, 'I must know all.' Yet even now in this desperate corner, my lady could not tell the truth. She mumbled, one moment denying and the next confessing a few less-wicked things, and he fuming, kicking the rushes, biting his nails and raving for the truth. 'Are you so black a liar,' he howled, 'that even now with ruin and disgrace and mayhap death before us, you must lie?' She tried to tell him but she could not. To unpack her heart and know that with each unpacking he would hate her more was too much to ask of any woman.

"Then he caught her by the shoulders and shook her, her head loose on the neck—for she made no attempt to stop him—bobbing back and forth while she hiccuped and her hair was flung up and down, to conceal and then to show her face glossy with weeping. He raised one foot as though to kick, to churn his heel upon her bosom, but held back, thinking most likely of the child. 'Tell me,' he raged. Sprawling she lay, no longer trying to take a pretty attitude but lying no-how, half on her back, her belly out-thrust and her legs spread-eagled, as though with this loss of love she recked not how ungainly and even ugly she might look, perhaps hoping to rouse his pity by her ugliness. He had no pity now. He caught her hair and twisted it and 'Tell me !' he cried in a terrible voice. 'Did you poison Thomas ? Did you weave witchcraft round me ? Did you fog me with drugs ? Enchanting me into lust ?

I must know each dirty detail of it if I would outwit Villiers. Tell me,' he shouted, dragging on her hair to lift her scalp so that her eyebrows rose as if she were surprised, like a child, and her mouth opened. But she'd not protest. And thus he dragged her over the floor, yelling that she must confess or he would kill her. And verily I believe he would have killed her, so mad was he, nor do I think my lady would have been sorry had he done it.

"Yet still he shouted for her confession and she with her head thumping the floor and her heels dragging through the dirt and the rushes, kicking up old bones and scraps and such that had fallen in happier times. ' I must know everything,' he sobbed and tossed her from him and sat down, panting, on a chair, glaring at her and rapping his fingers on his knees. ' When did you begin this devil's work ? Tell me, or by God . . . ' He raised his foot again, heel out, and poised it over her ; and she, within her hair, turned from him, began at last to speak . . .

"Little by little out came that sorry tale, and love which had seemed splendid looked tawdry then, passion becoming lust and dainty pleasures seeming horrible . . . She told of Mrs. Turner and how she had met Forman, Franklin and that crew. ' All for love of you, my lord ! ' she cried, but he'd not answer, shuddering from her. She told of Overbury's killing and of how she'd done it because she feared he'd wreck their marriage ; yet still her lord would not speak, but with big eyes of horror and amazement, as though he were stunned, he stared at her, no doubt seeing in her words the world tumble about him, leaving him unarmed and naked before his enemies. He saw the future which she could not. Loss of love was all that she could think of. Beyond that her mind could not move towards the Tower and a chill morning when she might have to bare her head to the axe. But he, knowing the hatred and conspiracies at court, saw the web in which he was tangled by her silly wickedness and he realised the disaster.

" 'We must save ourselves somehow,' he muttered. 'But how? Where are these images hidden, these conjurations and letters? They must be destroyed. There is time yet. I am a free man and I have the privy seals . . . ' Faint hope lightened his blue eyes and he began to breathe again more quickly. 'If only you're not hiding something more . . . ' he groaned, no longer trusting her in anything. She whispered names. There was Mrs. Hind who had been her servant but, wealthy now with the gold she'd bled from her mistress, had a house to herself ; and she gave other names. 'I must sew fig-leaves for our innocence,' cried he bitterly. 'O wretched woman . . . ' It was the way in which he said those words that struck her grovelling again while daintily he stepped over her and hurried from the room. With his going, she shrieked and shrieked again. Pray God I never hear such shrieks again. No damned soul in hell's lava could scream so terribly. It echoes in my eardrums yet . . . Then she lay sobbing, her body seeming boneless and shaking from head to heels, her hands and her hair covering her face. . .

" Busily went my lord to work but he was too late in most places. The chief justice had either been ahead of him or those that had the evidence concealed became afraid and gave it up. Hind's letters he got and they must have been terrible for him to read, being mostly written between my lady and Mrs. Turner. These he burnt but others had been found. O reckless fools were they to have retained such damning evidence ! There were your papers, Mrs. Forman. Why had you kept them ? That you might threaten my lady and get money from her, was it not ? "

" No, no," said Mrs. Forman, blinking cheerfully at the company. " I'd not destroy anything of my sweet husband's. There were spells amongst them. Anything might have happened had I put them on the fire. And had you seen some of the dear man's midnight visitors who came down the chimney you'd have been careful, too."

" Turner was taken," continued Nan, shrugging from Mrs. Forman and wrinkling her nose with distaste, " though my lady knew not of it. And now was the net complete. My lord was arrested by order of the king, and then my lady, too. Almost cheerful was she when the message came, relieved that the long long waiting now was over and sad only that she was not to be lodged with her lord, for which I was most grateful, knowing the bitterness of his hate for her. Yet even now she believed that she would win him back in time. ' It was a surprise to him,' she said, ' but in time, he'll get over it . . . ' And I looked at her amazed, wondering at her courage and her faith in her power over men.

" The earl took the matter less calmly. Furiously he wrote to the king, protesting at the injustice and the indignity of his arrest, for even yet he could not believe that his dad was bent on his ruin. But my lady was cheerful and troubled only by his absence, while she was lodged and well guarded at the Cockpit at Whitehall, and she was worried too because no longer could she see Mrs. Turner. Soon, the gentleman in charge of her fearing the responsibility, she was taken to Lord Aubigny's house in Blackfriars. Here she thought to woo her jailor, Sir William Smythe, such faith had she yet in her beauty, but Sir William feared the king's wrath more than he regarded her charms. When she offered to provide for him and his family while she was under his charge, Sir William stiffly refused, pointing out to her her poverty, which was indeed great, with her money taken from her after what her greedy pensioners had left. And he told her that she had too many attendants, more than she could afford, said he, no doubt fearing they might work a rescue. His show of coldness, however, was but a show. Plainly was he shaken and touched by her distress and loveliness. No longer did she wail and howl and pluck out her hair and kick her heels, but sat with melancholy cheerfulness, a sadly misjudged lady who would not repine at her martyrdom but accepted it with meekness and a few tears, and they only to brighten her eyes. To the end she'd not give up, such faith had she, not only in her own fascinations but in the stupidity of men."

" To the end do women keep that faith," growled the jester. " Else they die. Now, master," said he, turning to Will. " The tale has been long and clamorous and we near the end of it. Only must come the passion of the trial and we need not tell of that unless you wish it. Our friend the lawyer here has a bundle of papers which report that trial and here's the book that Mrs. Betty would have given you, will you read them now that you know what went before ? "

The pamphlet and pieces of parchment tied together with ribbons were laid on the table in front of Will, who shrank from them. Then when timidly he took them up and opened them, he found that the letters merged, blink at them though he did, and made no sense.

" I cannot read," he croaked.

CHAPTER XIII

At Bay at Last

TAKING the pamphlets and papers pushed to him in silence around the table, the jester cleared his throat while he untied the ribbons and opened them. No one spoke, while loudly in that silence sounded the rustle of paper and Will choking on his sobs. Embarrassed, all looked at their fingers or their laps or stared into the wine in their glasses while, mumbling to himself, the jester read, tipped back in his chair with his feet on the table, the long points of his shoes turning to end in little bells. Even Betty could no longer triumph in her young master's distress, but shared his sufferings, this tale of an old tragedy, of a woman's over-weening ambition which had brought such ruin upon so many, seeming to her sad instead of disgusting, as before she had always considered it. Something of her own youth, something that had begun to dry in her heart, stirred and made her shuffle on her chair with reminder of a black-haired lad in a garden of years ago when she had thought her future and the present both well lost for that moment in his arms. Impatiently, she sucked her gums and nodded her head to nod away such nonsense, while she frowned at Zenocrate, wondering if even behind that lard a young heart beat and dreamed of love. Behind all their ageing exteriors, she wondered, did such memories remain to disturb these guests? Did the dry-skinned lawyer recall some girl of his youth? And this staid physician? And the unhappy poet? The laughing soldier and miserable Mr. Nan? Did Nan Turner herself remember some lad of the past? The harlot had confessed to her repining. Now, old they had grown, snug inside their dry skins, but did they regret the comfortable, hopeless or dull lives they had toiled to attain by slaying the passion of their youth? Nonsense, muttered Betty, nonsense. And she tried to purse her lips yet could not stop them smiling when she glanced at the jester solemnly reading at the head of the table. So charming a man, she thought, and so amusing. A pity it was, she sighed, that he was not the marrying kind . . .

She blinked, furious with herself for thinking like a girl, like a fool, like this Frances Howard who had thought so much of a man . . . yet, when one looked back on life, what else was there to remember but men and the delights of loving and being loved? In those moments of desire, naught else had mattered but desire ; and had she been wrong to feel that way, shuffling awake to see that the stars over his shoulders were only stars after all, and the grass on her back was damp? Which had been the truth, the ecstasy or the awakening? . . . Honesty, she growled, and good living, and repentance for that sin, as she had always repented in the morning. That was the truth . . . until night came again. Yea, repentance, suffering, chastisement of conscience such as this Howard creature found . . . and serve her right . . .

"Serve her right," she snarled.

"Eh?" said the jester, peering at her over the papers. "Here speaks virtue, here speaks the heart of English womanhood that likes to kick another woman down ! Are you so very virtuous, dame, that you'd wipe mud up Frankie's nose because she was found out and never a rooster's feather in her hair to tell the tale?"

Betty flushed and instinctively clutched her cap as though to find a rooster's feather in it.

"I was thinking of those filthy images," she said, "and what she was doing in a closet with the wizard."

"Closet or fowl-house or bedchamber," said Archie, "all's one when one is in a hurry." He tossed the papers down. " I thought to read these to you," he said, " but the lawyers' gibberish sticks in my throat and much is repetition of what's been said. Here, first, is Dick Weston's trial. It tells naught new to us, save, mayhap, this at the end when Mr. Gore, one of the sheriffs of London, affirmed that he had heard the prisoner—that is Weston—say that ' he hoped he would not make a net to catch little birds, and let the great ones go.' The rogue was to have his wish but, as by then he was hanged, it could have been small satisfaction to him. All the birds were to be netted and clipped by Cokie before the end. Carr's friends rode to Tyburn and at the very gallows' foot tormented the wretched Weston, urging him to deny what he'd confessed ; but he'd not do it. He swore that all was true and he made a pious end.

" Next, here is the Lieutenant of the Tower, Sir Jervis Elwes's trial, and his evidence also gives little we don't already know. He died on Tower Hill, delivering a virtuous speech as is customary on such occasions. 'Tis a damnably long one and runs for many pages : a plague on such garrulity even at death's door ! The wizard Franklin makes but a brief appearance in court, and remarks that he feared that, in his turn, Frankie and Mrs. Turner would poison him to shut his mouth ; but there's no proof of that beyond his lying word, although I doubt not they'd have done it could they have enticed him to drink with them ; but the hangman sent his soul to hell instead. He, also, died most penitently, but, I fear, a little drunk. ' Wherever I dine today,' quoth he in jail, ' I doubt not but to sup with the Lord, and I hope to have the start of you all.' And he gave a friend a note that revealed the sport of witches and how best to snare them ; and he added that the queen had been bewitched three years before, which I doubt not, only her magic popped out of a bottle, the good lady not being often sober. Yea, the fellow must have been bezzled, or mad, for when he was told he was to die, he danced corantoes up and down his cell and talked in agony of three great ones, whatever that may mean : the devil, his dam and himself, mayhap. At the tree, he danced and smacked the hangman. Heigh ho ! a jolly wizard with the beard and the hair down his back, may he coranto it in hell with his partner, Forman !

" Now were the crew made to pay, and only the principals' turn to come. Mrs. Turner had been early taken and kept far from her mistress lest even now they might conspire together and conjure the devil to release them. Yet Satan made one notable attempt to save Mrs. Turner, as we heard from this gentleman, breaking the scaffolding when her images and other toys were shown in court."

" Here is the woman's trial," said the lawyer, tapping a packet on the table before him, " and I saw her there. Prinked like a whore, painted and powdered, she trotted with quick little steps to seduce justice with her yellow-starched ruff round her throat and her bosom poked out ; and the lord chief justice, being a sadly married man, gruffly told her that women must be covered in church but not when they were arraigned and so he caused her to take off that hat which was somewhat like a man's, having a peak in the centre and wings each side with feathers poking up ; and off she unpinned it and showed her yellow hair as though she were a maid about to marry the hangman. But it was with sullen reluctance that she doffed it, wrinkling her pretty snout, and she covered her head with her kerchief.

" After she had been indicted, letters from the countess to her and the late Dr. Forman were read and the filthy images were produced and the magical writings and, as before remarked, a note on parchment signifying what ladies loved which lords at court, and first amongst them stood the lord justice's wife's own name, the lady

Hatton's, and therefore he would not suffer it to be read, to everybody's chagrin. The evidence against the accused was not truly heavy but none present doubted that her white neck would be stretched by it, particularly when Lord Coke spoke so fierce against her, informing the jury that if a man be done to death with pistols, poniards, swords, halters, poison, etcetera, so he be done to death, the indictment is good, if but indicted for any of these ways. But if you ask my private opinion, ladies and gentlemen, as a lawyer myself, however guilty the accused may have been, this was not good law and Mrs. Turner was as directly murdered by Lord Coke's law as Overbury was without any law whatsoever. But that can be of no interest to you laymen and -women. It was on Weston's evidence that Lord Coke relied to prove her guilt. The accused knew nothing of that ruffian's fate, having been securely locked up during his trial, and when she heard what he'd confessed, she swayed and almost fell, her face turning to chalk, and only her painted lips and cheeks and her big eyes showed in the whiteness. That struck the fear of death into her guilty heart and it was evident that she gave herself up for lost. Merciless was Lord Coke towards her, for he hated whores, having married one. He told the prisoner that she had the seven deadly sins inside her : that is, she was a whore, a bawd, a sorceress, a witch, a papist, a felon and a murderess, the daughter of that devil, Forman, said he, and he besought her to repent and to become a servant of Jesus Christ and to pray to Him to cast out of her those seven sins.

" She licked her lips, and with a timid glance about the court, she sobbed. ' Be good to me,' she whimpered, and she said that she was ever brought up with the Countess of Somerset and had been for a long time her servant and knew not that there was poison in any of those things she had sent Sir Thomas Overbury. But her guilt was evident, even though the case against her was weak, and the jury was not out long before it settled her fate. When she was asked if she had anything to say why judgment should not be pronounced against her, she whispered that she only desired favour, but could scarcely speak for weeping. Lord Coke thereupon gave her another grave speech, exhorting her to repentance and telling her to prepare herself for death, she having little time now to live, as he warned her ; for she need not hope for pardon, being a witch, said he."

"She, too, made an edifying end," said the jester, "and the king respited her once to save her soul, she being a papist and he lustful to have her die in the Church, God only knowing the reason why. But the parsons he sent to her, I heard tell, were more intent on her sins than her soul and they fought to make her confess that they might have worse to bring against Frankie and the earl. Dr. Whiting, who attended her, swore that he wheedled her out of her religion, but parsons like to boast of such conversions and I doubt not that she died as good a Roman as she had lived. Only she begged not to be hanged beside Dr. Franklin. ' He is a villain,' quoth she, and she feared to die with one so foul. They granted her that wish and in a vast concourse of courtiers and their ladies, mostly her old customers, she travelled to Tyburn wearing starched yellow ruffs. They were of her own make, and on the scaffold she bitterly protested against the vanity of wearing such things, and doubtless her outcry was caused by her seeing that the hangman, in her honour, wore band and cuffs of that hue. As she went on her last ride she cast money amongst the people and her dying served one good purpose, apart from ridding the world of a two-legged monster, for it ruined that fashion, the Lord be praised, none wearing yellow starch afterwards. Of course, I must not forget to add, she made a pretty speech before her turning off and she cast all blame on Frankie."

" I, too, saw her die," sighed the poet, " and execrate her though I did as the poisoner of my well-loved friend and as a whore and a witch, I yet wept to see her swing, she being young enough and lovely to look upon, and as plump as any pigeon. A dreadful waste of womanhood, thought I ; but she repented. Ah, me ! if detestation of painted pride, of lust and malice and powdered hair, of yellow bands and all the rest of the wardrobe of court vanities ; if deep sighs with tears, confessions, ejaculations of the soul, admonitions to all sorts of people to make God and unspotted conscience always their friends ; if the protestations of faith and hope, to be washed by the same Saviour, and by the like mercies that Mary Magdalene was, be signs and demonstrations of a blessed penitent, then I tell you that this poor broken woman went in glory into heaven and now enjoys the presence of her and our Redeemer. I wrote a poem on it. Mayhap you've read it. If not, here are a few lines that might squeeze your hearts to tears——

> *O, how the cruel cord*, I wrote, *did misbecome*
> *Her comely neck ! and yet by law's just doom*
> *Had been her death.   Those locks like golden thread*
> *That used in youth to enshrine her globe-like head*
> *Hung careless down ; and that delightful limb,*
> *Her snow-white nimble hand, that used to trim*
> *Their tresses up, now spitefully did tear*
> *And rend the same.   Now did she forbear*
> *To beat that breast of more than lily-white,*
> *Which sometime was the lodge of sweet delight.*
> *From those two springs where joy did wilome dwell,*
> *Grief's pearly drops upon their pale cheeks fell.*"

" Most moving sentiments," groaned the jester, " to be spent on a notorious poisoning whore who seduced more women to lasciviousness than any man's fondling ! I also stood and saw her die, but I noted not her comely neck save to see how neatly the rope fitted it tighter than

any yellow ruff ; not did I heed her golden tresses or
her globe-like head, or her snow-white hand and lily-
white breast and pearly tears.   I saw only a woman for
once treated as she deserved and had I not feared a
beating I'd have cried Bravo to see her jig on air and
I'd have hanged a dozen or so of the wantons weeping
as they watched her, as examples to our wives and
sweethearts to keep their legs in one bed.   Thus went
that devil's dam, Nan Turner, and they buried her in
St. Martin's-in-the-Field more decently than ever such a
one deserved who should have been tarred and gibbeted
or dissected that the doctors might note the blackness of
her heart and liver."

" God have mercy on her," sighed the poet.

" She had no mercy on others," piped Kate, " and
with her last breath she blamed my lady when, had they
not met, my lady would most likely never have done
such ill things, being led by her example into wickedness,
from small beginnings of lewdery into murder.   My lady
was not cruel.   You'd have wept with her had you seen
her while she awaited trial.   Her fears were rarely for
herself but all for her dear lord who had spurned her at
the end after all the things she'd done to win him, and
she was frenzied with worry because she had been
forbidden even to write to him lest they conspire
together.   Ever was she asking how he did and did he
eat well and was he strong and so on.   Shut out of life,
guarded and spied on, she knew now what her enemies
had uncovered or what her servants had blabbed.   Yet,
as I say, so wonderful was her love that she heeded not
that and thought only of her lord while the time came
for her trial and child-bed both.

" Then she heard of Mrs. Turner's trial and doom
and death.   ' Poor Turner,' she whimpered and pressed
her breasts as though they ached, leaning a little forward
while she brooded on the woman's fate.   ' Dead ? ' she
said.   She did not weep but she gasped when I told her

what I'd heard, how at her hanging that wretch had
cried out on her as being the cause of her destruction,
and my poor lady wrung her hands to hear it. After
that, even her stout faith weakened and she grew afraid,
round-eyed and watchful. It was being kept away from
others, walled in with silence with little save rumours to
reach her, that sapped her spirit. I and other of her
servants learned a little of what was going forward, but
we, too, were watched and so fierce was the people's
hate against my lady that we feared often to go abroad
lest we be recognised and stoned and, mayhap, slain.
Little was the hope we could give her, particularly after
Dr. Franklin told such lies in hope to save his neck.
The wicked things he said I dared not repeat to her, and
I was sick that people could be so vile towards my lady,
and he having robbed her and given her false drugs
after the money he had taken from her ! But she heard
of them nevertheless. The dog even hinted that she had
poisoned the noble Prince Henry whom she had loved
in her extreme youth. True it was that she had been
hugely angry with the prince, as would be any woman
with a woman's pride, after he had refused her glove
before the court with such ungentlemanly a gesture and
cruel quip. But kill him, nay, never ! She might have
cried out against him, and so she did, as being ungrateful
to her and have wished that he might suffer for his
cruelty ; but those were only words : she meant no ill
towards him. Yet this charlatan-wizard, this so-called
Dr. Franklin who had bled her of gold and given only useless potions in return, told the lord chief justice that she
had worked Prince Henry's death ! Many others were
to be poisoned, the rascal swore : more than yet were
known, he said ; and he said that he had been offered
five hundred pounds to encompass the death of Princess
Elizabeth and others. All lies ! Even the king, he
hinted, might have died by my lady and her husband's
hands, and the queen, too. Everybody at court, it

sounded from his lies, had fingers in the poison-pot and a conspiracy more fearful than the Gunpowder Treason was being hatched. And all because my lady had rid herself of a spiteful enemy and had drugged her first husband who had suffered no harm from it ! Thus does the world take its revenge on beauty when it stands at bay.

" Her confinement respited my lady. Even Coke in his malice forbore from dragging her to the bar while she was in the family way. And woeful was my lady's state, she who had had a hundred servants running to obey a nod of her head now being reduced to such misery that she prayed that, in giving forth life, she might lose her own. With fearsome oaths she vowed she'd not survive the birth, that she would kill herself and the child with her. But they'd not let her do it. The king sent strong nurses to attend but rather to guard her and to see that she did no injury to herself ; and she cursed them, raging and weeping, crouching on the bottomless stool the midwives brought to ease her labour. And thus, from a mad woman—for at that time one would have thought my lady mad with her grief and misery— was the Lady Anne born and placed at her breast. ' Poor silly miting,' she moaned, ' to come at such a time to such a place. Why did you not kill me that I might have loved you ? ' The wee thing wailed and kicked in the midwife's arms, and my poor lady bruised purple after labour, yet, she moaned, still damnably alive, my lady called the child Anne after the queen, hoping that might rouse pity for her, but there were none now to pity the poor lass, only hundreds to exult over her misery and to clamour for her death as being a witch, an adultress and a poisoner.

" There were none to speak for her. In hovels as in great houses and palaces, in shops and taverns, all were stout against her ; high and low were loud for her death. Forsooth ! you'd have thought she was the only woman in England to have sinned ! And however heavy might have been that sin—I'll not defend it—truly in full did she pay the reckoning in the salt of her tears, with few coals to keep her warm in the winds of that autumn, with not a penny with which to pay her servants, and neglected by all save a few fools like me, and never one friend to visit her and wish her well. From the greatest power in the realm, fawned on by all, had she and her lord fallen until there were none too lowly that could not despise her and spit on her name. Her matchless beauty, her high lineage and her great family, all were now useless to her : indeed they roused enmity against her, most men and women joying to see pride and power and loveliness brought low.

" It was not Coke that was to try her but that sneaking rogue, Sir Francis Bacon, the attorney-general. He had grovelled to the earl in the old days, seeking favours, and at their wedding—you'd not let me tell you of it, sir— he had devised a masque of flowers at Gray's Inn, but it had never equalled the two made by Ben Jonson for those same merrymakings of which you did not like to hear. So I'll take no more of them now," she sighed, " but go back into the shadows with my lady. She was to appear at the city's Guildhall in the High Sheriff's Court, and in preparation for this they took her from her lodgings and carried her into the Tower, heeding not her lamentations at being parted from her child and her terrors of that dark fortress. Often I feared she would carry out her curse and slay herself, hang herself with her bed-sheets or leap from the window, so indescribable was her agony lest she be locked in that room in which Sir Thomas Overbury had died. Horror of his ghost transcended fear of the hangman or the axe. She could not walk, she could barely stand, and she cringed to the lord lieutenant, weeping and imploring him as he loved God not to put her into that chamber with that ghost. He promised he'd not do it and at first gave her his own apartment, but soon she was shifted into the lodgings

Sir Walter Ralegh had recently left that he might follow his brave dream to the Indies and his cruel murder by the king. Yet even there was she afraid and dared not sleep, seeing Overbury watch from every shadow and move amongst the moonlight. Ah ! those who once envied her should have seen her then, the once-haughty lady shrinking and chattering her teeth and shrieking at a mouse's scurry, weeping at a word. It would have made the hardest heart in Christendom bleed to see her as the days passed towards her trial and she never given one word from her husband."

" He was more insolent than ever," said the jester, " and made the king shake under his threatenings. God knows what secrets he held beneath his teeth, but many were the secrets Jamie dared not let his people know, and mayhap it was to do with his hated dealings with Spain. In miserable state was the king, even Buckingham could not console him, and had Carr hanged himself or cut his throat like a dutiful subject, he'd have danced at the funeral and wept while he danced. Determined was he to destroy this man he had once adored, but he wished to destroy him quietly and therefore pressed hard for a confession that the trial might be brief and nothing said that his people might hear. But Carr'd confess to nothing : instead, he threatened that he would talk, forgetting how that also had been his doomed friend's threat before his murder. Pardon did Jamie offer, anything, if only the loon would ask for mercy and confess his guilt ; but no bribes or promises or menaces could move him."

" They tried to make my lady accuse him," said Kate, " but that she would never do. Her own guilt loudly did she bewail but ever she swore that her Robin had known nothing of her wicked doings until it had been too late for him to stop her. And because she thus confessed, they tried her first, her plea of guilty making all things speedy; and it was to Westminster Hall that she was taken."

" We could not find space for all to watch," said the
lawyer proudly. " Seats were sold again and again,
great prices being bartered for them, such being the
people's eagerness to watch the prisoner. Four or five
pieces of gold were a common price that was paid, and
fifty pounds I heard were given for a corner insufficient
to hold a dozen. Yet the curiosity-mongers were
cheated and they loudly railed and blasphemed when
the trial was postponed for a week. Many were the
reasons given for this delay and most folk believed that,
after all, as Weston had feared, the great birds would
escape the net ; while others said that the countess was
too feeble and ashamed to appear, or was too drunk."

" In terror she was," agreed Kate, " and although she
drank—and who needed tipple more, may I ask ?—she
was ready to stand her trial, being, indeed, eager to be
finished with it that she might die, she said ; and with
unguents and paints she prepared herself to look her
loveliest, poor, lost, unhappy creature, but a true woman
to the end."

" It was heavy weather," continued the lawyer, " hot
and breathless. It seemed to press down on one's skull
and all were sweating in that crowded Hall. Since six
in the morning the sightseers had been pushing in,
brawling for their seats. They drank and laughed and
jested, making merry as though this were a wedding and
no hanging-matter. But not until ten o'clock did the
lord chancellor, who for the time was High Steward of
England, enter in his robes into the hall with six
sergeants-at-arms ahead of him bearing their maces, the
peers being present in their robes, with below them, the
judges in scarlet, in tiers each side of the lawyers' table
that had the judge and the prisoner at either end of it.
Then when all was prepared and the court ready to
open, the Lieutenant of the Tower, Sir George More,
brought in the accused.

" I am not one that cares for women overmuch. In

my long life at the law I have seen too much of their double-dealings and their rapacity ever to trust or to like them for long. Let them paint and perfume their carcases and their hair and parade their bosoms and show the length of their legs under satins and silks, it matters not to me who can never be tempted by such carnal, corruptible things. Yet when that day the Countess of Somerset entered the hall, I felt a rare emotion like to pity stir inside me. From the tales I'd heard I had expected to see some brazen harlot swagger in with bold eyes and lewd lips, and not this timid little girl who kept her eyes downcast while the clerk of the crown bawled at her : ' Frances Howard, Countess of Somerset, hold up thy hand ! ' Like a frightened child, she raised her little hand and she kept it raised until Mr. Lieutenant told her that she might put it down. Then was the indictment read, recounting Weston's evidence of Sir Thomas's murder and of how she had abetted him in the doing of it. While that indictment was being read, the lady stood with trembling underlip, white-skinned, and she shed no tears ; but at the first mention of Weston I noted that she put up her fan before her face and held it there half-covering her until the clerk had finished. Then said the clerk : ' What sayest thou ? Art thou guilty of this felony and murder, or not guilty ? ' and making an obeisance to the lord high steward, she said ' Guilty ' in a low voice, seeming wonderfully fearful.

" Here is the report," said he, holding up the papers, " but to read it would prove tedious as we know what had been done before. There are, however, details not recorded here, as not being legal, yet things which I'll not forget. Her sorrow, for example, her sober demeanour, which some thought was more confident than was fit for a lady in her distress ; but I have seen many prisoners and those that blubber overmuch and make a noise I do not trust. This lady's sorrow was not false because she supported it with dignity ; rather was it the greater because she disdained to show it before all those people gloating on each tear and seeing each frightened breath she took. One circumstance there was that made me shiver, used as I am to such things. I had been watching her closely, while listening to Sir Francis's powerful speech, and I noticed that suddenly she stiffened and, if that were possible, turned whiter even than she had been, while her eyes expanded. It was—I can put it no other way—as though she spied a ghost and, quickly turning my head, I saw standing amidst the great men immediately opposite her, a stern and melancholy young man staring fixedly at her. I asked another who he was that he should look so impertinently upon a lady, even though she were accused of murder, and he whispered to me it was the Earl of Essex, her first husband. Throughout her trial, he stood and never moved, staring upon her, not with hate, nay, nor with triumph, but with infinite sorrow and, unless I was much mistaken, with pity, too.

" Sir Francis was a skilful lawyer and he laid out the case against her with strong logic, then the king's instructions were read. His majesty desired the verity to be declared. So that was all, and the countess was again asked to hold up her hand and to tell if she had aught to say why judgment of death should not be pronounced against her. She answered in so low, so humble, so fearful a voice that many did not hear her, but Sir Francis had quick ears and he repeated what she said. She was so touched by remorse and sense of her fault, she had whispered, said he, that her grief surprised her from confessing, and she said that she could not excuse her doings but desired mercy. After which she was sentenced to death by the tottery chancellor and led back to the Tower. And the show of fashion for that day was over."

" Your father, my sweet sir," said the jester to Will, " sat there that day to judge her. Merciless and steady

had he been from the first in hatred of Somerset ;
always had he kept his nose to his fewmets to race him
down ; and I saw him smile when the lady, her chin up,
stumbled off. Her husband, young Essex, hid his eyes,
but your father smiled to see her destroyed."

Will shuffled from him as though he had not heard.
" Yet they did not kill her," he whispered.

" Nay," said Kate : " would to God they had ! But
the king and her other enemies, your father included,
with malice wanted her to live, condemning her to
greater sufferings than ever the grave could have given.
' I am so tired,' she said when she came back to the
Tower, and she lay down, dressed as she was, and slept
a while. Then when she woke again, she wept and
asked if I had tidings of her lord. And when I shook
my head, she sighed and—I was startled to hear her—
she talked of her first husband. Seeing him that day in
court had woken memories and, I think, regrets. Now
she pitied him and said it struck her to the heart to see
him look so sad. ' He must have suffered, Kate,' she
said ; ' poor man,' she said, and wanly smiled. ' He
never looked away from me,' she said, ' but all the time
he stared at me and ate me with his eyes. I could not
hear what Sir Francis said, O, dreadful things, but I am
used to that, for all the time I could feel him watching
me. I know he loves me yet and were I free I could
win him easily. Not that I want him. Pho,' she said,
' but he looked so sad . . .' Then she asked again
about her lord and when again I told her I had no
tidings of him, she sighed and murmured, ' My martyrdom this day is done. Now 'tis his turn to suffer.' "

" Bold to the last was Carr," said the jester, " unable
to believe that his king had forsaken him. He swore
that they'd have to carry him in his bed to court, for
he'd not walk there, he said ; but Jamie lured him to it,
sending him a message that he had naught to fear. And,
on that royal promise, he consented to go. But Jamie

was taking no risks. Throughout the trial, he had men
stand beside Carr with cloaks to muffle him should he
utter treason."

" It was unprecedented," growled the lawyer. " Never
before or since in any court of law have I seen a prisoner
so insolent, nor have I seen fellows with cloaks to muffle
him like that. As at his lady's trial, the great folk
flocked to watch, he being much hated and much
envied ; and he scorned them all with a shrug and a
glance. In simple garb was he dressed, wearing a plain
black satin suit with two satin laces in a seam, and a
gown of ancient velvet lined with unshorn wool. The
sleeves were laid with satin lace and his gloves had satin
tops. The Order of the George was round his neck and
he had his red hair curled and perfumed but his beard
was long from his imprisonment. Ill he seemed despite
his impudent air, white-faced, and his eyes sunk in deep
hollow, but nevertheless he was courageous and haughty
and showed never a wink of fear. Nobly did he defend
himself, but all in vain. Sir Francis had his instructions
from the king and nothing was to be allowed to save the
prisoner, although little beyond suspicion was proved by
law against him."

" Yet the king," said the jester, " was restless with
fears lest he say too much. All through that long hot
day he could not remain still but was sending to every
boat he saw that landed at the bridge, cursing all that
came without tidings, fearing lest Carr blab some of his
dirty little secrets before he could be hoodwinked.
Until at last came the message to say that he had been
condemned. Then the king smiled and drank deep,
being at last content, while he played with Buckingham's
curls. What he feared that Carr might blab has never
been revealed but most people thought that it was
because he had murdered Prince Henry and Carr knew
of it, although I doubt whether the craven would have
had the spunk to do it. Yet was Carr innocent of

Overbury's murder and his lady's witchcraft? Of her black guilt there can be no argument, herself confessed to it, but I who knew Carr and never liked him though brother-Scot do yet acquit him. His guilt lay in the breach of friendship and by suffering Overbury's imprisonment which was the highway to his murder."

"I care not if Somerset be guilty or no," cried Will. "It is her guilt . . . No! that cannot be . . . I've only your words for it, and her confession. 'Tis well known that prisoners will confess to anything if promises be made to them beforehand. How am I to tell what jealousies and rancours have twisted your stories?"

"Even now," groaned Betty, "you don't believe the blackness of her heart?"

"I know not what to believe," cried Will. "None but she could tell what really happened and she is dead. If she had been as wicked as you say, how could she have lived and slept at night?"

"She rarely slept, poor love," sighed Kate.

"And she was always ailing," said the leech.

"Tell us," said the jester. "Let her history be rounded to the end, through love and hatred to the grave."

CHAPTER XIV

Nails in the Coffin

" Now is it darkness to me," said the jester, " lit only by rumours. Out of life dropped Carr and his countess when they left the Tower. That they would be executed nobody believed, she being a Howard, yet the people were hot after their blood, particularly hers, while Carr, even with the axe against his neck, would not crawl to Jamie's wheedling and confess his guilt."

" For he was innocent ! " cried Nan. " Often and often I heard him cry his innocence, clenching his fists and gibbering with despair because, without tearing the heart from his breast to show its workings, he could not prove that innocence. In tears and penitence my lady would say that he spoke the truth, that he had known nothing of her conspiracies. Guilty he was of having had Sir Thomas imprisoned that he might be kept away during the divorce, but beyond that his guilt did not stretch, and nothing was ever proved against him, save through malice and envy. Of her conjurings and poisonings he suspected not a tittle until the trial stripped his lady of her vizard's innocence and showed her for a witch who had dabbled in abominations. His only crime was that the king no longer loved him."

" And that Buckingham hated him as a rival," said the jester. " A staunch hater was this new favourite and ravenous for gold. Those who had hoisted him, conspiring to throw down Carr, soon found that they had placed a scorpion over them, more dangerous, more petty-minded and more venomous than the pretty wasp they had destroyed. Not only did he hate Carr as a rival, but he could not forget in his monstrous vanity

how during his rising Carr had jeered at him and with
insulting words had spurned his offer of friendship.
Determined therefore was he on his humiliation. To
use the axe would have been too swift and noble an end
for either king or spintry to allow it. They wanted
subtler, more soul-destructive cruelties : life to be lived
out in contempt of self and brooding on what have been.
To such a doom they condemned both Carr and his
lady, leaving them to sweat in terror in the Tower, waiting
every day for tidings of their doom, having a few friends
visit them——"

"Not the earl," said Kate. "Few approached him.
As though he had the plague or the rabies and might
infect them with Buckingham's displeasure, all kept
away from him ; but my lady even in disgrace remained
a Howard and her father was still the lord treasurer.
Besides, Buckingham did not hate her as he hated her
husband. On occasions she was permitted to have her
baby with her, and that brought some contentment,
although long would she weep over the child, dandling
her or hugging her to her paps, because she feared her
future stained with her mother's sin and her father's
disgrace. You have all, save my lord here, called her
vile names, and in truth she was a wicked woman ; but
she was a loving woman, too. Rarely of herself did she
think but always of others. Even her murdering had
been done for others, to make her lord contented in her
arms, just as she had made conjurations and given her
lord potions to keep his passion steady and he content.
Now, locked away from her wizards, her vials and boxes
broken, her images destroyed and her magical parch-
ments burnt, she had naught beyond her beauty to hold
him, and that must die. Yet, for a little time, it seemed
to work.

"She was still lovely to look on, although grown pale
and thin, and her air of sadness, making her more gentle
in her dealings, added a melancholy charm which

touched the earl a little. His own deep misery, broken by sudden ravings and spittings on the name of Buckingham, left him remorseful and sick and in need of love and comfort, while no longer whimsical and tyrannical, his lady became timid and eager to please, waiting on his moods, and he seemed to soften towards her, cursing her less often, although he would not enter her bed again. The child, too, drew him. Often, sighing, would he gaze down on the Garter and the George which he wore continually, clinging to them as the symbols of his lost greatness, and anger again would glitter in his eyes when bitterly he looked at her. Yet he said little . . . for a time. I think he still believed that, could he see the king, he would win him back and unseat Buckingham. And he wrote many letters to him, protesting his innocence and pleading not to have his fortune taken away. But taken away it was, estates and furniture both, for Buckingham's delight. Not everything, however. There was undoubtedly some secret which my lord possessed—he sometimes hinted at it with a curl of the lip—which terrified the king and kept him from being as merciless as otherwise he would have proved, so that he gave my lord a manor in Northampton-shire and money, if not sufficient, for his needs. For nearly five years, however, were my lord and lady locked away, given no freedom beyond the Tower gardens, walking the parapets and sighing to see the happy people in their boats, the sailors at the wharves and the painted bridge over which the traffic flowed. And those were five years of growing hatred that was terrifying to watch. The tenderness which had touched him through the child faded when he began to realise that he was indeed ruined and cast off by the king while news of Buckingham's growing splendour came to madden him to futile threats and cursings on that name. Of everything had the new favourite robbed him, taking even his private secretary, that pious John Packer who knew by heart not only the scriptures but the psalms and proverbs and canticles, and who, uncontent with a Sunday sermon, listened to one at least each day, yet Buckingham remained unsatisfied in his spite. The countess was formally pardoned, she the guilty one, but not her innocent lord. For eight years was he left to hang by a hair, never knowing when he woke if that day should prove his last. Subtler even than that torment was Buckingham's insistence that this poor crushed enemy must plead through him for every favour ; even for such trifles as permission to receive a visitor, his signature must go upon the warrant."

" A great hater, indeed, was that Villiers," chuckled the jester, " and almost could I love him for it, so one-minded was he, so ruthless and so heroic in his lust to make himself and his family great though England be shamed. And he neglected nothing, not even that poor wretch in the Tower."

" It was money he wanted," said Kate. " He offered my lord a pardon if he would give him his manor of Sherbourne which was worth thirty-two thousand pounds——"

" Which was but justice," smiled the jester, " Carr having stolen Sherbourne from Sir Walter Ralegh."

" But my lord would not do it," cried Kate. " Spit-bubbles showed at his mouth's corners and his eyes seemed huge when he cried. ' I'll have none of that dog's service though I die for it ! ' And it was foolish of him to have refused because the king took Sherbourne without a by your leave and gave it to Buckingham."

" Magnanimously," said the jester, " did Buckingham refuse the gift to prove he'd not fatten on a rival's fall, but he got property to the value of eighty thousand in its place, so delighted was the king by his Steenie's generosity."

" All this had my lord to suffer," sighed Kate, " with regrets that gnawed him every time he looked upon his lady's face and realised that she was to blame for his ruin."

"Had he shut his eyes to Buckingham's advancement," murmured the jester, "he'd never have suffered. Not so much the enormity of his lady's crimes but his own haughtiness, and jealousy had tripped him. The king would have hushed the scandal had he accepted Buckingham, as the queen, good lady, accepted him. That was the true crime for which Carr suffered."

"Suffer he did, whatever his crime," said Kate. "The tenderness for little Anne, as I told you, which softened him for a time soon faded. Although he still loved the babe, his hatred for the mother grew great in captivity where he could not escape her presence. And she who had been all love for him also became embittered, hearing from his lips nothing but taunts with never a kiss nor a kindly word. 'When I am quit of this prison,' he would say, 'never will I look at you again.' Such insults could not be borne by any woman and my lady had ever a proud stomach. Soon she was answering him taunt for taunt and ceaseless became their quarrelling, their recriminations and abuse, until it seemed that deliberately they fed their hate.

"Yea," she murmured, "they fed their hate, they nourished it as if they feared its going. It had replaced their love and had become a passion equally as violent. I would see my lady when she was alone, sucking her fingers and muttering and panting to herself while she went over her wrongs and miseries, working up her choler till it flamed into her cheeks and shone through her eyes and puffed out her bosom, so that when my lord entered the chamber she would fly at him and he would fly at her, both screaming until their voices cracked or until, finding no further words to fit his hate against her shriller vituperation, like a cowardly man he would take refuge in his strength and beat her, trample her, yea, even kick her, that body which he had loved so well. Whatever terrible sins they had committed they paid for them in the end. They paid a thousandfold. Nor were they ever to be freed from that chain. When at last the king granted them liberty he made it a proviso that they live together."

" Wonderful in his cruelty was the king," chuckled the jester ; " Buckingham had little to learn from him when it came to spite. Both were remorseless in revenge. I warrant you that they laughed together when they thought of such a doom ! It would tickle both their hard hearts."

"The cruellest of dooms it was," nodded Kate, " that ever was decreed. In misery they lived and that great love which had defied the laws of both God and man was turned to the utmost loathing. In this woman still beautiful though lined with worry and growing thin, the earl could see only his own disgrace and ruin, while she remembered all that she had sacrificed to win him to the undoing of her immortal soul. Had they never met, I doubt not that she would have grown contented with her first husband and would have lived like most wives, finding solace in dreams and, mayhap, when her lord was absent—he being born a wittol—with a lover or two discreetly now and then to keep her spirit wholesome by proving she was still a woman and desirable. Now was she ruined, her name spat upon as that of a poisoning whore ; and all for love of a red-headed fellow she had grown to despise and detest as a fool and an ingrate. While he in his turn saw no longer her soft white body : he saw a witch who had studied excremental arts. Small wonder that he hated her and howled against this royal order which commanded that they live together in mockery of holy marriage. Even the satisfaction of quarrelling lost its delight as the years passed. They would not speak to one another but like two ghosts they passed when they met, their eyes averted ; and the child growing into girlhood, knowing naught of what they'd done, was puzzled by these separate households of father and mother under one roof. I could not bear to see it. Yet I'd not leave my lady and, while she lived her haunted life, I tended her, she being now rarely well yet with no sickness that had any name."

"In body," said the physician, "was she as hale as a ferret. Often was I called when she had a fit on her, and I am wise in my profession, but naught could I find to put my finger on. Heart, bowels, liver, kidneys, belly and lungs, all were sound enough. Yet I watched her die as though she were being eaten from inside, wasting away like a candle."

"Passion had taken its revenge," said Kate, "and having naught else to feed on, it fed on her."

"Passion is no word in my pharmacopœia," sneered the leech. "I physicked her and bled her, yet she would not mend. It was like a maid's green-sickness when she turns to womanhood, and I gave her therefore Hiera Picra in wormwood and Rhenish wine with syrup of mugwort ; but she vomited it up. She would smile at me and say that she was beyond my skill, but to that I would not agree, although I knew it to be the truth. Here, thought I, is a subject for dissection. Here can I make discoveries and become famous. But that was not to be. I never cut open her secret, the toad within her sucking on her heart. I have heard today how plump she had been when young, and how rosy. That was not when I knew her. One could see her ribs and her veins showed clear with no need to paint them, while her belly was slack and her legs lean. Yet her spirit remained strong, making her restless, for she could not sleep, no matter how I drugged her."

"She slept in fits," said Kate, "and would wake up screaming, thinking that Overbury breathed on her from the dead. Even after the king had died and she was permitted sometimes to go to court, new company could not save her. The ghost went with her."

"She stood godmother to my child," said Archie complacently ; then he gaped aghast to see the fury in Betty's eyes.

"Your child !" she yelped. "You did not tell me you were wedded ! "

"You need not be wedded," mumbled the jester, " to have a child."

"You need to be wedded to have a countess stand godmother," cried Betty, "that you might wheedle an expensive gift out of her. Woe is me if ever I believe a man again ! "

"Peace, peace !" cried Will, thumping the table with his fist, for now that Anne was entering the tale his interest began to grow again.

"But you did not hear what he told me," wailed Betty, "a little inn in the country and good food cooked by one so cunning as me and him to choke the fowls and draw the wine and all the court coming to us for custom——"

"Peace, mother, peace !" Will gripped her wrists. "Continue, wench," he said to Kate, while, her glittering gaze fixed on the jester, Betty sank back, mumbling ferociously, into her chair.

"There is not much more to say," sighed Kate. "Visits to court did her little good, but made her weep afresh with reminders of her youth and what her life might have been had she not met Mrs. Turner and been dazzled by Somerset. Back to the dark home at Chiswick would she have to go and, no matter how she bolted and locked her door, she could not bolt out hatred. One could feel her husband's nearness and his loathing of her."

"How poor Anne must have suffered ! " cried Will.

"Anne ? " said the jester, sitting up stiffly but avoiding Betty's baleful eye. " What do you know of Anne, master ? "

Will looked aside. "Only what I have heard," he

241

muttered. " It was said that she had a daughter and named her after the queen. For her to grow up in that household of hatred must have been bitter for a child."

" Yea," said Kate. " The tale was hushed from her and she knew so little of the world, being kept close at Chiswick, that she believed all wives and husbands lived apart. In looks she became like her mother, golden and chubby, her child's form giving promise of good shape ; but I've not seen her these many years. After my mistress's death I fled that house and came to this, knowing no other trade. In terrible torments did my lady die, her screams being frightful to hear. They lifted the hair on one's head and crinkled one's skin. Something was eating her inside away. Conscience, mayhap, regrets, or God's judgment on her for her sins. Scarce a moment had she in her latter years that was free from pain. Lean and shrivelled she looked, old before her time, even her golden hair turning dull and damp and grey ; and she was not forty when death took her, leaving her lord to live alone with his ghosts, save for their child."

" That child," said the jester, watching Will while avoiding Betty's eye, " would be now seventeen or eighteen, a marriageable age. Yet who would think to marry the child of a whore and a poisoner and a great fool like Carr who tossed away wealth, power and happiness for a wanton's bussing ? No doubt the wench is beautiful, but within . . . What could she have under her fair skin that was not evil ? "

" Yet this fool would marry her ! " tittered Betty.

" I knew it ! " cried the jester, slapping the table with his bladders. " I knew that there was more than idle curiosity behind your questions, master. You love the wench and your father was one of those that hounded down her father. He'd not approve of such a wedding."

" Yea," said Will, gripping his chair-arms as he looked up defiantly, " I love the daughter of Frances

Howard and Somerset and I am going to marry her. The tales you all have told are mayhap true or partly true. But who are we to blame this woman? Not a week since, I, too, would have brayed loud against her; but not now. Something has changed within me; pity has grown. Whatever anyone can say, she was a great lover and the evil she wrought was all for love. Had she had a husband to equal her, mighty would have been her achievement in the world. The pity is that she was caught by a coxcomb's beauty and was seduced to evil by a wicked woman, this Anne Turner. I am young and you are all older than I, and doubtless wiser, but would you say that you would have become the folk you are had it not been for some chance circumstance that set you on your course: a meeting, a word, a promise, a gift: some little thing which, had it not occurred, would have left you a different person? Therefore how dare you judge this lady? Loud have you been against her, all save this lady, Kate. Now will none among you pity her? Will none of you confess that, but for chance, you might have acted as she acted?"

"Never!" cried Betty, tight-mouthed, glaring at the jester as though she would spit at him. "I've had my temptations—what woman hasn't? and I was a noted beauty in the kitchen—but I've withstood all the filthinesses that I've been offered, knowing men to be liars, liars, liars, all of them!"

"God forgive me," whispered Kate, "I loved my lady and I cannot hate her. And, sweet gentleman, you have said the truth. I was reared in her household of wizardry and lust. Had I been like this dame, brought up in some good woman's kitchen, mayhap I too would have been as honest as she. In our youth is our future builded, although we do not know it at the time, and mine was tempted and I fell."

"The rest of you are silent," said Will. "I pray that in this silence you are looking on your hearts. This history has been to me a warning to set aside worldly ambitions and to be content with honest love, than which there is no greater happiness and contentment in this life. I go to seek my mistress, the Lady Anne Carr."

" And what will your father say ? " asked the jester.

" Already he has forbidden me," said Will. " But not if I wait for fifty years, will I abandon Anne. Nor could I do it if I wished, she being a part of me."

" God's blessing on you both," cried Kate. " May you bring happiness to that poor child."

" And damn himself in doing it," jeered Betty.

" Are we not all damned ? " said the jester. " Do we not each of us with care prepare our little hells while we dream of heaven ? Go to it, boy. The scandal'll rock the court and we have need of conversation there these days. 'Tis damnably dull since Buckingham earned his knife-thrust."

" Do none else bless my love," said Will, " save a strumpet and a jester to speed me on my way ? "

" You have a poet's blessing," said the poet. " I'll write your epithalamium for you, and write it cheaply, too, being myself so starved for love as well as food in my poverty that I am tender towards all lovers, wishing myself in their beds."

" Would I were in that bed," tittered Mrs. Forman. " You can have my blessing, too, boy ; and should a potion be needed . . . I have some yet of my late husband's books and know somewhat of his craft. Should you need a potion to fire you, come to me. I can make any wench, no matter how daft she be in her virtue, willing to any man ; and my fee is small."

" He needs no potions," scoffed Kate, " other than his bonny face and his youth and their love together. Would my poor lady have lived to see this day ! then would she have died happy in her pain ; but that, alas ! was not to be, unless ghosts have ears and she be listening to us now. Who knows ? She had Sir

Thomas's ghost always beside her to the very end, and
mayhap with love she haunts her daughter and smiles
upon us here."

" Who knows ? " repeated Will, and smiled.   Close
to him, her hand feather-light on his, he knew that
Frances Howard stood, no longer sinful and yearning to
thank him for her daughter's sake.   " I drink to her
memory," he said ; and all that company, save Betty
glowering at the jester and sucking her lip, drank their
wine to the dregs, then threw their glasses on the floor.

CHAPTER XV

Journey's End

LONG was to be Will's waiting, dark with despair were to be his nights of lonely anguish, bright with hope and faith were his mornings when he awoke to hear birds sing while he saddled his horse to ride to Chiswick by the river. Slowly the days drifted into months and the months to years, yet still was Anne withheld from him while he and she ached within the prisons of their separate bodies for the release of love. Even had he been less of an ascetic and, her mouth on his, had let his blood burn away caution with his virtuous resolutions, Will could never have had the chance to love Anne wholly, so narrowly were they watched, not only by her ladies but her father. And glad was he that he could not be tempted even while he raged against such restraints on passion. Yet pale he grew and at times dizziness shivered within his head so that he had to lean against a wall or clutch a chair-back, sickening with longing to possess her ; and she, although she concealed it from him, knew panic whenever he failed to visit her, becoming certain again that he had grown weary of merely touching and gazing, all greater intimacies denied them. There were also her ladies, yellow with virtue, to remind her of her mother's sin ; and there was her father whose sidelong glances told plainly that he dreaded to see in her her mother's wantonness. Even her mirror could not reassure her with her flawless image, so fearful was she now of the wicked harlot's blood bequeathed her, not only by her mother, but by her mother's mother who, she learned, had been rapacious both for gold and venery. Now that she had discovered the truth of her lineage, naught was hidden from Anne, her ladies taking a prurient satisfaction in telling her tales often untrue and some of them vile, which drove her to tears, to swooning and even to vomiting in disgust at her mother's villainy.

Corrupt beneath its fair surface seemed her body while, stirred by such lascivious talk, her mind, to her own horror and amazement, would startle her with forbidden thoughts when she lay betwixt waking and sleeping and drowsed into the devil's arms. That Will could ever forgive her mother and love her for herself alone she was unable to believe once he had left her and she was in that dark house haunted by dead desires and undying hatreds. Her father's painted, haggard face reminded her of his sufferings and his youth of lust. Plain to be seen was it that already he writhed in hell.

"In hell!" he screamed to Anne once, and the spit bubbled into his beard. "For I am damned," he wailed, "and damned and damned again! Look on your beauty, wench, and repent of it for it can lead only to suffering and the soul's destruction. You are your mother's golden shadow. Such hair as yours had she; and body, too; and eyes, and gait to torment a man. Get you to your prayers for God alone can save you if He will. And if God has pity let Him pity you that you were born of such a mother."

"A witch," said her women. "A whore. A murderess. That was your mother, child."

Printed in a book found by chance Anne had read the truth: or had it been by chance? Had her father or one of her women left it in her way for her to find? After that reading, she needed not their cruel taunts to remind her of her mother's wickedness. A Messalina, had that writer called her, a Circe turning men to hogs. He had written of how she had conspired with Satan to bewitch Anne's father, with her sweet Turner giving him potions to make him loving while making waxen images of her first husband to melt before the fire that he might die. The scenes that book evoked would never be forgotten, they had made Anne's soul writhe with disgust and seek some cranny within her flesh in which to hide for very shame.

"The rascal does beguile you, wench," cried her father. "His father always hated me and led the faction to destroy me. This is his viperish plot to set his son to ruin you and thus disgrace our name and make it a bawdy jest once more at court. But I am not deceived and I'll protect you. I am Argus to your virtue. Think not to hide with him and duplicate your mother. Where you go, what you do or say, is always overseen and overheard. Even your sighs at night are listened to, and the whimpers you make in the dark. If I must use the whip, I'll whip you into modesty."

Anne shrank from him, her eyes darkly shadowed, her skin turning olive, her soul's spring becoming autumn in its nameless terrors and love-longing. And seeing her thus, shy, unhappy, desperate, pleading for his pity, her father would veer from fury into tears. On his knees before her would he fall, swearing that he loved her and could not lose her even to a husband. She alone remained to him from the wreck of his world, he would sob ; and as though they were lovers, he would cling to her while she shivered from his touch, and he would kiss her as no father should, gazing with hunger into her large eyes, his wet beard dabbling her chin. Knowing that it was not her but her mother within her whom he sought, Anne did not fly from him but submitted in agony to his caressing.

Yea, for all that he might rage and curse her name, plain it was that the earl yet loved her mother, that woman who had snared and then destroyed him. Her memory could not be forgotten, while her invisible presence darkened the house. She was in the sighing of the wind and in the rustle of the curtains, in the scurry of a mouse and the creak of a board. If ever house was haunted it was that Chiswick house. More vital than the living was that spirit seeking, it seemed, forgiveness of the past, a poor sad ghost stealing out of hell to implore her daughter's pity. But Anne could not pity her.

" Yet," said Will, " she was your mother. I fought against her while I heard her tale. Until then had I, too, been stern in judgment, condemning sinners unheard, but afterwards . . . I know not why, but as I listened, I could feel her close, so lost, so pitiful, like a bird beating wings on the ground when unable to fly into the blue, and I was ashamed that I had dared to judge her, acting as our Lord did not act when the woman caught in adultery was thrown before Him. Has she not paid in full that we should hate her still ? "

" I cannot love her," said Anne darkly. " Because of her lusts have I been robbed of my youth, kept here hidden like a nun in this house. I have had to pay for her, I who am innocent ! Why should I have to suffer for her wicked doings ? "

" Yet," said he, " had it not been for her wicked doings mayhap we had never met. You might not have lived in Chiswick and I become the boy next-door. You might have been reared in luxury, been offered to temptations, taken when a youngling to court for men to lust after your beauty and for lewd women like that Mrs. Turner to steal your innocence until—yea, who can tell ?—little by little you might have taken those steps which lead down into hell."

" You have small trust in me, my lord ! " she cried.

" I know the world," he said, " the hating hateful world resenting innocence and goodness. But reared here, that dangerous age before one's spirit becomes truly formed and can be moulded to good or evil, that has passed. You have become a woman, Anne, yet you remain as innocent as Eve before the apple, and I am

grateful indeed for that. Therefore do I thank your
mother."

" Yet," she whispered, " even now she holds us apart.
Had it not been for her we might have married long
since."

That was true. The dead woman had condemned her
daughter to spinsterhood long beyond the time when she
should have married, and often as the months passed and
became years Will despaired because his father would
not let him marry Anne.

" Any woman other than her," said the earl. " Yea,
rather a base-born maid if she be virtuous, but not the
imp of that adulterous witch. My boy, sweet lad, are
there not ladies enough, honest women, chaste and of
good parentage, that you must seek a wife in that
adder's nest? The Lady Elizabeth, the Lady Dorothy
—their parents are willing and not a blemish on either
girl ; yet . . . O, I will not have it ! Never, never,
never ! Do you understand ? "

" And I," said Will, " shall marry none but she."

Wan with love-longing, sighing, Will went to court
and those who at first scoffed at his infatuation began to
wish him well. So strong and constant a love should be
rewarded, said both courtiers and ladies. Even Archie
Armstrong, before whose vicious wit all trembled,
ceased to scoff at him and proclaimed that such love was
a miracle and greater witchcraft than any worked by
Anne's dead mother.

" I only pray," said he, smacking flies with his
bladders, " that they might never marry. When he
discovers her to be a woman after all and tires of her, as
tire he must, our Troilus might become a Thersites, and
she a Cressida sneaking to the Grecian tents. Nay,
ladies ! if you would hold a man withhold your dainty
selves. Satiety oft turns to satire and then to saturnalia
with others ; or even worse, fie ! it might become
indifference than which there is no deeper insult to a

hard-worked lady. That's why these scurvy poets prattle of wenches they never get. Had they had them, they'd have writ no sonnets but lampoons. Diana and not Venus is the poet's true love, and never never Hymen, that destroyer of more than maidenheads. Therefore, say I, it would be wicked for this pair to marry and see themselves as they are."

None heeded Archie. They smiled and nodded to hide their fear of him, the women scorning such blasphemous philosophy and the men, desiring the women, swearing that the knave should be whipped. But jeer though he might, tiptoeing about the court that he might chance on a whisper that should not have been heard or might disturb some lovers in their nest, Archie when alone sighed and wished that he were young and handsome and able to love without always feeling the skull grin at him through the lips he kissed.

"Some day," said the queen, in her high-pitched yet pretty French voice, "we ladies will condemn you to a marriage, sirrah, with my monkey that you should rail against our sex which, by ruling men, rule all the world."

"Yea," groaned Archie, "'tis Satan's world and he wears a skirt to squat on it, it being notorious that women are his agents, as the holy fathers taught. Ay, we have failed, we silly men. We thought to jail you in a petticoat with whalebone, only to find that we have jailed ourselves instead. Is that not so, your majesty?"

"A jail we gladly enter," sighed the tiny king, gazing with adoration at his dark queen, "and one from which no true man would escape."

"I grant you it can be a compassionate jail," said the jester, "when the key is turned to the lady's satisfaction. Nevertheless, a jail it remains into which those outside clamour to get in and those inside clamour to get out. I speak of most cases. Your majesty alone refutes my argument, thereby proving it to be the rule. I was thinking of a youth I know, a silly lad who bleats for the moon as though it were a sucket, yet a handsome gallant of good lineage and wealth. Because he's free to romp in any flower-bed, he mopes to pluck but one he cannot have and his lass mopes with him, each of them sighing for that jail of matrimony. But it will never be. His father'll not have it, and one greater than his father, the greatest in all England, would forbid it if he heard of it. Yet the boy and the girl be all in a flame of love that has no fire to feed that it might burn out. I speak of young Lord Russell, your majesty, and Somerset's daughter."

Gripping the arms of his chair, the king stiffened and his eyes appeared glazed.

"We—we—we will not permit that name to be spoken here," he stuttered.

"Then, Archie," said the queen, "whisper it to me . . ."

She hated Buckingham who had stolen the king from her and had made her a jest with an empty bed, his murder at last having given her the opportunity to become the wife and mistress of her husband. Ruling the king, she ruled the nation, as Buckingham had ruled it before her, and enemies of the dead favourite naturally she fondled. On that tune did the jester play, dwelling on how Buckingham's plots had entangled Somerset to destroy him.

"Leave this to me," she said, smiling roguishly and tossing her dark ringlets. "He is a pretty youth and should not suffer for what her mother did. And I am always gentle towards true love, so rare it be."

Even the queen's urging, however, could not move the Earl of Bedford from his horror of the match ; even after she had coaxed the king to add his commands to hers, the earl pretended not to understand their wishes. To have the blood of that witch enter his family was to him an abomination, and even loyalty to his king and love of his eldest son could not move him from his hatred.

"Never!" he cried. "What egg hatched you, unhappy boy, that you should thus shame our blood! You are no Russell for all that you have my features, to dandle after such a harlot's whelp! You have grown sick on reading filthy ballads and romances until you think yourself a Paris and the world well lost for love. Or has she bewitched you with her mother's sorcery?"

"If I am bewitched," said Will, "a pure heart and a sweet voice are all the enchantments she has used. None other, sir. If you would only see her you would love her."

"I saw her mother," cried the earl. "She too had sweet looks and beguiling ways, she too looked a maid until the truth was known. A fair mask oft hides a rotten soul. Such are the devil's lures, my boy, not God's."

"Yet will I marry her," said Will.

Twist though the earl might from his king, he found his retreat made difficult when the king and queen visited Woburn and made plain their wishes.

"God forbid," groaned the earl, "that I who am the loyalest man alive should disobey your majesty, but I am a father as well as a subject, and O, your majesty, ask anything save this of me."

"Are not marriages made in heaven?" said the queen. "Therefore is it not a kind of blasphemy for you to stand against God's will?"

Hours on his knees spent the earl, weeping, when alone, and praying for guidance, hoping that with the passing of time this evil flower of passion might wilt in his son's heart. But time brought to it only nourishment; stronger grew Will's love and more stubborn he became. He had but to take horse to ride to Chiswick to look into Anne's eyes for any weakness to leave him and for him to realise that only death could rob him of such love. Yea, only death. Sight of Anne, touch of her, and he became enslaved, hot and trembling ; blinded by her beauty and his own desire, he would sit for hours, content to be at her side, to breathe the air she breathed and to hear her body move within its rustling garments. Thought of possessing such a goddess appeared at times incredible, like asking for the sun in his arms, a miracle which no man could deserve, almost a blasphemy, that those virgin-limbs could ever submit and be mastered. Whatever her parentage, however evil-living her mother and grandmother might have been, Anne had blossomed in chastity, a rose from a dunghill, too divine for any man's coarse handling ; that she, so rare a goddess, could love so awkward a booby as himself seemed a miracle which he could not truly believe when his fast-beating heart drove the blood to burn his cheeks, shaking all his limbs, until he feared he would swoon.

"Once I thought that poets lied," he said, "but even they've not told the truth entirely. There's never been such love before as mine for you."

"Nor mine for you," she sighed, gazing wetly at him, her lips parted, her bosom stretched beneath the cloth. Grateful she was to God while wondering how so handsome a man who had seen the world and countless lovely women could have chosen her in her simplicity.

Thus for hours, unspeaking, would they look on one another, never tiring, continually discovering fresh loveliness to adore until with hot mouths they kissed and moaned because, held apart by flesh and bone, their spirits could not mingle while teeth pressed behind lips, panting, sobbing with desire.

"It shall be done," said the king, turning to his queen.

"Yea," said his queen. "Such constancy must be rewarded."

Then no longer could the earl twist and plead.

" It is a royal command," groaning, he told his son.
" And may you never rue it. Please God this be not
devil's work. But stay ! " said he. " Although, to
please my king I submit to this disgrace, all rests with
Somerset. I'll not have that witch's spawn at Woburn
unless her dowry come near my own sacrifice ; that
have I explained to Somerset. See now if he loves his
daughter more than his gold."

" But he is ruined ! " cried Will. " His wealth and
honours were all taken from him."

" I doubt not," said the earl, " that one so cunning
and slippery as he hid most of his possessions from the
king. If he loves his daughter, let him vomit them
forth again."

" You have done this," cried Will, " in hopes to stop
the marriage, knowing that he has no money."

" I have asked a mere twelve thousand pounds,"
shrugged the earl.

" As well might you ask a million ! "

" I was being reasonable," said the earl. " I did not
wish to set too great a burden on the rogue."

Twelve thousand pounds ! Alone in his chamber,
Somerset sat and read again and again that demand.
Now and then he looked up at the faded tapestries
against the walls and at the worn carpet under his feet.
Twelve thousand pounds . . . Once he could have
snapped his fingers, like that ! and had ten times that
sum hurried to him from the royal treasury ; he had
only to ask and scarce a man in England would not
have run to offer it, and more ; such sums had he made
with the signing of his name when suitors had come,
cap in hand, to beg his favour with the king. But now
those days were over. James and Buckingham had
despoiled him, leaving little . . . Gone were his gilded
beds, his purple velvet furniture, his Persian, Turkey and
Egyptian carpets, his pavilions of cobweb lawn embroidered with silk flowers, his tapestries of the siege of

Troy and of Roman tales, of gods and goddesses and nympths and satyrs ; gone his many paintings, his jewels and his plate : all gone. Even his mules and his horses, his carriages and carts, had been seized to be given to others to please the king and Buckingham.

Twelve thousand pounds against his daughter's happiness ! What little he had saved and hidden would have to go, everything he possessed must go . . . Somerset crumpled the paper in his hand and, shutting his eyes, he groaned. Was the wanton ghost not satisfied yet ? Must she, the fortunate one that had died, yet seek revenge on him through Anne ? Love had brought him to this, his love for a witch, and now love for his child must steal from him the little he had saved and garnered. Twelve thousand pounds ! He could never raise so much . . .

But when he looked again upon his daughter and saw her wan and listless, hollow-cheeked and heavy-eyed, quivering at a sound as though her spirit, broken with despair and green-sickness, expected treachery even from the wind against the shutters, Somerset's heart smote him and he wept.

" You love this youth ? " he sobbed.

" How can you ask me that ? " she sighed and put her pale hands to her brows on which the veins showed darkly violet.

" More than you love me, your father ? " he demanded, stepping close to stare into her eyes.

" It is a different love, sir," she whispered. " I love you both, but differently."

" Would you leave me for him ? " he cried. " Would you abandon me to lonely misery in my old age, you, the one thing I have left from the shipwreck of my life ? Women were ever traitors to their loved ones, selfish, wilful, ready to murder if needs be that they might satisfy their unholy longings. Why should you be different from others of your sex ? Once I believed that ladies were chaste goddesses. I thought that of your mother once." He laughed and beat his breast. " I thought her honest although I knew yet would not believe that she had been the prince's whore. I shut my eyes to what was the jest of court when the prince threw away her glove. Thomas warned me and I destroyed him for his honesty. I killed my friend, the only one that ever loved me, as surely as though I'd used my dagger on him. One half of me was blind : but the other half of me winked. Why was I not surprised when he died so suddenly, so strangely, he who had no mortal weakness in him ? I knew the truth, I knew that she had murdered him, but I put it by with closed eyes, being glamoured by her loathsome spells. That was not I but the creature she had made of me, my heart struck through with a pin piercing a waxen image she kept locked in a cupboard. Yet, remembering all this and knowing how beauty can be a cheat, I still believed, I hoped, I trusted you, Anne."

" I have done no wickedness," she wailed. " Don't look at me like that ! I have done you no harm, it was not I . . . O, can I help it that I love ? Father, father, I am so unhappy that I wish I were dead."

" Dead ? " he cried fiercely. " Death is a boon I've craved these many years, but my detested body is too strong to kill . . . How long have you known this youth ? "

" Since babyhood," she whispered.

" Yea, yea, I know that. But how long since he came back to claim you ? "

" It was almost exactly two years ago," she sighed.

" Two years ? " repeated the earl. " That is most loves' lifetime ; yet he's stayed true all that long while ? "

" Yea," she said. " How could I help but love him, father ? "

" It must make Bedford curl," he muttered. " That's why he set so high a price. He hopes that I'll refuse it, wants me to refuse it. He thinks to humble me, his jealousy and hatred being yet strong, for he was a psalm-singing knave, a creature in black, jaundiced against love. With his cunning and treachery he helped to break me. This is God's revenge on him. Yea, yea . . . My child, do not weep. If your affections are settled on this lad, I'll ruin myself rather than that you should be unhappy."

" Why ? " she cried. " What is this ? "

" He sets twelve thousand pounds upon you, child. Think you that you are worth it. Twelve thousand pounds. That is the price the old dog asks to salve his shame in having a Carr bedded under his roof. What weight are you ? A featherweight now that you are skin and bone, wasting with longing, yet that's the sum he sets against your bones. 'Tis a fortune to us now, child, although once I'd have wagered double on a dice-throw. Love is priced, sold over the altar, nowadays as though you were some beast a farmer buys for breeding. In setting so high a sum he proves your value, the value of a Carr, though he knows it not. Would you have me sell you with twelve thousand pounds to your lover ? "

A faint blush darkened Anne's sallow cheeks and her eyes lightened as she took a deep breath and the tip of her tongue stole over her lips.

" I am sold already, sir," she said. " Love sold me long since and money has naught to do with it."

" Yet money must go with you to line your bed, money for the hound to spend on his own back and his estates. And I'll do it if only to spite him, for he thinks I can't. I'll do it if I have to sell the last stick and rag I own. None will say that Somerset stood before his daughter's happiness and bargained like a tradesman over her body. You shall marry him."

" No ! " she cried. " Not if it means your ruin ! "

" I am ruined already," said he through his teeth, " being but the wreck of what I was ; but I have pride

left in me and tenderness for you, my child. Prepare
yourself for the bridal. In silks and tags and laces shall
you go to him, and I . . . I'll not be with you. I
will be alone," he whispered, " with my ghosts ; " and
he cocked his head to one side, slyly looking from the
corners of his eyes, as though he watched a cunning
enemy creep near.

Scarcely daring to believe that love had triumphed,
Anne sank back and feared she would choke. Too
surprised yet to appreciate her happiness, she lay on the
chair, her eyes closed, hearing her heartbeats sound like
thunder in her ears, feeling tears move under her eyelids.
Her back was to the open window and the sun glossed
her uncovered hair and silvered her cheeks, deepening
the shadows in her lap and between her breasts.
Turning suddenly towards her, having heard her sob,
her father started and put up his arms, so like her
mother was she to him at that moment.

"You ! " he cried and gripped her throat. " You
. . ." Then at the touch of Anne's skin, he shivered
and drew back. " I am mad," he whimpered. " I've
lived too long with ghosts, and I am old, old . . .
Marry your Russell ! " he shouted suddenly. " Marry
the dog, breed for him, people the land with yet more
Russells, for there'll be no more Carrs this side of hell.
But never think to look on Me again ! Do you understand that ? Never ! "

Before Anne could speak, he had gone, hurrying into
the shadows, himself like a shadow, on silent feet ; and
she felt her throat which hurt from his grip and she wept
to think of his unhappiness and was ashamed of the wild
joy that trembled up her legs, making her wish to sing
and dance, while she wondered how she could possibly
live through the days that held her from her loved one's
arms.

Yet those days passed, although each night Anne
went to bed angry with dilatory clocks, and awoke

exultant yet furious that more hours lay before her to be suffered in exasperating tedium save when she dreamed of their love that must never die. Often Will rode gaily to visit her and they plotted a future of placid delights, of being always together, far from the court and London and Westminster, never seeing Chiswick again, their children about them and none to hurt them. Rarely did she see her father who remained amongst his papers, visited by lawyers and a few friends, and she knew that he was trying to gather her dowry. Terror lest he fail to collect sufficient money alternated in her moods with such love for him that she wept, helpless with longing to atone in some fashion for her desertion of him and for the sacrifices he was making for her sake ; but when he came to her or passed her in a gallery and she dipped into a curtsey, she sickened lest he touch her with those unwashed hands, still feeling his fingers on her throat. He was her father yet he had become a stranger to her and she feared him as she would a ravisher, her skin shrinking at the thought of his touch, her lips tightening lest he kiss them.

"All is arranged," he told her one day. " I am stripped naked that you might go naked to a stranger's bed, and I hope you're satisfied. My enemy has had to accept my offer : a thousand pounds in sterling and a further nine thousand within six months. This I can raise by mortgage on this house and all its contents, the few poor mementoes of my greatness I rescued from the wreck : some tapestries, some plate. Stripped bare it makes me yet your future father's still not satisfied. I must add another mortgage on those Scottish lands on which I have a reversion. On my death I've promised another three thousand, also to be secured on those estates. In return he'll give you and your husband two thousand a year with the proviso that his word'll not be binding should I fail to pay . . . Now I have nothing left, nothing at all. I who had everything, all

England for my toy, have nothing now, not even my child."

"Ah, sweet sir," she cried, "do not say that ! I will always love you ! "

"Love me ! " he laughed, "when you hide from me, shrink from me. See ! you'd not even kiss me, your own father, unless I asked it ! And faith ! you're right : my lips are poisoned, having once kissed hers ; and you are so like her that there are moments when I dare not look at you, seeing your mother in your hair, your eyes, in every wanton step you take, in the swing of your legs, in your bosom's insolent curve and in your voice. You are that woman born again. God's pity on your husband. May he find in you, I pray, the joy I never found in her. And yet I lie. Great was my joy in her at first ; therefore the greater was my fall from heaven into hell. From rare delights to utmost bitterness, to wake beside a wife one thought so innocent only to find that she's a witch, as in some old romance, the hag who took a young girl's shape to snare a fool in love."

"Can you never forget her, sir ? " Anne sobbed.

"Forget her ! " he cried. "Cut out my heart and you will find her name writ on it ; dig me from my grave when I am dead and what the worms have spared you'll find is hers. I am marked, doomed, scratched by a witch's claw, my soul sold to the devil without a by your leave. Such was my lady your mother : a very woman. You too are a woman and you have, I tell you, her eyes, her shape, for men's damnation and your own delight . . . Yet here's my blessing, child, for I've naught else to give, only this wretched life which God disdains to take that I might continue in penitence and memories and misery."

As though he feared to look at her lest he kiss or beat her, he swung away ; nor would he go near her again. Locked in his apartment, he remained while Anne prepared for her wedding at St. Benet's, Paul's Wharf, in July ; and only at last when she was leaving the house did he dress and perfume and paint himself with care to step for a few minutes into the sunlight to kiss and bid her goodbye. He smiled and waved to her, then when the coachman had whipped up the horses, quickly he turned and hurried indoors again like one who fears the light. Back to his ghosts he sped, blind with tears, back to his untidy chamber that would never again echo to Anne's voice ; and there he bit his nails, crouching in his chair and muttering to himself, nor did he stir to light a candle when night closed round him.

Anne's bridal-night. She had chosen an enemy to steal from him his last possessions. True woman who, to satisfy her lusts, would forsake her father. Like mother, like daughter : twice had he been betrayed now by woman : no ! by the same woman, Anne being Frances's butterprint. Stripped of possessions, even his soul sold to the devil, he had ever been the victim of women, he groaned, of mother and daughter, Howards both. Yet he smiled while he wondered whether her welcome at Woburn would remain so warm after it was discovered that he could not pay the dowry in full. To pay everything demanded would have been impossible, James and Buckingham, and later, Charles, having been merciless in plundering him. Yet he had given all he could scrape together, even his own happiness, for her happiness. And had he had the money, gladly would he have given that, too, finding a vicious satisfaction in his own ruin.

In young Russell's bed now would Anne be laid. The curtains would have been drawn ere this and the servants departed. Ah, God ! cried Somerset and he raised his fists and sobbed. This was a judgment on him for his sin, this was the vengeance of Overbury.

" Poor friend," he cried, " good friend, Thomas, have I not paid yet in full ? And you, you witch, are you not content to see the ruin you have made of me ? You whom I loved, friend and wife, will you not give me peace now that I am old and alone ? "

In the shadows they moved ; they spoke with the wind down the chimney, calling him out of life. Never, Somerset knew, would he be quit of them, these ghosts in his heart whom only death could release. Ghosts of the past. Around him in that dark chamber they came, strong once more in youth : lean Overbury laughing, reckless of the future and proud of his enemies ; King James slobbering into his beard, leaning with one arm about Somerset's neck and gazing at him with cow-eyes ; Buckingham in the splendour of cloth of gold and curling beard, haughty and mocking, smiling on his enemy's ruin, with fingers ever-crooked for money , and Frances with golden curls and tight-mouthed, secretive smile and bright blue eyes promising so much while her sweet Turner whispered lascivious promptings into her hair. Out of the past they stepped to act once more their roles in that tragedy which had been his life ; and clearly now, too late, Somerset saw what he should have done against what he had done. All for a white wanton, a poisoner, this shipwreck of his hopes, his honours, his pride, his happiness. That a woman's beauty and ambitions could destroy a world had once seemed to him a tale for poets with their Helens and Cleopatras ; but now he knew that the poets had not lied and that in a woman's scheming and sensual allurements could lie more powers and greater menace than in any army ravening after slaughter. They could wreck dynasties, they could destroy whole nations and could turn even God to mockery, beguiling men to blasphemies and murder that their pretty pride might be appeased and their dangerous flesh adorned.

Yet, he thought suddenly, and wept, besides calamities could they bring—were their hearts honest—such peace and such delights and such inspiration to men that they could be very angels on this earth. Beauty or the beast ? Was the choice theirs to make or were they, true minions of the moon, drawn to their fate by the pull of the stars, by the burning of their own blood, by their upbringing and tutelage, or by temptations too overpowering for their vain-glorious yet weak flesh ? Who could say ? Mayhap Anne might prove, he prayed, the other side of Frances, atoning for her mother's sins with rewards of happiness for her husband, redeeming a past of wickedness with her purity and selfless love ? Only the stars could tell . . .

But Will, taking Anne into his arms, had no such doubts. This was all beauty to him, this shy and trembling girl eager to prove her love and gratitude through loyalty and motherhood ; and the years ahead shone to him with rewards of happiness and peace : they together, always together, her mother's history forgotten, blotted out like this room when he puffed out the candle and closed the curtains on their perfumed bed, husband and wife, alone together at last.